Modern Jewish Literature and Culture

Robert A. Mandel, series editor

A House Too Small

and Other Stories

Ezra Hirschmann

Foreword by
Alan Berger

Texas Tech University Press

Copyright © 2013 by Ezra Hirschmann

All rights reserved. No portion of this book may be reproduced in any form or by any means, including electronic storage and retrieval systems, except by explicit prior written permission of the publisher. Brief passages excerpted for review and critical purposes are excepted.

This book is typeset in Scala. The paper used in this book meets the minimum requirements of ANSI/NISO Z39.48-1992 (R1997). ∞

Designed by Kasey McBeath
Jacket illustration by Anna Coventry-Arredondo

Library of Congress Control Number: 2013935173
ISBN (cloth): 978-0-89672-795-3
ISBN (e-book): 978-0-89672-796-0

Printed in the United States of America
13 14 15 16 17 18 19 20 21 / 9 8 7 6 5 4 3 2 1

Texas Tech University Press
Box 41037 | Lubbock, Texas 79409-1037 USA
800.832.4042 | ttup@ttu.edu | www.ttupress.org

This book is a work of fiction. Names, characters, places and incidents are the products of the author's imagination or are used fictitiously. Any resemblance to actual events, locales, persons (whether living or dead), institutions and the like is entirely coincidental and shall be construed accordingly.

For my wife, Marion

Contents

Foreword   ix
Acknowledgments   xv

Beggar in the Bahnhoff   3

The Clairvoyant   43

Fall of Grace   67

Hester's Folly   123

A House Too Small   141

Lady Dorothy's Dilemma   161

Ghost of the Ganges   197

Foreword

The Holocaust, as a historically anchored event, ended in 1945. The Nuremberg trials of twenty-two top Nazi criminals, which began in November of that year and ended eleven months later, signaled the end of official concern. The world turned to other matters. Postwar reconstruction, a future that looked bright with possibilities, the Cold War, the space race—all occupied public attention and newspaper headlines. But, as psychoanalysis has convincingly revealed, that which is repressed returns with a vengeance. This return manifested itself on two levels. On the one hand, there was popular culture's "discovery" of the Shoah, which frequently turned it into kitsch. On the other hand, there was the question of what it means to inherit the legacy of the destruction of European Jewry, which serious people dealt with. Psychologically, the effects of the Holocaust on this group did not and will not disappear.

A House Too Small, Ezra Hirschmann's debut collection of stories, places him in the category of those who take seriously the legacy of the Holocaust. Traumatic wounding refuses traditional healing. While more than six decades have passed since the ovens of the crematoria were destroyed, the psychic damage done by their existence continues. Although Jewish bodies are no longer being burned, memories of the tragedy continue to scorch the soul. But, like the biblical burning bush, the soul is not consumed. Rather, it is called to respond. Traumatic memory is passed on to generations who were not yet born at the time of the disaster. Nonetheless, these generations feel in the depths of their being the ongoing legacy of the Jewish genocide. This is a special type of memory, one that accrues to generations "untimely born" who nonetheless feel the ongoing effects of the past trauma.

However painful and necessary, we need to enquire into the nature of this memory. It is less personal than collective—although the inner discomfort it generates is very personal; and although it is a memory of a perished people, it comes *not through the eye of the witness but through the words* of one who bears the pain without the direct experience. In short, it is a memory constructed of a tragedy that casts an ominous shadow over all of humanity. Furthermore, this type of memory goes against the grain of a culture that prefers amnesia to reflection. The command *zachor* (remember) occurs over a hundred times in the Hebrew Bible, a text in which memory and identity are intertwined. But contemporary culture speaks more in terms of an amorphous humanity in which memory is frequently seen as at best prosaic and at worst parochial and divisive. Consequently, non-witnesses who engage in Holocaust memory encounter a vital question: How can one deal with the inheritance of the Holocaust?

In seven elegantly written stories, the author examines various dimensions of this inheritance. Heavily laden with memory, his characters vary in age, origin, nationality, and response to their complex legacy. All, however, are ineluctably touched by what happened in the kingdom of night. Together, their responses form a mosaic of Holocaust inheritance. Each of the author's protagonists seeks a path to a normal existence. But the reader soon realizes that a word like "normal" is oxymoronic following the Shoah. One cannot undo the past. Instead, the past threatens to undo and overwhelm the present. Each of these carefully crafted stories offers a discrete angle of vision concerning events that occurred during the Shoah and their ongoing repercussions. These include grappling with issues of restitution, recollection of Nazi cruelty, the continued existence of gratuitous violence, and instances of Gentiles helping Jews.

When read together these self-contained stories provide insight into the emotional and physical lives of those living in the Shoah's dark aftermath. An Israeli-born special operative acts on behalf of the second and third generations (children and grandchildren of Jewish Holocaust survivors). A Christian Viennese composer saves the son born to the Jewish woman he has raped. A mutilated man whose mother was repeatedly abused by a Nazi, and a child orphaned in the Shoah who is mistakenly killed after the war, seek to understand the past. Ezra Hirschmann's stories include those of three women, one Jewish and two Christian, whose lives have been indelibly imprinted by the evil of the Holocaust. The Jewish woman was sterilized. One of the two Christians is a decrepit widow of a Nazi-admiring fascist who had no use for her. The second widow saved a young Jewish boy from death at the hands of the Nazis. Cumulatively, these stories are a pastiche of post-Holocaust identity.

These stories are far more than a random collection dealing with the persistence of memory, although they do that as well. Rather, Ezra Hirschmann offers an extended meditation. He invites his readers to reflect on key issues raised by Holocaust memory. To what extent can one speak of justice in the face of National Socialism's monstrous crimes against humanity? This question plays a central role in "Fall of Grace," set in the context of a legal hearing. Justice does not come from any system. On the contrary, it is the result of individual actions. In this story, a barrister quietly enables a deformed man to learn that a crazed inmate killed the Nazi who had sexually assaulted his mother. The protagonist's name, *Ish Aval* ("man of doubt"), is itself symbolic. Has the Holocaust not raised the issue of the doubtfulness of the human enterprise? Can people live together without murdering each other?

Evil is very much with us. "Hester's Folly" reflects on the relationship between the words *live* and *evil*, reminding the reader that humanity and evil are coterminous. The tale's protagonist, a semi mute child survivor, lives in England following the war. Seeking to deliver a message of hope to the Queen, the young woman is inadvertently killed by a British soldier who mistakes her for an intruder in the royal garden. During the Holocaust one lived by accident but died on (Nazi) purpose.

These stories implicitly remind the reader that, as Elie Wiesel has observed, "for survivors the Holocaust continues after the Holocaust." "A House Too Small" takes us inside the tortured emotional world of a sterilized Jewish woman, who nevertheless insists that she needs a bigger house in order to provide room for the children she will never have. Her situation has left her suicidal and incapable of fully experiencing life. Yet the stories recall the righteous Gentiles who helped their persecuted Jewish neighbors. "Ghost of the Ganges," a complex tale of violence and brutality, recalls the life-saving action of a German woman. The boy she saves subsequently becomes a registered nurse who devotes himself to saving the lives of others.

This volume teaches many important contemporary lessons. Writing itself is an act of mourning (even for those whom one has never met) and of *rebellion* against evil, and against those who delight in its perpetuation. Remembering the victims is as well an act of rescue. They should not remain anonymous. Moreover, these stories remind their readers that forgetting the Shoah is the ultimate form of Holocaust denial. This is a crucial point in a world where genocide is still occurring, and where distortions and lies about the Holocaust accompanied by outright denial continue to spread their poison. Finally, this volume also serves as a warning. The Holocaust was a murderous assault on Jewish existence. It has been followed by an assault on Jewish memory, no less murderous. Whose memory will be next on the executioner's chopping block?

Ezra Hirschmann reminds his readers of the need to be aware of the obligations imposed by inheriting the Holocaust as well as the imperative to remember. But there is more. His stories portray the near autonomy of memory. The protagonists, both Jewish and Christian, do not so much summon memory as are summoned by it. For some, this summons is an imperative to act. For others, it requires meditation on events long past. But all the protagonists discover that memory is the linchpin of their identity in the post-Shoah world.

Alan L. Berger
Raddock Family Eminent Scholar
Chair of Holocaust Studies
Florida Atlantic University

Acknowledgments

Without the encouragement of dear family and friends, this book may not have come into existence. My appreciation of them and their lives is abiding, even if they are not named here. With respect and gratitude, I also acknowledge: Robert Mandel PhD, the Director of Texas Tech University Press, my esteemed publisher who consistently believed that *A House Too Small* should be in print and dedicated his talent and energies to fulfilling that goal; his Assistant Jada Rankin; the Editorial Board, Faculty and Staff; Alan Berger PhD, eminent Scholar and Professor at Florida Atlantic University who wrote the Foreword and is counted among my close friends; Joanna Conrad the Managing Editor; Kasey Mcbeath, the Production and Design Manager, and my Editor Mary Beth Hinton, who worked tirelessly. My thanks also go to several of my colleagues whose names (for professional reasons) I do not mention here, but whose wise counsel is greatly valued. My admiration, above all, is extended to those who experienced (and still do) "the holocaust within"—beyond my imagining—and whose memories I attempt to perpetuate in this work of fiction, with honor, in a creeping "Age of Forgetfulness".

Ezra Hirschmann

A House Too Small

Beggar in the Bahnhoff

> My very chains and I grew friends,
> So much a long communion tends
> To make us what we are—even I
> Regain'd my freedom with a sigh.
>
> **Lord Byron, "The Prisoner of Chillon"**

"He will be the breath of God," the old man said, speaking softly to his dying daughter. Her strength failing, Ruth clutched the infant to her chest. Her bones protruded through the flimsy nightdress. Her father's words were spoken as if he were carving carefully, like an artist working in the wood of words.

Manfred Isaacs was a towering figure. An icon of the state, famous throughout the Holy Land and beyond; he was large in frame and reputation. Now, though no longer young, he still practiced his profession. He had survived the Nazis, with others on board a rickety immigrant ship during the last years of the Mandate, ignoring the British naval blockade as if it were a trifling nuisance. It was he who led the exhausted group of remnant survivors onto a deserted Jaffa beach, and he who headed a small brigade of ragtag soldiers in the War of Independence. Never in his life had he bowed to brutes. In one of "the camps" he had stopped a German officer with a look that said: You can kill me, but I will haunt you forever! The young, ignorant peasant of the Reich, who had been elevated for sheer brutality, feared the hulking man. Manfred Isaacs, though wasted from starvation and scarred by beatings, had never succumbed. Instead, his strength seemed to grow through suffering and challenge.

With his head held high, then and always since the day of his "return," as he called it (for, like Ben Gurion, he considered that his life had begun anew), he devoted his mastery of psychology to helping any and every "survivor" who sought his aid. He practiced his own methods of hypnotic transcendentalism; dietary substitutions (for many prisoners had suffered great harm caused by malnutrition); and vulpine touch techniques, even allowing patients to attack him verbally and physically in order to expiate their demons. He let his adult patients be children and his juvenile patients be adults. He dug deeply, excised, absolved, repudiated, reattributed, and restored. Manfred Isaacs became his patients and allowed them to become him—for, above all, he was one of them! He was a son, a husband, a father, a soldier, a founder, a writer, a grandfather, a distinguished alumnus of the Hebrew University . . . and a man.

Manfred Isaacs would not thunder in a place where his only flesh and blood had been brought to give life and to lose hers. He would not rend the air in the strident voice of a prophet. He would not tear his garments. He would not don the sackcloth and ashes of the bereaved.

She will pass on, according to His will. I shall plead with God, but I shall never denounce Him! The suffering is not hers alone! It is mine too! Manfred's voice, like the roar of a lion in a den of defiance, sounded within his being. Ruth's sunken eyes stared unblinkingly at her father, whom she loved for his kindness, his tolerance, and his soaring knowledge of the human mind.

Manfred left the room, walking backwards, his eyes resting

on his daughter's stricken face. With a vast effort of will, Ruth turned away so that Manfred could not see the tears on her hollowed cheeks. Nor could the infant boy (who had not yet been named, as this was the first of eight days prior to circumcision) feel his mother's tears fall.

The doctors had told Ruth that she would not survive the arduous birthing; but she did, albeit for a few moments—just enough to see the infant.

She hugged the baby weakly. Then she released him into the attending woman's hands as she whispered her wish for him to be passed to her father.

Thus, Ruth let go of her only child, knowing that her father would protect and nurture him. "He must live!" She tried to shout it out; but only a whisper emerged. Manfred Isaacs, who had heard screams, wails, and whimpers in godforsaken places far from the ears and eyes of all but the victims and the pitiless, realized that *the soul soars momentarily when the dying body releases its essence; it becomes light so it can fly; its sounds are numerous and none.* He knew this, having buried his wife. Now he began to prepare himself for the task of burying his only daughter.

During her illness she had gazed through her window. She saw the sun setting over Jerusalem, where stone took on the fluid pink hues of dawn and dusk—just as it had appeared to Viscount Allenby in earlier days. Millennia after seers of old sang the Song of Songs and prophets shouted their outrage, it was much the same as it had always been.

Her husband had been killed months before by a concrete beam that fell from a crane at a construction site, crushing him down into a dust-filled hole. That is why the attendant placed the baby in the arms of Doctor Manfred Isaacs, the only one who could care for him. The baby's little body felt like soft, raveling wool.

After waiting a suitable time in the hospital's corridor, without asking permission, Manfred strode back into the delivery room. The nurse had gone out in great haste to fetch something. In one of his powerful hands, Manfred Isaacs held the baby's cranium, resting its torso in the crook of his elbow, which looked as if it were the size and shape of an axe's head. The boy's legs dangled, his plump toes touching his grandfather's chest. With the lightest of caresses, Manfred stroked the nape of his daughter's neck. He pressed slightly as she took her last breath and "passed into the Temple of Peace," as he later told his grandson, who would be named Abel. Manfred uncurled the infant's fists, which until that moment had been tightly and boldly clenched. He looked closely at his daughter. Ruth's sightless eyes stared back. He pressed the bell next to her bed, released it, and closed her eyelids. Turning away before the nurse re-entered, Manfred left the ward, shunning the entourage of melancholy that sought to accompany him.

The old man's face had a sober look of longing that his grandson loved. It transported Abel to another dimension—a secret, but not isolated, place. When he was just a boy, Abel wished he could reach that special destination as his grandfather's traveling companion. And sometimes he could, with a little assistance. But all of that came later . . .

Manfred Isaacs signed his articles in the *International Journal of Psychology* "Apostle of Pain." When asked why, he replied, "Because it seems right to do so for one who has amassed painful confidences."

Now he whispered to himself and the child in his charge, "I am the repository of many hurts, lost hopes, and dreams." He continued, "Some men collect objects. I accumulate the suffering of my people. Stories that have been told to me in sorrow and guilt. They are the inheritance of our people. I am an archaeologist of the human psyche."

Little Abel could not yet realize that these tales were his grandfather's personal "ingathering of exiles" on which "Hok Hashvot," the Law of Return, the bringing home of a scattered nation, was based as a fundamental tenet of the resurrected State of Israel. Abel was content to play, surrounded by Manfred's powerful presence, which filled the rooms of his apartment in one of the world's most ancient and august cities.

One day a patient asked Manfred to explain the concept of *return*, enshrined in the laws of the Holy Land. Manfred paused, because it seemed that the question did not have a logical connection to therapy. But he never considered any question to be trite or stupid and he never left a concern unaddressed "lest it become a festering mental sore."

Having pondered for some minutes, he replied, "It derives from the historical desire for belonging." Whether intended or not, the reply calmed the patient, and the session continued.

Naming operates in reverse, one generation perpetuating memory by transferring names to another. Some say it is "tradition" at work. Perhaps it is? But more likely, we all experience a deeply rooted desire for reincarnation, Manfred thought, on the day that his grandson spoke for the first time.

The toddler, who talked in words of his own fabrication and scooted four-limbed on the hard terrazzo floors, suddenly stopped. He hauled his chubby bottom onto his grandfather's favorite pouffe and looked directly into the old man's fathomless eyes. Later, Abel would describe his grandfather's eyes to his beloved. "They were profound and luminous, evoking Solomon's pools." Fascinated as always by youth's irrepressible energy, Manfred observed Abel. He waited, sensing that a miracle of human evolution was about to reoccur. He was right.

"M . . . a . . . n . . . n . . . y."

The diction was clear. From the mouth of a toddler, letters cohered to form a name. The old man felt as if his grandson had awarded him a special title, more valuable than his multiple honorary doctorates. Each sound was punctuated by precise gaps. From then on, he would always be "Manny" to his grandson who would come to regard his grandfather as the epitome of the finest qualities of humankind.

Children create language anew, he thought. *They count in different time. To them, we are all ageless!*

The toddler saw his grandfather beaming, which thrilled him into action. Pushing himself off the pouffe, he continued his crawling. His grandfather had a name! Until then, he had just been a shape of towering love and a source of fluid babble. Now he was a friend, a guide, and a confidant who would conduct him through the pitfalls of youth.

Abel had spoken his first word. He and Manny were joined by the bond of language. *Old and young, an unbreakable chain,* the elderly man thought. Though Abel could not recall his mother's face (except from a faded photograph), through his grandfather's abiding love and steady hands, he encountered her warmth and tenderness.

Many years later, when he left a magnificent hotel on the banks of a lake in the heart of Europe on a boat named "Black Cat" with the tanned girl of his dreams, Abel thought: *My mother's spirit dwelt in her father's touch . . . in his twinkling eyes, which could penetrate anyone and anything . . . in the subtle patterns of an old man's unwavering compassion despite what had befallen him and his people, and all who have suffered through the ages.*

Sometimes the pain of his patients dripped like a slowly measured liquid drug hooked hypodermically into a vein. Some cried on the soft pillows of his couch. Others revealed their untreated wounds in extreme grimaces and unsightly twitches. In spite of all his efforts, Manfred Isaacs knew that some were beyond healing. He called those "the adamantine ones," applying its literal and mythical meanings. Shuddering in the embrace of the old man, a woman once said to him, "My baby was murdered and its fat boiled to make soap." The words ripped out of her. As soon as her catharsis began, so it fled. Despite the hold he had on her, she collapsed in the hallway of Manny's apartment, never to regain either her equilibrium or her sanity.

He did not ask for payment from any survivor. He taught Abel that "victors have been vanquished by the futility of claiming ownership of God." On a fragile antique table at the door of his home near the Jaffa Gate, a brass plate lay. Some, but not all, left money there. At times Manfred Isaacs (who had seen "clubs of humiliation wielded by youths drunk on the alcohol of bigotry" and heard the breaking of glass storefronts shattered by "rocks of ruin") returned donations to those whom he felt could not afford to pay.

A recollection came to the psychologist. *Money from a theft,* he thought. *I traced it before it became fungible and I gave it back to a woman from the poorest part of the city when I heard the confession spluttered by a man on the couch. Then I told the patient that, although peace may never come to him, I would aid and abet him to locate the devious impulse that lurked in his mind so that he could "arrest" it before it could escape to commit more crimes.*

Applying a softer voice than usual, Manfred spoke to his little Abel, "Cain slew his brother and was forced into a lifetime of wandering in shame." The boy listened well each time his grandfather spoke and kissed him on his cheeks. "Remember," he added, "pain is the perception of pain. If the perception is removed, then pain itself follows meekly through the exit." Doctor Isaacs knew that *children understand much more than adults think they do.* Thus lessons passed from grandfather to grandson, like the whispers of far-off winds.

When approached by "a person of stature" from the Office of Nazi Investigations who came to ask if he would be an expert witness, Manfred Isaacs replied enigmatically, quoting Sigmund Freud's comment on human aggression.

"It is," he said, his brow furrowing into deep trenches, "an original, self-subsisting, instinctual disposition in Man . . . the greatest impediment to civilization."

Then he nodded his agreement. The official was elated, for he knew that in Manfred Isaacs, the renowned Jerusalemite who was considered the preeminent expert on the psychological effects of trauma and shock, he had achieved a triple result. *Eyewitness, doctor, patient,* the emissary thought. *New condemnatory evidence. The Lion of Judah will be calmed!—but only when Justice is finally done.*

What Manfred Isaacs, the distinguished psychologist, demanded was most unusual, almost unheard of, and certainly not readily sanctioned by precedent. But he was an exceptional personage and he was needed for the trial. It was not easy to refuse the paramount "Holocaust Healer" in Israel.

"Not permitted!" the chief prosecutor told him.

"If you do not agree, then I shall not be a witness in your court!" he replied adamantly. His thick foreign accent shook the air.

The resulting silence did not disturb Manfred, who was used to all the contrivances of communication.

"Alright." The reply was reluctant. "I shall grant an exception, only this once."

Thus the price of testimony had been paid for the privilege

of attendance . . . and a child named Abel, dressed immaculately in a scout's uniform with a scarf around his throat, came to be seated behind his grandfather in the highest court of the land. Manny's back was upright, the wide neck rigid and the straight shoulders set squarely. His long beard's irregular strands trailed onto his chest. The old man projected an aura of silent dignity. His arms were folded on his protruding stomach. His eyes gleamed with the penetrating brightness of moral conviction.

The courtroom was austere. Bereavement seemed to hang in the corners like bats. *Truth spits out of dark lips!* Manfred Isaacs thought, *Until this trial, Evil shrank beneath the skirts of cowardice.* Soon he too would enter the witness box. He had always been ready for such a moment. *My testimony will be like a single grain in the multitudinous sands of the Negev desert. I shall walk on a moving surface of drifts, heated by the suns of torment! But though I burn, walk I shall!*

In the early days, before he went up to Jerusalem, when he was a farmer-soldier on the Kibbutz, from the spout of a silo he had seen grain pour in fluid currents of seed. *Such are the stories of our forebears*, he thought then, and again when he received the call from the chief prosecutor.

Before taking the stand, Manfred Isaacs formulated his statements, which would be more than answers. In his voice of conviction he declared the monster in the dock to be "insanely sane," based on his examination of the imprisoned patient, whom Manfred would have killed with his bare hands had be not been acting as a doctor, convinced that the justice of the Holy Land would prevail for this now-pathetically unempowered, thin, bespectacled, uprooted, unrepentant, man, alone amongst those he wished to annihilate. Manfred elucidated his opinion. His diagnosis would not only counteract any defense of "unfit to stand trial by reason of insanity," but also "insane at the time of commission of crimes." With the two words "insanely sane," Manfred encapsulated the enormity of the prisoner's responsibility for the unspeakable perpetration of horrors against the innocent.

The prosecutor rose and a hush spread through the room.

The accused sat ramrod straight. But his face twitched uncontrollably, and his eyes bulged behind his lenses. The sparse oily hair on his scalp adhered in pencil-thin lines to his almost-bald head. Despite the prosecutor's inner rage, the prisoner reminded him of an admonition in Deuteronomy: *The Chosen people shall not become like the pagans around them who discolor their skin and decorate the bodies of their dead.*

The man in the dock seemed as rigid as a plank. Beside him, watching his every nervous tremble, two policemen in blue, the sons of survivors, stood at attention. *Their right hands have not forgotten their cunning*, the prosecutor assured himself, recalling an extract from a biblical psalm. *They hold the cold iron handles of pistols. Their fingers itch to reach the triggers of their weapons. We shall not be passive victims again! Never! Never!*

Drawing a breath, he hesitated a moment, before stating, "This man . . ." he pointed stiffly, his short arm acting as the proverbial "long arm of the law," jutting from the wide arc of his robe, "is charged with horrific, almost indescribable, crimes against humanity! He was the architect of 'the final solution,' the mass murder of millions of Jewish people!" The immensity of the prosecutor's outrage struck all who heard the accusation.

Retribution, like hawks, seemed to circle. Wind ruffled their wingtips. Even the large blades of the turning fans could not alter their flight. A great stir rippled through the audience, the jurists, the witnesses, and the leaves of the law books.

"We seek the death penalty, especially promulgated by the Knesset for this trial! We ask for it in spite of its limitations, for death is not a punishment! It is the ultimate price to be paid for his guilt! It is the only and the ultimate tool we have in this case. 'An eye for an eye!' He must be removed from the face of the earth. The gibbet beyond the gates of our city shall serve the purpose!"

Transformed by the awesomeness of his responsibility, the prosecutor felt elevated, as if hoisted upon the shoulders of the dead whom he represented. Almost shouting, almost weeping, he had become the public ventriloquist of slaughtered multitudes.

Representing the *Bleitung*, a newspaper of the town of Berchtesgaden in the Obersalzberg region of Germany, not far from the Austrian border, a young journalist tried to expunge collective guilt by attending the trial. At its conclusion, he wrote of the opening address:

> Cowering in the corners, Death's lonely Messenger seemed to hear the prosecutor's words. A gloat of triumph choked in its throat. Sounds like hammers nailing a scaffold blared in its ears. Then, escorted by ushers of the deceased, for the duration of the accusation the Messenger flung itself furiously away from the court. Deprived of its assigned role, it caught and rode the uproarious wind that rose like a banshee in Jerusalem. But as it fled, the Messenger stopped to test the rough rope of the noose. It was too strong to be broken, growing tighter with each word, firmer with each pull. On damaged wings it passed over the Church of the Agony overlooking the Garden of Gethsemane. It did not see the flowers blooming there. When it reached Heichal Shlomo, the Great Synagogue on King George Street, it hesitated as if the Old Temple were raised high again in gilded stone. Millions of fluttering souls impeded the Messenger's flight. It waited as if gathered up by the crowd that demanded to know the reason for its presence. Then, suddenly, the souls were gone, scattered to the four corners of the earth. Resigned to its expulsion, the Messenger opened its gaping mouth and, in a voice of failure, declared: "'The Trial of Denunciation' has begun. Nothing human or inhuman can impede it!" Then it fled in shame and humiliation!

∞ ∞ ∞

"Close your eyes."

The boy obeyed. His grandfather's words never inflicted any anxiety.

"Tilt your head toward the sun."

Manfred Isaacs took the boy's face in his hands. Abel felt their cool firmness. In that grasp lay the surety that children crave from a grandparent, even more than from a mother or father. They were sitting on a small balcony. The old man and the boy had a direct view of the Temple Mount in the Old City, which Grandfather often said was "bathed from morning to night in supernal light." A cloud hung high. It formed into an anvil, shaped by the condensation of vapor at a high altitude. Then it began to disassemble. Despite intervention by the restive cloud, the sun shone brightly in the sky over the City of Peace. Manfred Isaacs directed the boy's head upward and outward, turning it gently.

"When I tell you, stop squeezing your eyelids. Let them be loosely relaxed, but not open." Manfred waited, squinting to avoid the direct penetration of the sun's rays into his own eyes.

"Now! Tell me what you see."

Abel did as his grandfather told him.

"Bright red," he replied, thinking this could be a game. He loved to play games with his grandfather.

"Remember that color," the old man said. "It is the color of the blood of all who suffered, and still do, from generation unto generation." He spoke in an ancient voice.

"But be not blinded to it, or by it!" His words were as kind as his hands, for despite his size and influence, he neither scared nor punished with language. Instead, his words, though not fully understood by one so young, seemed to soothe.

The boy, who became a man far quicker than his grandfather would have liked, remembered what he had been taught by Manfred Isaacs. He remembered, too, the dead look in the eyes of the monstrous convict when the sentence of hanging was handed down by the presiding judge. The memory dug into Abel like spurs into the flanks of a wild horse, and he knew that he had to do something about it. So, like his grandfather before him, he determined that he would become an agent of justice, in his own way.

Despite the immensity of suffering cast upon him, and even until the day he died a hushed death while the sun reflected its glorious rays through the windows and glass doors of his apartment that lay open to anyone who would enter, a benevolent smile still graced Manny's face.

He spoke his last words, the names of his beloved wife, Rachel, and his daughter, Ruth (both of blessed memory), and his grandson, Abel, now the youngest captain in the army. Then, as a last gesture of faith and confidence in a will greater than his own, he raised both hands to his face and closed his own eyelids in submission to and welcome of the inevitable.

Thus Manfred Isaacs—survivor of three concentration camps, counselor to hundreds of patients here in his own land and from other lands—took his last breath without allowing torment a final intrusion.

"May the Almighty rest his soul and may his grandson, Abel Isaacs, who took his grandfather's last name, be comforted among the Mourners of Zion!" the Rabbi of the Mount said.

All present moved nearer. They waited their turns to cast earth onto the body lying six feet below, wrapped in a simple shroud without a coffin, as is the custom. A clod of soil from a shovel tumbled onto his grandfather's body. Abel heard it thump. He thought he could see the smile that graced the old man's face and the sparkle in his eyes whenever his grandson embraced him. In that moment he felt the lined, steady hands on his face as he turned to the sun and saw the crimson that Manny had told him was always there, "if you look for it." He had learned the lesson well.

"Rest in peace," Abel whispered, wanting so much to cry more. The galloping cavalry of Manfred Isaacs's courage thundered past the cemetery of hope. At the saddest moment of his grandson's life, optimism rose like a wall and defended him against the onslaught of grief.

∞∞∞

The electric train glided out of Zurich's Haupt Bahnhoff.

At first it moved slowly. Then it gained speed as it wended its way through mazes of tracks and webs of switching points. On either side, kilometers of factories, warehouses, and buildings of glass, steel, brick, and concrete drifted by.

Abel looked out of the window. He was pleased to be traveling in Switzerland to his new job as chief of security for an esteemed hotel group. He had been picked from a group of foreign applicants because he had exceptional military training and experience. He watched the structures, which seemed personified as if they were staring at him with primitive purpose. Despite the urban threat, he felt calm, as was his natural inclination, especially when facing the unknown. Having experienced sniper fire from invisible sources, he knew how to guard himself. His grandfather had taught him: "Do not act impulsively. Act properly in all circumstances."

"And, remember to breathe, expanding your lungs sideways so that you may be calm in all ways when you do."

Buildings gave way to pastures. Farms and small villages clustered around central churches, their steeples needling the clear summer sky. Occasionally a medieval castle blustered on a hilltop. Millennia may not have dented their permanence in the countryside, but the fast-moving train ripped them out of sight remorselessly. Like unwelcome weeds invading fertile soils, they soon were gone.

Inside the first-class compartment, save for pleasant vibrations, silence prevailed. Discreet signs forbade noise of any sort. Rippling lighted notices and the occasional artificially produced lilting female voice announced the toilet locations, beverage and food counters, and passing stations in four languages. Everything occurred in subdued perfection, as if decibels were the enemy of refinement.

The train rounded a corner. An elongated valley appeared. Rolls of plastic-covered hay dotted the landscape. Farming implements, open-sided sheds filled with puzzle stacks of triangularly cut firewood, vessels, and tractors appeared and then disappeared like vanishing dominoes. But Abel saw no people. Only occasionally a distant car moved on the roads that meandered before connecting like blood vessels to arterial highways. Ribbons of roads rose on stilts. Highways perched on arches. Like ancient Roman aqueducts, bridges leaped across deep ravines, sparkling crystalline streams, and seemingly endless farmlands of celadon green.

Abel tilted his head back against the white cotton cover on the headrest before settling deeper into the plush velveteen of his striped seat. He looked at the passengers. Diagonally opposite him, a man dressed in an expensive silk suit slept through the magnificent scenery. Abel wondered, *How can anyone be bored in an environment like this?* He thought for a moment, then concluded, as his grandfather had once told him: "The price of neutrality is detachment from reality."

He looked up. Concave Plexiglas windows curved the light into panoramic vaults. Through a pane high above he saw a glider. Its wide-spanned wings appeared to rest in the sky like gossamers. It was riding thermal drafts, at ease with its environment. Adrift in a sea of blue between two opposing massifs, the powerless aircraft began to gain impulsive momentum. Temporarily master of its domain, thrust by the unseen hand of wind, it rose and fell as if on a tide of air. Then it spiraled beneath the dome of sky in wide, circling patterns. Its fragile frame, like an illusion, seemed to bend with elastic grace. All of a sudden Abel noticed something.

Astonishing patches, he thought as he stared. When the glider pitched at an angle, one shape appeared as another disappeared. Alternating as if by graciousness, red seemed to emerge, radiate, and then depart as white superseded it. Squinting for better focus, he recognized the markings. *Squares with central intersecting lines*, he observed. *Audaciously simple!*

Abel had always been fascinated by the symmetry and significance of flags.

"Do they represent patriotism or pigment?" he had once asked Manny, showing off his youthful articulateness. His grandfather did not answer immediately, as was his habit, for he believed that the silence between words often had the greatest impact.

"Show me a flag without blood on it, whether visible or invisible, and I will show you a nation of deceivers!" the old man replied finally.

How blessed I was to have him, Abel thought, as the glider drifted from view and the valley passed along the glinting steel rails.

The train did not stop at the stations of small towns along

the route. *Express trains of the famous, ultra efficient Schweizerische Bundesbahnen, known as the "SBB," ride fast and with hard determination through the Swiss countryside,* Abel decided. *They benefit from a privileged right of way!* This one had taken to burrowing at high speed into the railway channels cut into the slopes of hills. The terrain had changed—subtly at first, then more definitely.

Now vineyards appeared, from the hilltops to the watery edges of a huge lake. In some places their gnarled stems and persistent stalks had taken hold, clinging to the soil. Through cracks in concrete retaining walls, between rocks, on the borders separating houses, and right down to the flat concrete platforms, they emerged in defiant determination. They even crept up the sides of canals built to conduct melting snow into the gushing torrents that feed the grand lake's insatiable thirst.

> For centuries vintners, who trace their heritage back to Benedictine monks more than eight centuries earlier, have faithfully worked their family plots. When the light is right, a visitor may be forgiven for imagining the orderly land arrangements becoming blocks of polished jade or of burnished gold before liquefying in the rush to the shores of Lac Léman, which divides and links two nations, Switzerland and France.

Before he left home, Abel had read that descriptive passage in a guidebook about the area. He felt excited. *A new beginning*, he thought, feeling the press of history around him as the train slowed for its approach. A frisson of exhilaration ran up his spine. As the train drew to a stop with a slight hiss of halting steel wheels, a sign came into view:

MONTREUX

On the buildings, across façades, and upon metal, glass, stone, and plaster, he saw spray-painted graffiti. The ugly evidence of gangs, the slogans of immorality, blighted old and modern buildings alike. *A metastasizing cancer.* Abel wondered how such desecration could be permitted in a country of exemplary principles and tolerance.

For three years of full-time duty and more in the reserve forces, Abel had fought, protected, drilled with his men, marched, attacked, defended, crawled, climbed, rushed, shot, and held ground under the extreme conditions of war. He was no stranger to the challenges of violence and yet, at heart, he was still the gentle boy who had played with his grandfather.

His idyllic trainride contrasted in Abel's mind with the cardinal experience of his life as a soldier in his home country.

"We live in a tough neighborhood. Don't worry. Follow my orders!" his commander had told him on more than one occasion of potential ambush. Abel had learned how to control his thoughts and actions under duress.

The brigadier, known to his soldiers (even the religious ones) as "God," was fond of making up his own clichés. "Don't be heroes," he liked to say. "I don't like to bury my boys with medals. But do your duty every time!" A career officer for decades, he had a mission to accomplish and the soldiers he needed to implement it. But he never forgot: *They are too young to die!*

The commander's voice rang clearly. Gunning the engine, he led the way forward. Behind him Abel and his small platoon approached a white blockhouse not far from the zigzagging border. In the air above, a projectile whistled ominously. The infantrymen heard it. Then the blockhouse disintegrated, just yards ahead of their position. Dust filled the air. Within the cloud, flames erupted; then, smothered by dirt and smoke, they vanished.

Abel's cell phone squawked once. He caught the signal and went in. A metal case lay on its side, battered and warped by intense heat. Its lid was still sealed shut. Several bodies lay amid the debris—ghostly pale and still. The rest of the platoon was checking the area. *There seemed to be no survivors!*

Abel knelt beside the locked container. It was too hot to touch. Withdrawing a small fire extinguisher from his backpack, he swathed the case in foam. Metal popped. In the dirt, something moved. A small hand reached out. The fingernails were gray, the skin ashen. It reached for something. Abel recognized the *L* shape of an improvised pipe bomb.

It took only a second for him to release his pistol, obliterating the silence. The click of the safety catch coming off was deafening. He pulled the trigger several times, very fast and calculatingly, but not in anger, just in defense of his men and of himself. The movement ceased. Blood leaked and soaked. The riddled body on the ground was a worthless memorial to the collapse of normalcy.

Abel put his weapon back in its holster and pulled a listening device from his pack. He went to work. When he was done, notebooks and plans, diaries, sketched maps, and confessions filled plastic bags. Abel's mind went numb. His duty was done. Not far off a bulldozer's engine growled in readiness. He withdrew. With the records of aborted casualties weighing heavily in his satchel now, Abel announced clearly into the specially configured "God phone" on loan to him from the brigadier: "Done!"

He did not know that his commander, whose huge nose plagued him constantly, had quite a few such phones—all for different purposes.

The *Gare* stood at the base of a hill that led to a mountain, which led to another mountain, until they became the chain of the Alps. He exited on Platform One and walked the tunnel, amazed by the contrast in cleanliness between the Bahnhoff where he had embarked and the Gare at which he had just arrived. *But even in this perfect country there are "unfortunates,"* he thought.

Abel remembered the image of the woman on the concrete floor of the Zurich station where he had seen her before boarding the train. Her head was bowed, her hands barely strong enough to plead, her legs missing. As an officer charged with cracking safes and opening metal trunks under battle conditions, he was keenly observant. With absolute clarity he could recall every detail of her clothes, her face, her dirty fingers, the emaciated look of her forearms, even the number and the denominations of the shiny coins in the soiled beret that lay in the folds of her tattered dress. He did not know her history. *Could she be a survivor,* he wondered, as if they were a special species of humankind. *Is that possible? She looks too young. But one never knows.*

An escalator took him to the Avenue des Alps. On the way down, an artificial ceiling with squares, constructed and suspended on ultra thin wires held small pots framed in each aperture. Flowers bloomed, making a dangling garden that floated above one, when going up, and hovered below one, when going down. *Admirable use of space,* he observed, *like a miniature version of the Hanging Gardens of Babylon.* In this small, beleaguered, but proud country where *every inch counts,* Abel liked what he saw.

In the army, he was used to duffel bags. The canvas straps were thrown over his shoulders so that the weight would be distributed evenly over his upper body. Abel walked confidently along the declining avenue. He did not need a map, having memorized the layout of the town from the information board at the station. The back and sides of the sprawling Fairmont Le Montreux Palace Hotel showed distinct signs of age, yet it still clung to its dissipating dignity like a faded dowager.

There will be plenty time to explore later, he thought as he continued with a determined stride, albeit on a route longer than was necessary because he was not yet familiar with the winding alleyways of the old town that the locals used as shortcuts. Reaching the "C" corner, where the Rue du Lac and the Grand Rue greet each other in a permanent handshake, he continued in a northwesterly direction. On the Rue du Lac itself, just a short distance ahead on the right, he saw the four-storied villa.

Flowering trees stood before the building. It looked rich, frothy, and abundant, like two Italian wedding cakes joined in the center. As he gazed up at the building's façade, the high arched windows seemed to call for attention from pedestrians. A pillared terrace accented the rooftop. In the small passage to the left of the structure he found the door, rang the bell, and walked in.

"Fabienne," she announced, without being asked. This was the young woman who worked as a receptionist and a public relations assistant manager in the hotel buildings.

Immediately, Abel was struck by her beauty and dazzling

smile. Her accent was as French as her name, and her voice had a tinkle like ice clinking in a glass. Its rhythm and timbre thrilled him. Her hair flowed in dark curling waves. Her skin reminded him of ripening olives on the ancient trees growing out of dry soil in the hills of Judea, where he had spent many days walking and picnicking with his grandfather, who had taught him the meaning of life.

"Bonjour, Monsieur."

Although he could speak some French and German (Manny insisted that "linguistic skills enhance intellect and promote thought"), Abel realized immediately that the lingua franca of the famous international hotel school where he had come to take up his position would probably be English.

"Thank you," he replied, lowering the canvas bag and extending a remarkably dry hand in greeting. Despite the heat, he never perspired much.

"You are beautiful."

Like a slippery fish, the compliment slid off his tongue before he could catch it. The color of her cheeks darkened. He expected a reprimand for his effrontery. But she just blushed her acceptance. Almost imperceptibly, her eyelids fluttered. *The frangible wings of a butterfly!* He caught the sign. Something exploded. This time it was not an artillery shell on a blockhouse in a damned place.

The blooms on the curved reception desk seemed to surround her in a protective embrace, but they could not hide her delicate perfection, which sent his soldier's heart running amok into unidentified territory.

Abel's attic room in the villa held a secret, which he soon discovered.

Ironically, the simple accommodation of the *chef de sécurité* for the Lac Léman Hotel group of the finest hostelries in the city allowed a glimpse of the water and the mountains beyond. A crack of space between the buildings may have been the result of a municipal accident or an architectural intention. Either way, Abel could look beyond the traffic on the avenues, see the gathering of waves on the lake, and stare in wonder at the chameleon colors of the mountains, as sun, clouds, rainbows, and moonlight cast their magic upon sloping woodlands, naked rock, and snowy caps.

Nature's exploits moved him deeply. "They are compliments to the Almighty," Manny said. Those words had become his own.

Although Abel had fallen in love with Fabienne from the first moment he saw her, and she with him, nothing prepared him for the disintegration and reconstruction of self that were the by-products of their steadfast love. They relished their free time together. At night, they crept into each other's rooms and lay chest-to-chest throughout the warm hours of darkness—entwined, melting like candle wax, until the emergence of premature dawns.

When nightmares tore at the fabric of his subconscious (especially when the thin gray hand of a child reached for an explosive device), she rocked him back to reason. She would rise, returning with cool compresses to wipe his face, to soothe him, and to restrain the devilish memories.

When their paths crossed in any of the four premier hotels where they were employed, they exchanged simultaneous flashes of yearning. All they wanted was to be together. On holidays, when others deputized for them, they explored Lavaux, called "a region between water and sky." On their journeys among the old castles in the hilltops, they examined their love without conscious investigation. They let it lead, following as willing disciples of its supple but determined power.

From Château d'Ouchy to Château d'Chillon (where, in Lord Byron's poem, a prisoner languished in a dungeon, chained to a pillar as were his brothers, who died near him) they explored old towns, vineyards, trails, and watercourses.

They took ferries, trains, and buses. On the promenade that runs the full length of Montreux's shoreline they strolled, thrilled by magnificent arrays of summer flowers. In manicured parks they lay on soft, fluffy grass and fooled like adoring adolescents among the statues, or pretended to tease the busts of great musicians, or watched dogs plunge into fresh water pools. They rode funiculars. In small cafés they ate sugary and aromatic crepes, and licked creamy gelato from brimming cones.

But most of all they cherished the hours of walking with fingers intertwined like the vines that filled terrace after terrace of the *poudingues*—ubiquitous rocky plots that clung to the hillsides and extended to the shores of the lake. Together they tasted the wines of Dezaley, Villette, St. Saphorin, and Chardonnay. In the hills and valleys they discovered the foods of delight and the delicateness of feelings, which would become the ingredients of their lasting memories. On particularly hot days they swam in the cold water of the lake and sunned themselves on the smooth-pebbled beaches of sheltered alcoves.

Their skin grew brown and shimmered in the tremulous light.

They spoke of life, of love, of freedom, and of the gift of children.

They were happy.

"Our love is full to bursting, like grapes," Fabienne said, as they nibbled cured cheese, which left a tangy aftertaste hardly diminished by a fine blush rosé wine, at La Maison du Gruyere, the last stop of the "little train" at Pringy—an almost midway point between Fribourg, where history and chocolate coexist in abundance, and Lausanne, a city that celebrates in the splendor of French trimmings.

It was there they learned that the noble English poet had stayed in the Hotel d'Agleterre, inscribing verses about captivity in the dungeon of the Château d'Chillon. But they were alive, free, and filled with the joy of togetherness.

Fabienne had an unusual hobby. She would light aromatic candles and then watch them burn down until the wicks snuffed out and the perfumed tendrils rose, which she captured in wide-necked glass containers.

"Bottled smoke," she answered, when Abel asked her what the collection on the window ledge of her room was.

"Why do you do that?" he asked.

"So that when I release it, it can blow away," she said.

"May that never happen to our love!"

On the day she told him about a certain event that would soon take place, they had just come from the "Marche," an open-air market in the old city of Vevey. The flavor of summer fruit still lingered on their lips with subtle persistence. In a small square on an incline, orchestral music escaped from a church. The compulsion of the sweet sounds drew them to the church's Gothic heights.

Linked at the elbows, as Fabienne enjoyed doing—she called it a "chain d'amour"—they began to stroll through the cobbled alleyway that led up to the church. Broad stone stairs paved the way to a fountain in the middle of the square, its water tumbling from the spigot formed by a swan's jutting copper head. Ahead of them lay heavy wooden doors inlaid with black crosses. As they approached, they passed a young mother breast-feeding her infant in the shade of a cherry tree. Its green branches were laden with fruit and festooned with yellow streamers to dispel marauding birds.

The interior was blessedly cool.

The back pews in the nave were vacant. But where the transepts intersected, the rows were full. Parents were taking photographs. A music teacher led children, from two to five years old, all holding miniature violins. "Frère Jacques" echoed off the concave ceilings. In the choir stalls, under the direction of a young woman dressed in a long dark-blue skirt and a finely embroidered white cotton blouse, the children played.

"Close harmony," Fabienne whispered as she squeezed Abel's fingers, emphasizing her double entendre. The sound of the instruments en masse rose and spread through the chambers. Bells rang. The clanging was interspersed with the music of the children. It made everyone smile, inviting applause by the town itself, which seemed to have stopped to listen to the accomplishment of its very own *petite ensemble.*

Abel and Fabienne were delighted by the children's disciplined talent and the range of their playing. Under the guidance of their teacher, the group ended the familiar tune. Immediately a four-year-old girl prodigy rose and played the last stanzas of Mozart's hauntingly beautiful Turkish violin concerto.

Just then, Fabienne whispered hoarsely into Abel's ear. In place of her usual bright tones, an edge of concern made itself evident. She spoke about the forthcoming event: A group of old Nazis would be meeting in the Grand Hotel, the crown jewel of the hotel group.

"I heard about it at the Department of Public Relations . . ."

Her voice trailed as the final notes drifted off almost indiscernibly. Abel felt the swell of excitement that precedes a rare opportunity. Perhaps it was the music of children, or a sudden recollection that would come upon him unexpectedly, as it did now. He thought of the caramelized ginger squares and alluring notes that his beloved would leave on the pillow where her head had lain, after a particularly bad nightmare had beset his sleep and left scars on the pockmarked surface of his disrupted slumber. The culminating words were always: "Endless Love."

The little girl violinist lowered her miniaturized replica of one of the most famous violins ever made—the del Gesù, created by Giuseppe Guarneri in the first half of the eighteenth century from wood chilled by a particularly cold winter. At one time, the original had belonged to Henri Vieuxtemps, a Belgian violin prodigy, composer, and court soloist to Tsar Alexander II.

The girl's father, a cabinetmaker from the outskirts of Geneva, had copied it in a quarter of its size and placed it in a wooden box beside the crib of his daughter on the day she was born, "so that its beautiful sound may be the lullaby of her dreams," he whispered to his sleeping child.

Its music had now fallen silent as the child allowed it to rest quietly in her small hands.

Back in his room in the attic of the villa in Montreux, Abel sat, shrouded in a black cloak. His mind churned relentlessly like ingredients being mixed together in a steel urn. Then, fury planted a seditious seed. It began to root and grow like a poisonous, unreachable weed. Abel wondered if it would seek to strangle the creeper of love into which it wove. As the internal struggle waged, he realized with rising relief that *ahead lies a day in history*. It would hold the presence or absence of consolation, and he felt compelled to see it through, without anger and with the cautious, meticulous planning that he been trained to carry out.

Near the famous casino where rich and ostentatious patrons gathered in the salon privée, away from the public eye, the legendary Rose Room of the Grand Hotel du Lac sparkled in brazen magnificence. Pristine white tablecloths covered the dining room tables. Silverware and fine china glittered. A smorgasbord of trout, salmon, sole, crab, ragout of lamb, beef, venison, wild hare, eel in aspic, other exotic meats and seafood dishes, salads, rare celery in wolfberries, fruits, custards, soufflés, and jellied pastries were displayed on long trestle tables spread from the arched entrance to the bay windows overlooking the splendid garden and glimmering waters below.

Uniforms and long dresses, predominantly in red and black, flowed in cotton, chiffon, and silk.

Medals flashed. A toast to the leader who committed suicide in a bunker was proposed. The decrepit general guffawed, raised his glass, and clapped one-handedly against a wasted thigh so that his flared breeches puffed out.

"Today is the anniversary of the Leader's rise to power!"

"*Prost!*"

"*Trinken!*"

"*Essen!*"

The toast seemed to constrict his voice, which no longer held the power it once had to praise the paradigm of wickedness.

Men tried to stiffen their scoliotic spines in vain attempts at glorification. Rickety arms shot out in salutation. But they wavered and shook with age. In Bavarian cut glass decanters and long-stemmed glasses, Muskattrollinger red wine, like blood, shimmered through the helical grooves of cut-glass flutes. Elderly women drank Gewürztraminer and Kir Royale as they tried to hide their sagging bodies inside whalebone corsets beneath their gala gowns.

The Rose Room lived up to its reputation as the most splendid venue in all of Montreux. Inside its luxurious hall hand-selected soft blooms wept with color, as if they remembered the days of transient glory.

None of the members of the Order of Guido von List or their spouses or mistresses wore rings, necklaces, brooches, or other jewelry, all of which was locked away in their hotel rooms' safes. Only General Heine had a small, single insignia pinned into one broad lapel of his uniform, having left his magnificent bejeweled iron cross, presented to him by the Leader himself, in custody as directed by the security chief. In his mouth, when his lips, darkened to purple by angina pectoris, curled back, a gold incisor glinted. Martial music boomed. Horns and drums rattled the glass windows of the solarium. Passersby, down below, looked up at the light of the ballroom, enjoying the celebration vicariously and wondering what was on the menu that night.

An old woman paused on the promenade. She was permanently bent over and did not have to lean to smell the perfume of rambling roses near the walkway.

Before the light of dawn garlanded the lake that morning, a note had been placed under the door of each room of the Grand Hotel du Lac, starting with the splendid suite of General Otto Heine, founder of the order. In flowing typescript, it read:

> Dear Guests: I regret to inform you that we are aware of a robbery plot in the hotel. Therefore, management respectfully requests that you place all jewelry and other items of value in the safes located in the closets of your suites. The head of security will visit each guest today to inform you in person of the new code to be used. Please call Reception to arrange your appointment. Only a few minutes will be required to explain the situation. This is a temporary measure, until the threat is removed. Management apologizes for any inconvenience, but is confident that you will agree that the security of our residents and their valuables is our utmost priority. We assure our esteemed guests that all measures are being taken to eradicate this unusual situation and we emphasize that no interruption of functions in the Grand Hotel du Lac shall occur as a result. Thank you for your understanding and cooperation.
>
> Chef de Sécurité, Groupe d'hôtels, Lac Léman.

In a guesthouse on the other side of the lake from where the group of hotels stood, the proprietor was speaking to those present. "Six days the vichy collaborated with the invaders of

France. On the seventh, they rested. It was a rancid respite, like wine turning to vinegar!" The Frenchman spat in disgust. None among the "Twos" or the "Threes"—second- and third-generation survivors of the Holocaust—responded to his caustic remark. They merely listened to him say what he wanted to say—this man who, with his wife, owned a plain establishment, simply called *La Maison*. He went on to remind those present of a headline in the German newspaper *Völkischer Beobachter* after the Evian Conference in July 1938, in his hometown:

Nobody Wants Them!

"I am as ashamed of the collaborators as I am of the perpetrators," he said, then added, "on both sides of this celebrated lake!"

The proprietor—an old resistance fighter—felt heat in his cheeks. It was not the by-product of wine, although he held a glass of claret from the Bordeaux region and thrust it out to his guests in a gesture of hospitality. His face flushed in anger.

Many years had passed. However Claude still carried a concealed weapon, tucked into the broad band of his leather belt, beneath his ruffled shirt. *Just in case I come across one of them! It is never too late to kill a rat, lest it spread the plague*, he thought for the thousandth time or more. His gun had a name. "The Gem," he called it, thinking of how polished it was.

The weapon was unholstered. Its cool metallic touch felt good against the loose skin of his hip. The gun was in immaculate condition. He remembered the last time he had fired a bullet directly into a man's heart. Infamous words of hatred, quoted in an interview that retired Major Josef Hell obviously felt privileged to hold with Adolf Hitler in 1922, had echoed in the Frenchman's head. The statements had stood like trees in a forest of ignominy. Pulling the trigger to kill a high-ranking collaborator had been an act of eager defiance.

The owner of La Maison was not Jewish. He was a retired jeweler who now ran a small establishment listed in a travel guidebook with a white rolling logo on its cover. It contained a rather exaggerated description of a humble boarding house. But it was clean and comfortable, and it offered haute cuisine on account of the fact that his fat and jovial wife was "a magician of culinary delights," as a Tour de France official once wrote in their visitor's book.

Claude knew what it meant to stand firm.

The national motto of France rang in his ears: "Liberté, égalité, fraternité."

"For France . . . for freedom . . . for all!" he declared, not translating but pronouncing. "It is my honor to accommodate you! *I* want *you!*" he said.

They looked at him, as one. "Viva!" came the united chorus of the Twos and the Threes.

Claude's color heightened, this time with pleasure, as he thought of what *resistance* really meant. Laughing, he said, "I know the difference between a Jew and a jewel!"

Some looked puzzled. Others joined him in the joke. All rejoiced in the true meaning.

Abel met with Otto Heine first.

If I convince him, the rest will be easy, he reasoned. The general greeted him with a resounding click of heels on the marble floor of the vestibule of the Purple Fuchsia Suite situated on the penthouse floor of the Grand Hotel. All the suites were named after flowers.

Otto Heine stared through his gold-rimmed monocle. Neither of his rheumy eyes blinked. Abel thought that the lids appeared brittle and hairless. The teeth were yellow, except for one upper incisor, which fluoresced with an inlaid precious metal. A counterclockwise crooked cross glared malevolently from a buttonhole.

"Jawol, ich verstehe," the general replied, responding to the notice that he and the others had received, though with a disparaging note of shrillness in his voice, as if testing the limits of acquiescence, and speaking in German inside a French Swiss hotel.

Otto Heine had taken and given orders all of his life. Thus it was in character for him to accept the new numerals to be entered into the safe's electronic panel as given to him, the leader of the visiting group, by a man who, although young and "Jewish looking," nonetheless acted and spoke in a highly authoritative manner. "For good reason, Monsieur!" Abel told him politely, speaking in French and not elaborating further. All the other members of the order and their female companions in turn heard from General Otto Heine officially. They too did as they were told.

Fabienne and Abel's earlier discreet reconnoitering of the rooms when the guests were out had begun to yield results that suited their forthcoming purpose. But the fruits of their labor were not yet fully harvested. *The followers of von List are a disciplined lot, after all,* Abel had thought as he left the last suite, checking that he had not omitted any. *If they can adopt a symbol of peace as the emblem of their rotten evil, it becomes them.*

His grandfather seemed to be speaking to him.

"There are no benefits to cruelty," he said.

Abel nodded. He had never contradicted Manfred Isaacs.

In the Rose Room, the music grew louder. A river of alcohol flowed. Faces shone. Powder and lipstick loosened and streamed into the grooves of old skin. Reminiscence flamed. Stories lengthened. Tears of glory fell upon the order like manna. The rapture of a past era glowed in the coals of narration.

Toward the rising peak of joviality, the chef de sécurité had returned to the rooms and was now patrolling the upper floors of the Grand Hotel du Lac, pulling a wheeled suitcase behind him, acting like a nonchalant guest arriving for a vacation, although this time he had more than a cursory search in mind. He knew exactly what he intended to do.

Silk gloves covered his dry fingers. He slid a plastic master keycard, with a magnetic stripe on its face, into the slot of each door lock. The fit below the bronze handles was perfect. Immediately he was inside. Abel quickly opened every safe, using the identical code. With a rapid sweeps of his palms, he cleared the contents, dropping the items into the suitcase. It grew heavier, but did not slow his movements. He was used to bags filled with the accoutrements of a locksmith and the weaponry of a soldier. His muscles were toned and strong. Working swiftly and deftly, he left no traces of his presence. Even the soles of his shoes were covered with strips of silencing sponge.

He went into the service elevator and left the building by a side exit. The gloves came off. He wrapped them into a ball and stuffed them into a trouser pocket. On the corner of the Avenue des Alpes, a Smart car waited.

Fabienne opened the door. Abel thrust the mobile case into the back, forcing it into the small space. They drove off, heading toward the Château d'Chillon, where a gleaming speedboat waited in the seclusion of the moat, its engine idling. On its prow it bore the name *Chat Noir*.

"Black Cat indeed," Abel said.

"Let's hope it catches good fish!" Fabienne replied conspiratorially, her voice spiking with excitement, a sound that Abel loved most of all. The buoy to which the "Cat" was loosely tied served another purpose as well. With persistent labor, a duck family had turned it into a floating nest of interwoven twigs and feathery flotsam.

"In Montreux, for the right price, anything is available."

Fabienne injected one of her inimitable smiles. Abel's expression began to change. He was calm, inertly at ease, just like when he went into the blockhouse to do the gory business of war.

It had to be done. If not by me, then by another soldier. If he had to apologize to anyone, it would be to Grandfather. Manfred had said something else that now stuck in Abel's mind. "There are ways through guilt, but not around it."

As they rode they saw bright yellow awnings shading the lake hotels and palatial homes of the city, dotted with clinics and spas devoted to the health and harmony of wealthy patrons. As dusk descended, the malleable sounds of electrical motors whirred. Early evening light began its intrusion through the windows of hotel rooms, apartments, mansions, and lakefront restaurants.

Church bells pealed in the steeple that towered over the cape promontory. A rising moon added icing to the mountaintops in the east, converting lancet tips into molten glass. Soon that color too morphed into the misty grayness of hunched silhouettes, as tricks of illumination played out the sly catastrophe of visual disintegration.

Klarens, the boatman, was barely out of his teens.

His youthfulness showed in traces of acne on his florid

face. He was exuberant. *Probably a product of life in a small country's frivolous city*, Abel concluded when first they met.

In his wooden boat, Klarens felt liberated.

The thrill of an adventure in the night sent shivers through his lanky frame. His eyelids blinked continuously, betraying his feelings. He chewed gum mindlessly. But his gums felt inflamed where wisdom teeth were erupting, and the pain radiated to his temples.

Abel was adept at recognizing signs of gullibility caused by large appetites. So he used a little of his abundant charisma—and a tight roll of clean, large-denomination paper money—to elicit the charter that he needed to cross the lake. Exhilaration lit Klarens's eyes when he saw the crisp notes. A glint was all that Abel needed as the assurance of secrecy—sealed by the hardest handshake that the boatman had ever felt. *The art of confidentiality is embedded in all who live here*, Abel thought, as he handed over the cash.

Klarens threw off the tethering rope, startling the sleeping duck family, which squawked out indignation. He gunned the inboard motor. The Chat Noir's prow rose as the stern dug in.

Twin brass propellers thrashed. Silvery bubbles ripped across the glossy hull's sides, emerging and disappearing in submarine translucence. Fabienne watched them in excited fascination. As they formed inchoate shapes, she imagined the face of a Breton boy in silhouette, *like on a Faïence ceramic plate from Quimper on the Odet River in Brittany*, she thought, remembering a romantic weekend spent in the quaint town of the Finistère region when she was a teenager on the brink of womanhood. It was there that she kissed a boy for the first time.

The black powerboat struck farther out into the gathered darkness, heading rapidly and confidently for the coast of Evian, not too far distant. Klarens gripped the knob of the throttle until his knuckles whitened. The moon had quickly shunted the vague dimness of nightfall aside as if it were an unwelcome gambler at a baize-covered table of fleeting fortune.

Sitting on the low plastic bucket seats in the stern, Abel and Fabienne pressed the soles of their shoes firmly down on a duffle bag. It was the same one Abel had carried when he walked from the Gare to the hotel school on the day of his arrival and headed for the villa where they met.

Inside were hard objects. The suitcase, now filled with all the discarded clothes of a young man and a young woman, lay in the back of the Smart car that they had left parked at a jaunty angle in the lot of the medieval château. The castle's thick walls and spiked turrets gloomily upheld its symbols at the crossroads of punishment in the center of Europe.

Behind the sleekly speeding boat, memories lingered in the folding wake.

Fabienne spoke a few soft words. Abel's heart leapt like a wolf when he heard her voice. *Love becomes prey! Prey becomes love*, he thought, realizing that *when one is in love*, as his grandfather had told him, *it is important to distinguish between the two*. More stars emerged. The moonlight pushed most of them aside. He gazed at those that remained visible. In their formations Abel imagined the outline of Grandfather Manny's face. It was calm, as always he remembered it, devoid of the burden of painful recollection.

He reached for Fabienne's hand. Her fingers were yielding and pliant. They seemed to absorb his flesh. Their breath settled and then harmonized. He wondered fleetingly if his nightmare would recur before realizing that it was a futile concern because he did not yet know where they would lie down to sleep that night.

"The unknown has its way with us all."

Manfred Isaacs had said that. He was speaking, again.

Klarens throttled back and brought the speedboat smoothly to berth at the dockside in front of La Maison. The windows of the old restaurant and room establishment looked down at the already gathered group and the new arrivals. In the reflected moonlight, the folded shutters were like the unfocused eyes of elders gazing upon progeny who had come for a surprise visit.

However, the company was not unexpected.

As Fabienne greeted him in French, Claude immediately remembered the inflection in her pronunciation from the telephone call he had received. Her speech was fine textured.

It reminded him of music written by Charles-Camille Saint-Saëns as he watched the lovely young woman step out of the boat, handed up by her handsome companion.

The Twos and the Threes formed a close knot of heads.

Claude opened a pair of bottles. The rare clarets came from his carefully guarded cellar. He would use the Gem to shoot anyone who intruded there. For many years he had stored the large bottles away in the cool confines of the basement where their olive green patina had dulled as dust collected. The owner had waited patiently for an appropriate occasion. Now it had arrived, and on the French shore of Lac Léman.

"Shalom!"

They had all gathered in the salon of La Maison. Each held a glass goblet, only partially filled with claret. The wine shone like liquid rubies in precious chalices. Claude left the room briefly and returned with a brown raincoat. It was the one he had taken off a dead body nearly a half-century ago, in a frozen forest where branches cracked as loudly as gunshots. It had been so cold that it hurt to breathe.

Kneeling, the elderly hosteller unbuttoned the front, reached inside, untied a string, and unrolled a small Persian rug. Its silken tassels lay along the dark wooden floor. The woolen weave was tight, the colors deep, the surface shiny. It seemed transformed, emancipated, flooded with light, and blushing at its release from the once-sodden coat of a fallen enemy. He had used the coat to cover and store the carpet, which was, as Claude recalled, *war booty from an "unknown" source.*

Abel emptied the contents of his bag onto the scarlet rug. Against the sheen of the rug, created by the small hands of a child or woman from a far-off land, the piled jewelry sparkled. He touched the pyramid, almost reverentially. The items tumbled and separated as if no longer willing to be connected.

Fabienne knelt beside Claude and Abel.

Around them the Twos and the Threes closed their circle tightly.

All were silent, awed by what lay before them.

Claude said, "There is a mountain somewhere deep inside

Germany. In its cavernous, cool heart, loot is stored. Within a huge safe, inside a vast strong room hidden by an immense outer chamber, resides a priceless fortune of jewels and artifacts, such as silver candlesticks, finials of embroidered scroll covers, and pointing-finger instruments that once marked the lines and pauses of holy texts. These treasures were all looted from the Jewish communities of dozens of countries and held secretly there. When they were much younger, the Nazis in the Grand Hotel du Lac had taken their fill of jewelry for their mistresses and wives from this hoard by intimidating its guards, using seniority of rank to steal already-stolen property." Abel already knew it from the brigadier and he had told Fabienne. The forebears of the Twos and Threes—those who survived—now knew it too.

"What lies on this carpet on the floor of La Maison this moonlit night in the French town of Evian is just a tiny fraction of a theft too great to measure," said Claude. Abel and the others remained hushed.

In silent obedience to Claude's gesture, first the ten members of the second-generation survivors, along with Abel, Fabienne, Claude, and the brigadier (an unannounced but most welcome "military guest" as far as Claude was concerned), who had given his captain a "God phone"—began to sift through the magnificent pieces.

It took a long time during which nobody spoke.

As the Twos withdrew, the third-generation survivors were ushered forward. Their gestures were diffident, but not apologetic. Sorrow did not dim their faces. Their memories were constructed of stories told by those who now stood back and watched their children select, until nothing was left on the carpet—except for one crossed piece of black, polished metal. A magnificent, single diamond lay trapped in its intersections. It shone against the carpet. Abel lifted the piece, wrapped it in a white serviette from the laundry room of the Grand Hotel, dropped it into a pocket of his shirt, and left the room with Fabienne at his side.

"*Merci. Au revoir.*"

Claude nodded. Uninhibitedly, he finally shed a quiet, single tear for those who had been tortured and robbed of life and possessions. The brigadier remained respectfully silent.

Abel walked back to the small dock at the end of La Maison's lawn.

Klarens was sitting on the bow of the Chat Noir as it bobbed like a dark cork on the waves of the lake that had grown restless in the grip of a sudden wind. *Monsieur Isaacs only told me that he is coming back to give me something and to instruct me what I must do.*

Abel beckoned Klarens forward.

He handed him the object in white cotton cloth and spoke his instructions firmly into the youth's ear. Gripping Klarens's hand tightly like a vice, he forced Klarens to wince. The warning was clear. The boatman cast the mooring line off from the round post and put the boat on a course back toward Switzerland.

The disturbed wake failed to wash away his troubling sense of not having been permitted to witness something exciting, *perhaps even historical.* Often when he boated out on the lake, unseen by anyone, he dipped his hands into the water and scooped it to his lips, relishing the fresh taste. Near to the midpoint, he slowed the Chat Noir, thrusting the knob of the throttle to neutral, reducing the engine vibration. He followed his habit. But this time, the water tasted bitter. "Like devil's wine." He repeated words he had once heard from a disgruntled priest who, he later heard, was excommunicated.

That morning, a train skirted the edge of the lake, twisting along its shores like a serpent. Abel looked back across the blue water. Fabienne was reading a French magazine. She had seen enough of Lac Léman during her years there. In the distant haze, before the train rounded a corner and left it behind, Abel observed the faint outline of Montreux as it clung to sight, its fine buildings pale against the clip of puritanical mountains.

Then it was gone.

On the windowsill of her vacated room in the villa, the last bottle remained untouched. It was sealed. Even if the actual smoke had disappeared, to Fabienne and Abel when last they saw it, it seemed that the contents still swirled as if trapped inside, seemingly driven by a mystical force.

The young boatman entered the Zurich Bahnhoff.

Abel had told him where to look amid the rushed activity of the platforms, booths, luggage carts, uniformed SBB staff, and multitudes of passengers coming and going. Near the information and sandwich counters, just as Abel had said, he saw her. She appeared to have no lower legs. She wore a tattered gray smock. In front of her downcast eyes lay a soiled, upturned beret, its mustard-colored headband gaping like a fallen halo.

As he approached, Klarens reached into the pocket of his jacket. Clutching the object in its white wrapping, without a word he bent at the waist and leaned forward, so close that he could smell the odors from her hair and the dirty garment that hid her missing limbs.

He released the parcel into the halo, knowing that it would be difficult but not impossible in a city of wealth for her to redeem the value of the item. He knew too that beggars have a way of arresting attention and, in some bizarre manner, getting what they need by triggering responses from the able-bodied and the employed. Klarens would not dare to cross Abel. If he did, he knew that he would not live to tell the extraordinary tale of what he had been ordered to do.

She did not look up. If she spoke any words, they were too faint for him to hear.

General Otto Heine's iron cross, set with a pure white diamond, boomed out its message. The frail body of the beggar in the bahnhoff gave forth a shudder that for some reason Klarens could not fathom. It made him think of a fleeing ghost. Then she rocked back and stopped as the sounds of the Central Station—a constantly moving microcosm of rattling affluence that seemed to become still when the iron cross dropped into the soft container—blustered back to life.

He tried to straighten up promptly, but felt immobilized, as if something had burst suddenly within his gut. Until the sensation of inner disruption abated, Klarens, the boatman of

Lac Léman, was afflicted by inherited remorse over the crimes of his ancestors.

At the ticket office of the Fondation du Château d'Chillon in Veytaux, just a short way up shore from Montreux, impatient tourists were lining up. Children and adults chatted and smiled, eager to enter the castle, descend to the dungeon, and view the place where a prisoner of a bygone era had been chained to a post beneath the surface of a lake surrounded by immutable, silent beauty.

Although it was not a custom, on this rare occasion, at the request of a brigadier in the defense force, an air force helicopter took off from its base not far from the broad white beach of Herzlia on the Mediterranean coastline just north of Tel Aviv, the "Hill of Spring." Inside the helicopter's clattering fuselage, Abel and Fabienne sat next to "God," who, as usual, was issuing orders on one of his special phones used for different military security purposes. He lowered it to speak into the microphone and give the pilot the coordinates.

Above the sea, in the air, the helicopter stopped and hovered.

"There!"

The brigadier pointed, looking down, past the bulge of his huge red nose, which was perennially afflicted by allergies. Abel and Fabienne followed the line of his index finger, wondering how he knew the closest spot which he had in mind. "The special phones," Abel whispered, reading her mind. Nothing visible on the surface of the sea marked the exact spot, as that was only possible by vectoring the coordinates. All the waves looked the same as they rippled beneath the downwash of the rotors. But Abel knew what his grandfather had told him about how the convicted monster's body had been cremated (which would be against Jewish custom, were it not for the fact that the killer was a Gentile) and the ashes placed in a loose-fitting cannon cartridge.

It was there that a deliberately weakly-welded shell case had been flown out beyond territorial waters, hit the surface, split open, and spilled out its ashes, years before. A tear formed in Abel's eye as he remembered Manfred Isaacs and felt honored that the brigadier had brought him with his beloved Fabienne to this area, which was the brigadier's uniquely calculated way of saying thank you to Manfred and to his grandson for their service to the country. Fabienne saw it. She cried as she sought to conjure the image of the old Holocaust Healer whom her beloved always described with such respect and adoration.

    The brigadier's face seemed set in stone as if chiseled by Jerusalem's masons. Like a dragonfly drawn irresistibly to liquid, the helicopter hovered for six minutes above the watery oculus. It seemed to stare back an ominous warning. Then, in a blur of noise and power, the helicopter rose higher above the water, tilted at a forward angle, and flew off on its return to land.

Beyond the eastern horizon from whence the helicopter came, a dense and dark cumulonimbus cloud formed—the forerunner of a storm, which seldom occurred at that time of the year. Some isolated drops of rain streaked across the helicopter's bulging windows.

    The streaks were like blown tears.

    As the Mediterranean, the "Sea in the Middle of the Earth," disappeared from view behind the occupants of the helicopter, Abel wondered if any of the other men present had read Lord George Gordon Noel Byron's chronicle of suffering. But both the question and its message of uncompromising justice in the end remained rhetorical when his grandfather's finger of warning appeared in his mind, wagging at the accused in the trial court . . . when he was just a child.

Abel and Fabienne walked hand in hand to the Jeep.

    They climbed in with the brigadier and drove away—heading to the main road that led to the Judean Hills and the city beyond. As the dust settled behind them they smiled. In each other's eyes they saw the future. It was filled with shared hope, happiness, and the bounty of wonders that their united lives would bring.

    Fabienne entwined her slender fingers with Abel's. He felt their confidence and he thrilled to her beauty, her loyalty, and her radiance. *Nothing can add to her perfection*, he thought, as he squinted through the trailing dust particles at her and paid homage to his good fortune in having found her.

They reached Jerusalem.

"Please drop us off at the Jaffa Gate," Abel said to the driver.

The Jeep pulled up sharply in front of the huge ramparts.

"Shalom," the brigadier stated as if he were bidding welcome and farewell simultaneously.

"God sends His good wishes."

Abel knew that the brigadier spoke for himself and the Higher Power. He was not self-deprecating. Nor was he being blasphemous. He was just being what he always was—a brigadier.

The couple walked through the cobbled alleyways.

They came to the Jewish Quarter. Ascending the stone steps, Abel and Fabienne arrived at the door. Abel removed a large iron key from his satchel. They entered the apartment. On a fragile antique table at the door, the brass plate lay. A few coins rested there. The Arab housekeeper had done a good job. The place was clean and tidy.

A few paces inside, they stopped and stood still, greeted by the glowing vista of the Western Wall and the Temple Mount, ancient images seen through the glass windows and doors of the balcony.

Peace prevailed.

After a while, Abel linked elbows with Fabienne, as she loved to do.

"Chain d'amour," she whispered.

Abel led her into the bedroom. Grandfather Manfred Isaacs seemed to rise from his bed as he had each morning when the sun came up and Abel was a child in his keeping. Abel thought he could see the old man smiling a deep, serene smile when the couple stood before him, as if waiting for his approval . . . and something else. Grandfather Isaacs was raising his hands above them, his fingers formed into V's in symbolic bestowal of the priestly blessing.

Watched by Fabienne, Abel lowered himself onto his grandfather's favorite pouffe, where he had spoken his first word.

"M . . . a . . . n . . . n . . . y."

The diction was clear, although it came from the mouth of a toddler. His grandfather's image began to dissolve, then fade away. But Abel had seen it long enough to feel, at last, worthy of the old man's infinite love and devotion.

He turned to Fabienne.

She was poised and beautiful. He took each of her hands, raised them to his lips, and kissed them as a sunbeam reflected off the huge stone blocks of the wall of old Jerusalem, which spoke the secret language of eternity

∞ ∞ ∞

The Clairvoyant

> Now I feel thy power
> Within me clear; not only to discern
> Things in their causes, but to trace the ways
> Of highest agents . . .
>
> **John Milton**

Summer swept across Austria.
With warm and soft fingertips it caressed the bases of tall mountains. With supple arms, it hugged the plains. Nimbly it tickled the surfaces of deep lakes. From the Neusiedler See in the east to Feldkirch in the west, and from Villach in the south to Gmund in the north, the Motherland bathed in the glory of temperate sunshine.

Nights were clement. Stars shone brightly. Clouds rippled across velvet skies in tidy masses, and benign moons followed radiant suns. As long as no one looked too closely, the days seemed tranquil.

More than three decades of the twentieth century had already passed, and strife raised its predatory head once again, biting the tendons and tearing at the flesh of Europe like a rabid animal.

Within the confines of a friendly tavern, one audacious patron dared to whisper, "Who but madmen make war?" His was the anonymous voice of wavering protest. Its timbre grew less steady as he continued: "Despite the passing of millennia, the continent remains a collection of hostile tribes mired in old vendettas."

Festooning beyond the city, out in the countryside, the silent audience of ash trees was a constant reminder of Nature's seemingly infinite tolerance for the foolishness of humankind. A dreadful and tragic drama was at play—one in which the central protagonists ignored the extent of the impending calamity.

"Morale is bad!" the Kommandant announced, as if speaking to submissive underlings. The accent was Viennese. The voice was quietly controlled, almost serene. "Something needs to be done!" He sat in his office at the concentration camp, staring out of the windows at the drab surroundings. Tapping his knee with a swagger stick, his tone had a strangely lilting quality, as if maleness struggled in vain against the influence of femaleness.

Outwardly there was no indication of any such internal conflict. The fascist uniform prevented candor. By projecting a vividly pretentious authority, it masked the source of internal disgrace. The Kommandant did not consciously engage in self-vilification. Deceit lay concealed in his heart, which had hardened to the torment of others. The clothing afforded expedient concealment to a ruined officer of the Third Reich.

In the city center of Vienna recitals were not usually held outside the protective confines of a cathedral, and it was rare indeed for the event to take place in the basilican quadrangle. But the lethality of the orders brooked no argument. In any case, Herr Direktor was not given to obvious resistance. *In these times that would be suicidal,* he thought. His displays of idiosyncratic belligerence were seen, not in public, but only inside his large estate and at his *Schloss*, where his employees treated him with reverential awe, as much for their own well-being as for the inbred conviction that the upper class was far superior to the peasantry . . . and would always be so. The choir was gathered and he was ready to begin.

The Direktor, Count Hermann von Stübler, was the aristocratic heir to a venerable European title. His inherited fortune included vast land ownership and social respectability. He had the means and opportunity to follow his love of classical music and fine art, and his adoration of young male voices.

"I am merely the interpreter, not the composer," he was fond of remarking to journalists who sought his opinions before the war. His turn of phrase, pretentious mannerisms, and recitals conducted in the finest venues distinguished von Stübler, whose reputation was legendary throughout the land. He had perfected the art of separating immaculate interpretation from ideal composition.

Outdoors . . . never! he thought as he replied to the messenger wearing a black tunic, flared pants with crimson piping, and high glossy boots.

Nonetheless, given the peculiar circumstances, he replied: *"Jawohl, mein Herr."*

As the choristers sang, all traffic seemed to still. The clangor of the city surrendered to a brief pause. From within the crowd a woman spoke.

"Hymns of peace in times of war," she declared.

Her words filled the vacuum left when the song ended. The elderly speaker was part of a spontaneously gathered audience temporarily oblivious to the dangers of remaining in one place instead of scurrying into cellars. None responded. They may have mistaken her plain speech for some unanswerable profundity . . . or perhaps their silence was the result of fear.

It was midday. *Not a good time for crowding, when bombs may fall!* the Direktor concluded. Rumbling was heard above the city. "Aeroplanes," he said, but in a soft voice so as not to alarm either the choir or the audience, which he now faced and watched warily.

Nonplussed, von Stübler wondered, *Can it be that the grandeur of song transcends the wretchedness of misery?* His rhetorical curiosity was ripped away when he stared at a boldly written note handed to him by the provocative messenger.

"Horst-Wessel-Lied!"

The Direktor gasped as he saw the three words. They seemed to be linked like soldiers in a platoon, epaulet to epaulet.

It is false what some say. I am neither a sympathizer nor a collaborator! Despite rumors to the contrary, which came to his ears via incautious means, he believed his own denial. Although such allegations stung him, with a contrived air of apparent nonchalance he let them pass, leaving his detractors wondering about the implications of cowardice.

Gott!

Dumbfounded, he tried to reject the fragmenting thoughts insistently beating his mind into turmoil. *Fallen peoples. The broken nations of dead conquerors. Victims and victimized, all thrown together in a barbaric age of insanity.*

Someone knows about my boy . . . who his father is, who his mother is! The realization struck. His hands shook.

But how? I paid handsomely to have all traces erased! They use the boy's Christian name! Raising his hands to signal commencement of a song, Hermann tried to hide the tremors.

"We shall sing the anthem." Its repulsive name exited his mouth in a tremulous hiss as he thought, *Angels hide when the Devil beckons!*

The boys have had to practice it. That was some comfort, although he still had to use one hand to steady the disorderly other.

"Sing well, my children," he pleaded, almost as one would urge softly in the private supplication of the confessional.

Die Fahne hoch! Die Reihen fest geschlossen!
SA marschiert mit ruhig festem Schritt.

The voices lifted.

All twenty-five boys of the small touring group, varying in age from ten to fourteen, sang in the voice of a single being. The ensemble of superlative singers, whose tradition began in the late fifteenth century, was approaching the last stanza. It was identical to the first.

The Direktor brought the national hymn of belligerence in

stern harmony towards a halt. The final phrases soared, then fell. Like exposed bodies dangling beneath nooses, the notes hung momentarily in the air before settling back in imperceptible patterns.

> The flag high! The ranks tightly closed
> March in spirit with our ranks.

Being a consummate master of chorale, the Direktor was acutely aware of the inflammatory and propagandist power of music. *Just consider Wagner!* he thought.

The interventionist flash struck his mind like a blow. He dared not utter such a remark. Gesturing with the point of his chin, his head pulled back sharply, perspiration accumulating in the thin folds of wrinkling skin just above his clavicles, Hermann gave another downbeat to restore the song.

In case the boy, Horst, might have missed the signal, he plunged his index finger into the space ahead of him, as if striking at the music itself. A self-protective vacuity seemed to fill Hermann's head, supplanting the pestilential thoughts that had begun to spread disease among the hosts in his mind. He almost toppled from the dais as an intrusive fear of losing his son came upon him. It felt like the shock wave from a bomb, which although falling far off, is still frightening. Under stress from his body's shaking, the small platform shook, then rocked back to steadiness.

Hermann sensed that he was being watched closely. If a stare could be made to materialize into hardened substance, he believed it would inflict wounds in his back. Pausing, certain that the disturbing presence was just within the portico entrance of the Gothic church's imposing structure, he braced himself. Born with a caul, von Stübler had possessed extrasensory perception from early youth. The passing years had not entirely diminished his ability to predict events, although superstition sometimes spited the rare aptitude. Now flaring, the contaminated presence was bold and possessive.

The man is hidden from my view. Lofty flying buttresses ... pinnacles and spires ... stained-glass rose windows set in lead and stone ... shimmering crystals of refulgent light ... the grand

beauty of the basilica . . . none can conceal the wickedness present!
Within the fissure between reality and futility, his troubled thoughts returned, hammering persistently.

Horst was a bright boy.
The skin of his face glowed translucently pink. His red lips glistened moistly. The blue-and-white striped pinafore that he and the others wore on that bright day matched the limpid color of his eyes. Inherited from his father, they never seemed to blink, as if he intended to be awake at all times, seeing and comprehending.

Before the Direktor's protruding finger stabbed strictly, the boy caught the implication of the man's head as it tilted to one side.

At thirteen, Horst already projected an air of perfection, only surpassed by the quality of his voice. In all of his years as the chorale master, Hermann had never encountered such excellent rendition by any alto tenor. *His falsetto range is unequalled!*

The boy's voice took flight.
Like a bird sweeping on a thermal wind, high above the cliffs, a mere flick of wingtip, a ripple of feather casting it into a circling motion of splendor and form. Thus von Stübler perceived his protégé's range. *It is extraordinarily superb, especially in the increasingly resonating and productive notes of the passaggio.*

The hair on the back of the maestro's wrists rose, like an applauding audience brought to its feet. With his exceptional sense of hearing, the Direktor could separate a single unique voice from the chorus's swell.

Von Stübler had considered having the boy's voice analyzed by leading Viennese musicologists. But that was before war tore the fabric of old, steady normality apart. A remnant of his erstwhile intention struck him. *No wonder* tenor *derives from Latin* tenere *. . . to hold*, he thought.

Hermann von Stübler's education was extensive. His privileged background assured him of classical endowment. Latin, Greek, German, French, and Hungarian were as familiar to him as was the orthodoxy of his musical repertoire. *I, too, was a choirboy in the same old school housed in the palace. Now I am its Direktor.* His recollection flashed. By force of will, he mustered the faltering passion of dedication in a world of disintegrating and confused reactions.

The words of Friedrich Nietzsche—*who was born,* he realized with a start, *almost one hundred years previously and died just forty-four years before all this madness began*—came to him in a rush of truth. *Without music, life would be an error!*

Then, just as his hand lifted to prompt the commencement of the solo, as if a secret accomplice were at work, a piece of von Stübler's own life revealed itself in the staccato frames of memory. Its rampant energy stampeded in his mind. Although just a frisson of recollection, it seemed longer, more potent and unnerving as it struck a blow, stopping the breath in his lungs.

Clutching the railing of the podium, part of his brain reverted to the past as another staggered intoxicatingly through the present. Hurled back forcibly by figurative power, Hermann von Stübler receded into another era—one that he usually suppressed. But now it emerged with ill-timed urgency.

Not very many hours' travel from the capital city itself, which in its antebellum condition sparkled like a rare European jewel in the once-endless-seeming glory of the Habsburg reign, lay a rural settlement.

Like many others along the Danube, this one was not much of town, but rather more of an old, outlying village. Beyond the center with its cobblestone streets and quaint shops, a road wound its way up a small hill. At the top it came to an abrupt cul-de-sac, its progress interrupted by a large gate hanging on enormous iron hinges between gray stone pillars. Above the warp of the frame that held stout wooden sections in place, an imposing sign in Gothic letters proclaimed the name of the castle: Schloss von Stübler.

A turreted medieval citadel stood behind the imposing entrance. Although small and well maintained by the standards of the larger castles that dot Europe like bastions of artificial permanence, the fine Schloss stalwartly declared affluence and authority as it overlooked the small dwellings below its high station.

The interior of the castle incongruously contrasted with its exterior. Modern era furnishings had replaced old oak closets, worn leather settees, and dark brocades. The rooms were filled with white ceramics, interior support columns of fine alabaster, marble floors, and concealed sconces that seemed to multiply light in profusion. Starting at dusk and ending at dawn, a rosy glow emanated from Bohemian crystal chandeliers, setting carpets and balustrades alight in varied degrees of illumination. Fine antique appurtenances and magnificent paintings filled the modernized interior of the ancestral home that Hermann von Stübler had inherited from his father.

A continuous line of male succession traced the family's lineage back to the earliest origins of Austrian nobility. Despite the castle's opulence—all the rooms of the Schloss were replete with accessories of great wealth—the possessions were arranged so as to render a superficial illusion of understated elegance.

At the base of the grand staircase, ascending in a semispiral from the interior of the house to the private apartments above, Hermann's favorite collector's piece stood in pride of place. On the velvet-papered wall above it, his second-most-valued possession appeared in an ornate gold frame. Brass-encased lights in the top corners, so small as to be almost invisible, cast lustrous beams on the contents.

Hermann had established a habit. Following his peculiar routine, he never ascended to his bedroom without first paying attention to those two special items.

First, he would read the letter written in fine style on paper yellowed by time, marveling at the ability of the ink to retain its clarity for one hundred and sixty-seven years. The long-dead author of the memorandum had written to his father explaining why he had, until that time, so loved the instrument that he called a Klavier.

When he, the current head of household who had followed in the footsteps of all prior male von Stüblers, read the letter as he had hundreds of times before, a thrill crept up from the base of his spine to the ridge of his shoulder blades. *It was written by Wolfgang Amadeus Mozart himself! This is the writing of a mastermind. He was merely twenty-one years old at the time, when he referred to his favorite "fortepiano" built by Franz Jakob Späth!*

How such a famous letter had come into the possession of the von Stübler family was a mystery. But, despite the secrecy of acquisition, it was there, protected behind handmade glass in the gilded finery of its frame, written simply, almost childishly, so that the reader had to detach the author from the genius so as not to be disappointed.

On finishing his reading, although he knew the wording by heart, Hermann turned to the piano itself. Also by some unknown means, his father, the late Count Der Zählimpuls Friederich von Stübler, had acquired the very piano that the great composer had played.

This heirloom is priceless!

So the Direktor had its feet embedded solidly into the marble floor of the Schloss. At the time he instructed his artisans to take the greatest care with the rare instrument's fine qualities. *If any thief makes so bold as to enter my house without detection to steal my piano, he shall have to remove it in pieces!*

Hermann recalled sitting alone on the posh stool. Every day that he was in residence in his private fortress, he set his fine hands to the keys of the delicate instrument. As he began to play, a tentatively benevolent smile creased his lips. Although he loved them, he did not choose one of the many sonatas. Instead, that night he decided to play some bars from the composer's unfinished masterpiece.

Notwithstanding that the piece was scored for instruments, Hermann took the liberty of playing the first of the fourteen movements on the old piano without any accompaniment. Mozart's haunting *Requiem* was his favorite piece. He loved the alto and tenor sequences for choir. The entire work was locked permanently in his memory, right through to its moving finale, the "Lux Aeterna."

It mattered not to Hermann that controversy surrounded the composition, for some experts said that the Austrian composer did not pen the entire work, having died before completing it. In its profound beauty, the aristocrat heard the inner voice of a young man whose genius came from mind, heart, and hand . . . even as a boy!

That same night Hermann von Stübler's life changed drastically.

His wife had died many years before. *She left me too soon! We were then both young! She was beautiful, but so very fragile.*

Edwina's frailty had caused her to succumb to the complications of severe pneumonia. When she passed away, Hermann mourned in ferociously intense solitariness. His sorrow seemed endless, his spirit inconsolable. However, with the passing of time, the pain of loss began to blunt a little until it arose again, jagged and severe when least expected.

Over the years, despite his ardent desire to cling to the physicality of the unblemished image, his delicate late wife seemed to have transformed in his mind, from the perfection and embodiment of beauty that she had been in the flesh into an amorphous and spectral legend of ephemeral timelessness. Thus Edwina would appear to him inchoately, beckoning tantalizingly with her slender arms in dreams that refused to depart when he awakened. The images haunted him relentlessly. Only when he played on Mozart's piano could he expunge them.

Sometimes, seized by a contradictory impulse, he played not to drive his dead wife from his mind, but to bring her closer so that he could have her again. Yet her spirit refused to obey; her image would dissolve into a deceptive swirl of ectoplasm.

This night, when the last note died away, fading into reprised nothingness, the replicating void began to molest his soul, casting it into deeper anguish, beyond the reach of grief's disorderly arrangements. So, he climbed the long, sweeping flight of stairs.

He entered his spacious bedroom chamber. With a sense of rising frenzy, he cast off his expensive clothing. Not being a slovenly person by nature, such behavior was uncharacteristic. When he inherited his father's patrimony on attainment of majority, he effortlessly accommodated himself to the customs, traditions, and behavior of the aristocracy.

They escort expectation and attend entitlement, he had long since concluded. The privileges of wealth and exploitative land ownership had settled easily upon him. Yet that night was different and unnaturally cogent in its demands.

Naked, he compulsively reached for his dressing gown. Draped in the red folds of fine Chinese silk, he stretched out his tapered fingers tipped by manicured nails. He took hold of a framed picture on the bedside table.

A white candle, braided from several strands of expensive imported wax, burned on three wicks. Each intertwined with the others, so that they became one. Hermann loved the mellow glow yielded by the soft disintegration of the melting wax. It added strength to his increasing sense of weakness, which quickly gave way to distress, anger, confusion, and then, suddenly and unexpectedly, to a rising sense of unappeased salaciousness.

Conflicting emotions rippled through von Stübler. All airs of refinement seemed to desert him as a base, plebian urge gripped him and refused to let go.

Like a challenging shadow, the glass surface of the framed photograph reflected his face. In his likeness he saw an alien expression. He looked beyond it, staring intently and silently into the grayish image as if trying to reject the choking authority of his own imprisoned temperament. A handsome upright nobleman looked back at him. The man was dressed in the regalia of an Austrian count complete with top hat, tailcoat, cummerbund, starched white shirt, black bow tie, and a single magnificent medallion brooch in one lapel. The heraldic badge of his ancestry shone, even through the smudges of old sepia, as if teasing the past into the present.

His gaze turned from the likeness of his lost youth.

Now it focused on the small bride standing beside her groom. Despite the vintage of the photograph, the young woman's face shone with ageless beauty as if the inky wash rendered her lovelier with time. Her slender body was decorated with a magnificent wedding dress.

She was, he thought, *more gracious, attractive, and innately more desirable than Sandro Botticelli's tempera on canvas.* In his mind's eye, she surpassed the unclothed goddess Venus who rose otherworldly from a fluted shell. She floated from depths to shore, observed by the vesper winds. Although an angelic attendant hovered protectively nearby, Venus seemed oblivious of any need to conceal the purity of her nakedness with raiment.

Hermann saw beyond the comparison to the Italian work of art that he considered to be the most profoundly beautiful in the entire world—past the bride's clothing, the long swirling train hiding her delicate feet in satin shoes, and her legs in white stockings. Instead, like Praxiteles's Aphrodite, his own idol, *the short-lived divinity with which I was temporarily blessed*, appeared defenseless. Yet, too, she seemed strengthened by her inimitable loveliness.

She was Venus, her right hand placed between her small breasts, not hiding them completely; her left hand softly holding long auburn tresses that only partially hid the virginal apex between her thighs in timid modesty.

Arrested by the memory coiling audaciously within him—for, most often, he dared not recall such an image lest it became too hard to bear—he remembered what Edwina had so often implored him to allow.

"Permit me to fly with the wind," she had urged, especially toward the end, when her illness had claimed its investment with avaricious purpose. The words caught in his throat; he knew that she was destined to be borne away by the very substance of her longing.

She had treasured the sound and feel of air streams. Their restless energy seemed to renew her failing strength, imbuing her with an impermanent reprieve from the distress of her ailment.

"Take me up, *Liebschen*," she would request, even on sultry days when it would have been more comfortable to remain in the cool environment of the salon or bedroom. Hermann always complied, carrying her in his arms, feeling her lightness of form and her radiating warmth; her elegance and frail loveliness piercing him like a molten spar.

Flaming desire could never be smothered, never doused, and his thirst for her beauty could never be quenched.

She was my essence, he thought, for never before or since had he achieved such unfathomable happiness. Now, to express profound emotion would be like speaking into a vessel that swallows sound. So he remained silent, trying to still his rampaging heart and dislocated mind by diaphragmatic breathing, as practiced by trained singers.

But the interval did not last.

I shall go to her room, he thought, then said out loud, "The belfry tower of the Schloss, her favorite, secret domain, like the hideaway of a child."

"There she loved to listen to the sounds of the currents rushing past, and finally she tried to grip stone—only to be pried loose from it, set adrift, and borne away by the irresistible whims of elemental strength!"

Within him a tempest raged. He grabbed the candleholder, disregarding electric light, and rushed to the far end of the corridor, beyond his bedroom. Hurrying through, he flung the door aside, his bare feet ignoring the cold iron of the staircase that spiraled up. He climbed higher, although, strangely, he felt as if he were descending.

Until that moment he had forgotten completely about the woman who now slept there. He had become a distraught soul, the discipline of responsibility, the tidiness of nobility having forsaken him in his untamed rush for the unattainable love he had once known.

Thus Hermann crashed impetuously into the chamber of his housemaid. The door was unlocked. The servant had obeyed an order that he had given her, although he had forgotten it. The room was intensely dark, obtrusive moonlight held back by heavy curtains.

He lunged toward the bed that had never been removed—the one on which his *Sweet Angel* had lain during what she had so daintily, but aptly, termed "the last of my voyages."

In a desperately vain attempt to eradicate the demons within him, he ripped back the covers to expose the woman who lay there, lost in a deep sound sleep. Before the housemaid, whose silenced well-being lay in the hands of her employer, could react to the presence of the man looming over her, it was too late!

He was upon her, tearing frantically at the material of her

nightdress, ripping the flimsy protection of her reticence, thrusting her legs apart. When he reached for her breasts, it was not with tenderness but with importunate need.

The acts that he performed passed very quickly. At the moment of fleeting satisfaction, the phantoms within receded. With an internal explosion, the exquisite image expunged itself. He felt liberated—not from love, but by his impulsive carnality. Edwina had disappeared.

Quietly, respectfully, with a sense of being re-willed, he lifted himself from the supine body of his maid. Then he whispered with an air of refinement, most gently in her ear, *"Danke, Junge Frau."* He did not wait for her response, for he expected none.

∞∞∞

Outside the basilica, in the city's center, the recital continued. The boy was singing in the highest register. *A female soprano cannot reach such elevated and pure tones,* von Stübler thought. However, as the last stanza of the loathsome anthem ended, a brooding and proximate malevolence intervened.

The Direktor heard a strange, ominous, heel-tapping sound on the stone paving. To his trained ear it had the offbeat and unevenly metronomic thump of a boot. This time the black-uniformed man who appeared beside the dais was not a lackey.

The Kommandant was the most immaculately dressed soldier the choirmaster had ever seen. Yet Hermann could not avoid feeling the stab of ineradicable cruelty that came from his eyes. *It is,* he thought, *true, but of no comfort, that one who hates attracts loathing in greater measure.*

The voice belied the speaker. The register was too high to be normal. Hermann had only heard such vocal production by castrati. The choirmaster was right, although he had no way of knowing what had caused the awkward gait and the high-pitched voice.

In a bizarre accident, the Kommandant had suffered hideous injuries.

Gottlieb Wilhelm Daimler, from the old Kingdom of Württemberg, was considered by some to be a great inventor as well as a superb engineer. The Kommandant admired the man and the products of his company: the Daimler-Motoren-Gesellschaft.

It was therefore not surprising that he insisted on owning one of "the vintages"—a splendid collector's piece. The "60 model" was so named because of the exact maximum speed that it was capable of reaching at the turn of the century.

One day when the weather was inclement, the high-ranking officer and his subaltern had an accident. Squalls, worse than usual, ripped across the countryside. Nonetheless, because he liked to see and be seen when driven, the Kommandant urged his driver to make speed for the camp as he sat in the back of the automobile with its top down.

The chauffeur obeyed, as the Kommandant reclined into the yielding leather of the rear seat, pulling the broad collars of his cape around his high cheekbones to arrest the blasts of chilly blustering wind.

They were nearing the gate when a herd of squealing pigs rushed out of a hole in the hedgerow beside the twisting road, just ahead of the grand car. The driver reacted reflexively. Instead of hitting them out of the way with the large fender, at the last moment, as he saw the pigs and piglets running on their stubby legs, he pulled hard on the steering wheel.

The vehicle veered violently, skidded, bounced, and lurched. Tearing metal screeched in menacing announcement of the inevitable. The Daimler crashed through the hedge, tipping to one side, as its tires lost purchase. It hit a low wall and went over it. The side where the Kommandant had been sitting ripped open. When the automobile came to a wheezing halt, almost upside down, he was still alive. He was lying sideways, halfway through a torn rear door.

Beside him, almost face to face, a large pig stared at him through dead eyes. Its head had been severed. With bile rising into the back of his throat, he reached out a gloved hand and swept the hog's head from his sight, leaving a curling trail of blood.

The driver was dead. That didn't matter to the Kommandant. He grabbed the holster of his pistol. It was a treasured gift from a general, given to him when he visited Weimar. It rested on his right hip. Although shocked and confused by the hellish impact and shaking as if seized in the grip of an epileptic fit, he managed to unclasp the flap. Pulling out the weapon, without a word and not knowing the condition of his driver who had been hurled backwards and sat crushed up against the front passenger door, the Kommandant fired a single bullet into the back of the man's skull. It penetrated just beneath his black cap. The subordinate's brains spewed out of a gaping hole in his forehead, onto the remains of the shattered windscreen.

"Idiot!" he tried to growl, but the word and the cursing outcries that followed emerged in a voice which, although his, sounded different, unfamiliar, and weak.

The Kommandant had decided that it was not enough for his driver to die once on a wet and winding country road that day; he should die twice, firstly because of the errant hogs, and secondly at the hands of the superior he served.

Feeling better and sure that he had fully executed his subaltern, the Kommandant tried to raise himself out of his awkward position. It was only then that he realized, with a profound sense of enveloping shock, that his flared pants were stained and a dull pain had begun to give way to an insistently terrible throbbing. With increasing awareness, the Kommandant was returning to the present. Looking more closely, his focus improving, he saw the hemorrhage and, incredulously, observed a transparent splinter protruding through the material of his pants.

He stared in disbelief! Then he lapsed into unconsciousness.

It was only later, in the hospital of Linz, that he was told.

The short glass swagger stick, which he used as a symbol of power on parade, had been thrust from his lap by the potent force of the impact. It had plunged through his testicles and penetrated his groin. So much anatomical damage had been done that a surgical castration was imperative.

"You were lucky," the surgeon said, "to have avoided a penectomy, although some intervention there was also necessary," the doctor hastened to add as quietly as possible in the hope that the patient would not hear too much, or at all.

"Hand over the boy!"

The Kommandant was now standing right next to Hermann, though slightly below his level. The Direktor's tongue cleaved to the top of his palate, which, at that moment, seemed to divide his intellect from the remainder of his body and shut down his power of speech. Yet, despite all instincts to the contrary, he obeyed the order.

"Horst, *bitte*, please come here," he said, summoning his reluctant tongue to speak politely and unthreateningly. The boy separated himself from the choral group and came forward as bidden.

At that moment von Stübler's mind closed. What he witnessed was transient, as if he had entered an alien dimension of incomprehension.

The Kommandant simply took the boy by the hand as if he were a kindly schoolteacher leading a gullible pupil to class.

Hobbling off, the Kommandant headed back, out of the sunshine into the darkly beckoning entrance of the basilica, which seemed to gape, then swallow man and youth in an instant gulp.

∞∞∞

It had been a year since the incident in the turret room of the castle, after which Hermann's housemaid disappeared. One day his personal valet, standing in locum for the butler who had the day off, answered an unusually insistent knock at the front door of Schloss von Stübler.

The servant wondered how the visitor had gained entrance through the looming outer gates of the estate. However, as soon as he opened the door the answer was obvious. He recognized the young woman. But not the infant she carried in her arms. Even so, with a gracious bow of greeting he ushered them into the parlor.

The woman remained standing near the priceless piano that had once belonged to Wolfgang Amadeus Mozart. In the high belfry tower, its music had reached her on many nights, although the player had not realized that she was his only audience. A shudder passed through her, but she held onto her composure tenuously as Count Hermann von Stübler entered the room to the announcement of the substitute butler. The exchange of conversation that ensued was brief. Von Stübler tried to greet her. She cut him short.

"This is your son!" she declared, her face set quite placidly, but her lips betraying a slight quiver as she looked directly into her former employer's ice-blue eyes. Hermann staggered, as if struck by a challenging gauntlet across the face. He took a step backward, feeling a wave of nauseating incredulity lurching into his stomach. He could not speak. Words froze on his tongue. All he could think of was: *Where has she been all this time? Has she been hiding throughout the pregnancy? Who looked after her?* Before he could voice his thoughts, she continued.

"The boy is Jewish! Any child born to a Jewish mother is Jewish! That has been the law from the time of the Crusades, when our ancestors were raped by knights and minions and any other evil men who could heave themselves onto us!" She spoke as if she were a female nation of one.

A barrier had been raised. Von Stübler's silence divided them. His face looked gaunt—the result of having practiced unhappiness for so long. Then, quite unexpectedly, he did something that surprised not only himself, but also the young woman.

He reached out for the baby. Without resistance she surrendered the child. Hermann took him and walked to Mozart's piano. The woman remained standing as she watched, rooted to the spot, like the heirloom instrument itself.

Hermann sat down gingerly on the luxurious stool. Placing the baby in his lap, he stretched out his elegant hands and began to play. It was an extract from the "Requiem Aeternam," selected spontaneously. Something told him that the news he had just received called for this haunting music in which the souls of the dead seek the ultimate comfort of repose. When he stopped playing, three evenly spaced words came from his lips.

"My dear son," he uttered.

In that moment a poor Jewish servant woman and her child fell beneath the protective mantle of Count Hermann von Stübler. Suddenly she understood that he would hide their identity as long as he could in the terrible times that she knew, with absolute certainty, were descending upon them! From such dangers, escape seemed otherwise impossible.

Sleep had been elusive. When it came in fits and starts, it was filled with implausible dreams, grotesquely vivid forebodings of the future. While awake, which was most of that night, Hermann thought long and hard about how he would save them.

In the early misty hours of morning, just as dawn was breaking over the manicured lawns, walls, and spires of the Schloss, Edwina seemed to appear before the Count again, in all her haunting beauty.

Then a solution came to him.

He saw the outline unfolding before his very eyes. It was not the diminishing shadows that fled in the encroaching light of daybreak, but rather an entire pattern of saving grace that unraveled and revealed itself.

Later that day, when the servant woman brought the infant a second time, Hermann instructed his staff to accommodate her and the child, telling them that she could resume her position as a housemaid at the Schloss. After explaining to the other servants that "the father, being an unknown workman, had dishonored and abandoned a mother in the distress of childbirth," a dangerous thought struck him.

"Is the boy circumcised?" he asked the woman.

Unswadling the infant, she exhibited his tiny body. "No, he is not! Look for yourself."

A sense of intense relief flowed through von Stübler. Following his plan, he arranged for the boy to be baptized in the presence of a full congregation from the village over which he largely held dominion. The priest was ignorant of why the child was given the honor; but he asked no questions, money being the procurer of lasting silence.

"I baptize thee Horst." The priest stressed the name as he spoke in a formal manner.

Hermann had given the woman and child new Austrian identities. *Horst means* wood *or* thicket *in German*, he thought.

What could be more common? And to have this beautiful young woman working in Schloss von Stübler . . . that is good!

So he let it be known, "The woman and the boy will live here."

I shall see to it that none shall question their presence, he assured himself.

Von Stübler's motives were far more about his own reputation, which was at stake over his illegitimate child, than about the assembling storm clouds of conflict that had billowed since the end of the First World War and were now at a bursting point.

It never really ended and it will never be over fully! He felt the vicissitudes of the changing times. More so, the fear of his indiscretion being discovered dwelt like a live obsession within him.

Horst had a naturally beautiful voice, which von Stübler cultivated. The boy had private lessons within the cloistered confines of the Schloss, and when he was old enough von Stübler quietly arranged for him to be admitted to the Palais school. From kindergarten Horst remained there, nurtured, trained, and disciplined until he turned into the finest boy soprano in the ensemble.

Fame preceded the choir in the civilized cities of Europe and beyond . . . until that day, outside the basilica in the capital city of the Motherland! Had it not been for his father and his school, Horst might not have developed an astounding ability to recall music and lyrics. Count von Stübler realized that his own amazing faculty to see objects and people in situations and states that were not discernable via ordinary senses had been transmitted to his only son. He was not sure whether to be relieved, proud, or alarmed that the boy had discovered the propensity as a student in the original home of the choir at Leopoldstadt, which had been so badly damaged in recent times by Allied bombing that the choristers had to be temporarily housed in alternative accommodation. *Better some place to be than none,* Herr Direktor concluded bitterly.

After "the accident," as he called it, the Kommandant had sunk into an abyss of self-loathing. Abnegation came in ever-increasing acts of brutality. He supervised killings without remorse—a leaden man, emotionless, dead but yet living, carrying out his "duties" to the letter and beyond.

His final day of life was the fifth of May, nineteen hundred forty-four. When he rose from his bed and dressed in his black uniform, struggling to pull up his boots and strap on his pistol, he did not fully realize that within a few short hours he would be standing before an American officer at the gates of Der Konzentration Lager, over which he had been the sole ruler.

Before breakfast, he summoned his orderly and had him bring "the boy" to his quarters. The Kommandant's penchant for croissants derived from some time spent in Vichy, France, where he had perfected certain "skills" and acquired his liking for "pre-breakfast delicacies," along with methods for satisfaction of other unspoken desires. By the time the boy was marched in, the Kommandant was already enjoying a full meal of hot porridge, ham, eggs, and toast taken with a first cup of coffee.

He listened in silence as the boy's alto voice soared in the aria of "Ave Maria." Whenever the falsetto soprano reached a high note, the Kommandant's free hand went to his own tight buttocks, as if seeking assurance there of his personal power over all underlings and inmates.

Magnificent! he thought, admiring his foresight in keeping the boy fed enough to be able to sing and entertain him and senior Waffen-SS.

The orderly cleared away the fine Hutschenreuter breakfast set, leaving behind only a steaming cup of black coffee and some more ham on thickly buttered toast. He placed the items beside a small porcelain vase containing a few sprigs of early spring flowers. The Kommandant took a sip of the hot liquid. Then, swirling it down his throat, feeling satisfied he uttered an order.

"Get out!" He threw half-eaten toast and scraps of meat onto the floor. The boy did not scrounge like a hungry dog. For some reason, which the Kommandant did not care to consider, he made no attempt to gather the discarded food.

Lifting a pen, its cap bearing the menacing, inlaid gold emblem of a Swastika, he paused to admire the handcrafted gold-milled Meisterstück instrument from the Schanzen district of Hamburg. Then he began to write in bold block letters:

"MEIN LETZT WILLE UND TESTAMENT."

But he was interrupted in recording his will by the sound of gunfire and the unmistakable deep-throated roar of diesel-driven tank engines. He lifted himself up, laboriously, his injuries aching deeply.

He limped out to the camp yard. From there he continued unevenly to the gates, where iron letters curved high above them, having deceived multitudes of innocent victims who were forced to walk beneath them.

A single battle-begrimed officer walked toward him. Behind the American, a row of vehicles lined up.

Enlisted soldiers looked out toward where the two very differently uniformed men approached each other—one with a tired but confident gait, the other with a severe disability that forced his heels to the ground and seemed to pitch him forward in a rollicking motion accompanied by foot dragging. Even in his lurching progress, the Kommandant appeared immaculately turned out, as if he were deploying on a mission for which his orders were clear.

The American looked at the approaching figure, placing his hand on his sidearm just in case, although the abundance of defeat all around was unmistakable. They stopped beneath the cruelly deceptive sign that proclaimed, "Work Makes Free."

"Gruss Gott!"

The American major did not reply or return the salute from the Kommandant who had come forward to surrender. The German lowered his stiffly outstretched arm.

The American was wearing darkly tinted green sunglasses, which prevented him from seeing the German's face too clearly. The Kommandant thought he smelled something awful—like the sour, fetid breath of a hog exhaling before the moment of slaughter. His mind traveled backward, to the accident on the wet road years earlier.

Damned swine! he thought.

Suddenly he wasn't sure to whom he referred. Then, as if

he were drawing water from a deep well with a long rope, in slow motion he pulled his Walther .32 pistol from its holster as he had done often before to kill inmates. Only this time, he raised it to his open mouth, bit down on the steel barrel between his teeth and squeezed the trigger with the index finger of a gloved hand.

He fell at the feet of the liberator.

The major looked at the fallen man. What he saw on his face remained with him for the rest of his life. Although the bullet had carved its trajectory through the Kommandant's brain, and the gun had slipped out of his thinly puckered scarlet lips, in its place there remained the glowing coal of an arrested smile. It was surrounded by a ruddy, indelible expression, as if the corpse possessed the final, awful, deadened pain of unexpressed shame!

That night, in the cavernous master bedroom of Schloss von Stübler, an older man with silver hair and a younger beautiful woman lay in a tight embrace on the huge antique four-poster bed. They clung to each other, their arms intertwined after making love.

Tears ran in a steady flow down Count Hermann von Stübler's aristocratic face. In his arms Frederika, the Jewish housemaid (whose real last name he still did not know), felt wetness descend from her cheeks to her bosom. For reasons that they both understood, they wept until dawn, drawing vicarious strength from one another—even as they shook together in wracking spasms.

Although the count had expected Edwina to appear as she did in times of his anguish, this time she did not.

An American colonel stared at the young boy entertainer from the camp who stood before his bare table. The boy seemed surprisingly healthy compared with the skeletal survivors whom he had seen in the past days. The colonel, a trained psychiatrist who did not speak German, was puzzled.

He turned to his interpreter, intending to have the corporal ask the question that bothered him: *Why is he here and in seemingly good health?* when suddenly, after having been silent all the time since he had been escorted into the room, the boy began to sing. His voice was high and clear. It maintained its own resonance in crystalline perfection.

The song was unrecognizable to the colonel, who had an adequate knowledge of vocal compositions. *Even more disconcerting, the words have no apparent meaning,* he thought.

They are extraordinary, like the sounds of Babel!

The boy appeared to be in a surreal, transcendentally inspired state. It was not awareness, not consciousness; it was not grounded in the present reality of the proposed interview. Instead he seemed to be airborne—as if his mind were carried by a strange, dreamlike wind.

The colonel wondered whether the boy was in a traumatically induced trance in which he may be seeing ghostlike images. His training had impressed upon him the dangers of interrupting such abnormal behavior. *What he has seen may be beyond my ability to alleviate. It seems paranormal. Certainly he will never be entirely cured!* the colonel thought.

Suddenly, Horst's voice changed, transmuting into that of an old man ... then a young man ... an old woman ... a young woman ... a boy ... a girl ... even the mewling cry of an infant! With a start and no longer in need of translation, a realization came suddenly to bear on the senior American officer.

"These aren't words," he said. "They are names!"

"Many, many, distorted names!"

∞∞∞

Fall of Grace

No peace this side of the grave like the peace of Doornkloof . . . here I sit in the study hearing only the dull subdued hum of silence in my head . . . and the companionship of books.

Jan Christiaan Smuts (May 24, 1870–September 11, 1950), field marshal, privy councillor, member of the Imperial War Cabinet, a founder of the League of Nations, and prime minister of South Africa during some tumultuous years

On a winter's night, the stranger came to Figlands Park.

A man with a single good eye, a bad leg, and many pains called his home by that name because, he said, "Once fig trees grew abundantly in the garden." The house was adjacent to a park. The lawn was dry, wilted, and brown in the cold Highveld chill. Remnants of invasive weeds infiltrated the flowerbeds. Dead vines crept up the stone walls and entered the chimney. Although moss had begun its clinging descent into the fireplace, hindered by soot and by logs burnt to the core, it had stopped its journey. Creeping ivy, thyme, and phlox had been defeated, ripped off walls and slopes of brick by the onslaught of wind. Growth, it seemed, had lost its tenacious fight and had surrendered to the daunting power of bitter purpose.

Frigid gusts blew across the grassland at an elevation of almost six thousand feet above sea level and four hundred miles from the waters of the Indian Ocean where the Mozambiquean current flows warmly, even in the cold season. It seldom snowed in Johannesburg. When it did, a public holiday was declared officially.

Before the man arrived, snow had fallen copiously.

It began at dawn and continued throughout the day, into the evening. At the end of autumn in the southern hemisphere, the swimming pool had been drained. A frozen cover of shimmering cold—like a pristine shroud—covered the gunnite cement shell. It was no longer blue, just gray. In the park, a pane-like glassiness topped the small lake's surface where mists rose like wriggling wraiths. Ice mirrored the frosty stars in a blinking sky of inky blackness.

When its disabled owner had entered the house for the first time with his timid little wife from Uganda clinging to his good arm, he closed the shutters. Since then they had not been opened. At the end of the driveway, a fanciful gazebo had broken down with time. The garden of Figlands Park had grown weary of inattention.

So it faded, and almost died.

Having rung the bell repeatedly, the unannounced visitor waited at the front door. He removed his rimless spectacles and wiped away the condensation that clung to the lenses in deference to frosty weather. Just as he was about to turn back to his BMW parked in the driveway, which rippled from fissures beneath the snow, he heard the tap-tap of a cane on a bare wooden floor.

Accompanying the metronomic beat of the stick on parquet, the heavy footfalls of a severe limp announced the occupant.

Before he introduced himself, the stranger looked back at the vehicle in which he had been driven to the house. In the driver's seat, a blue uniformed policeman—Sergeant Blackfoot (one of the few white officers whose first language was English)—sat smoking, even though it was against the rules to do so while on duty.

"I am Attorney Yustus Toledano," the visitor said, summoning a mixture of solicitousness and simulated gravitas. He used his nickname because his first name, Gonçallo, was unintelligible and unpronounceable to most who heard it, especially when pronounced with a Portuguese accent. "Mr. I. Aval?"

"Yes." The voice sounded almost apologetic at the admission.

"In the extraordinary circumstances of the inquiry in which my firm has been instructed, I have been authorized by 'the authorities' to do two things."

Not revealing who granted him such power, he looked out at the flakes that had commenced falling again. He pulled his scarf tighter around his narrow neck and flipped the lapels of his coat so that they lifted enough to cover his fleshy ear lobes.

Yustus Toledano shifted, discomfited in the presence of a fairly young man who, he thought, *is so damaged that he is dependent on prostheses.* He had noticed a metal crutch with a plastic elbow support propped against a creamy wall that swarmed with flickering shadows. Nearby was a three-footed cane. An old painting hung on a long wall. Depicting a bucolic scene on farmland somewhere in the cultivated lands of Europe, it was framed in gilded wood chipped with age and suspended on an exposed rusted chain. The paint was cracked, its sheen lost as if complementing the stark gloom in the interior of the house and the bleak austerity of the grounds outside.

Silhouetted in the doorway in a no-man's-land between threshold and lintel beyond which the weak glow of candles leaked outward, the attorney continued.

"A subpoena to attend court in the town of Doornkloof on the date mentioned in this paper." As he waved the demand, he glanced at the BMW. The sergeant appeared to be nodding in agreement, although he was out of earshot and blowing blue smoke through the crack of an open window. In an instant the cold night air grabbed the smoke, wafting it away. "And," the attorney hesitated, "I need your statement, actually an affidavit, to be sworn before me. I am an *ex officio* 'commissioner of oaths' by virtue of being an officer of the court." He did his best to sound important.

But Ish Aval was not impressed.

With eerie overtones, a piano was churning out harsh nocturnal sounds, the keys being hammered hard, like heavy tools—as if the player wished to eradicate harm.

"Who's there?"

A woman's voice in a high register trilled in the living room, rising above the music. *Like a brass bell being struck with a pounder to summon attention,* Yustus thought.

"No need to fret," the crippled man said. He seemed to be speaking to his wife and the stranger, his voice steady and devoid of unctuousness.

"I have been expecting this. I knew that one day you would come."

He turned, swiveling on his rigid bad leg, steadying himself with the cane, and reaching shakily for his gray crutch.

"You had better come in." It was less of an invitation than a request. A ridge of ulcerous lesions that never seemed to heal tripped across his brow as if in lively competition.

The Law Firm, Toledanos, comprising three generations of Portuguese descent—Eliézer, Manoel, and, lately, Gonçallo "Yustus" Toledano—was represented by the visitor to the austere premises at Figlands Park. The law firm was one of a kind, for there was no other such Sephardic Jewish partnership anywhere in the country.

Eminent Queen's Counsel Elijah Sweet, who had been briefed by the Toledanos in the matter, unsubtly quipped to a newly admitted advocate of his group at Hofmeyer Chambers in the city's central business district, "They sound like restaurateurs, rather than attorneys. If they must insist on being lawyers, they should rename their firm!"

"'Heed, Tell, and Wit,' otherwise known as 'Hear, Speak,

and See No Evil,' would be more suitable. Three musketeers of illustrious criminal defense lawyers." Elijah Sweet, the renowned barrister, whose reputation allowed him to accept or reject briefs from attorneys at his whim, nonetheless held most of them in contempt, and when he spoke of "some lawyers," his voice was thick with sarcasm.

"Yustus, his byname inexpertly altered to facilitate daily usage," counsel added as a derisive postscript, "is the youngest, with a long road to travel, professionally and personally!"

The person of whom the grand barrister had spoken now stepped into the forbidding lobby of the premises. Immediately he noticed that the interior was shabby, having the drab appearance of subjugation. *Like its owners,* he thought wryly, wondering if polio had claimed the man as a victim. Then he reminded himself of what Elijah Sweet had told him. *Of course not,* he thought, correcting his suspicion, *Aval is the casualty of a terrible accident!*

The woman, who had stopped her frantic playing, rose and now hovered like a protective though ineffectual mother pigeon with wings outstretched as her husband spoke to the stranger. She waited in silence for a while. Then she returned to a recessed niche of the salon that accommodated a black baby grand with long scratches across its sides, as if it had been clawed by feral cats.

At first Yustus heard her weeping. Then the music struck up again. A nocturne by Béla János Bartók squealed from the piano. It sounded frenetic. Although not familiar with musical renditions, instinctually Yustus felt the impact of something more profound than the rampant night sounds projected by insects of the Hungarian hinterland. However he did not make the connection between the piece that the woman was playing and the painting on the wall. It depicted the surroundings of Lake Balaton in the transdanubian region through which the River Zala's streams have flowed for centuries and cows have grazed in idle submissiveness as time washed by.

The briefcase in the attorney's hand suddenly seemed to drag him downward. *Its heaviness derives from a source other than gravity,* he concluded without realizing that solemnity would become the ultimate mark of his visit.

It was time for him to leave the house, albeit without the oath in hand. As he exited the high door of Figlands Park, the son of Manoel Toledano, grandson of Eliézer—whose fate of having been early refugees to Brazil, from Portugal, and ultimately immigrants to Africa—had kept them far from the horrors of Europe, failed to notice the mezuzah. The small case nailed to the doorpost was made from a piece of polished driftwood. It contained a kosher scroll inscribed with holy text from Deuteronomy, its surface smoothed by the manifold rubbing of fingertips. Guarding "the going out and the coming in," it served its given purpose. Somehow, by the sly slippage of custom, the meaning and benefit of remembering the fragility of life on every departure and return to home had been eradicated from Yustus's consciousness. For him, tradition and faith had been broken on the barren rocks of apathy. In their place lay the desolateness of abandonment.

As he returned to the BMW, despite his warm clothing, Yustus felt damp cold collecting in the hollow of his elbows, settling uncomfortably behind his knees, and seeping inside the caves of his clammy armpits.

"This man and wife have perfected loneliness!" he declared as he drew up to the vehicle.

But the policeman cared not for his comment. He continued to blow cigarette smoke out of the window as the car belched white condensation from its exhaust pipe. The BMW made its way through the snow, down the twisting driveway in slippery caution to the gate and the street beyond.

∞∞∞

"For the record, state your name."

"Ish. It's short for Ishbak."

"One of the six children of Abraham's second wife, Keturah," the witness added voluntarily.

"Because my mother could not name me when I was born, I named myself."

"The Crimean nurse who delivered me called me 'Zalanköy.' She said it reminded her of her Tartar home, left behind to smolder in the forgotten territory of nothingness."

All present in the courtroom were silent.

"I changed it by writing myself a 'document,' a kind of 'deed of poll' that bound me to my new and chosen identity."

"A 'Promise of One.' I still have it!" His forehead crinkled into lines that accentuated his burn scars and untamed ulcers. Over the lost eye a black patch, held in place by strings that ran across and over his head, ruled like a sinister eparch. As he spoke of his arrival into a world of chaos and confusion that followed the end of World War II, his voice altered. Praetorian authority seemed to replace prior reticence, albeit briefly.

I am the product of my mother's rape! He wished to scream the declaration of despair. But the court's walls closed in, and the chamber of enquiry stilled his mental eruption.

Observing closely, Elijah Sweet, the famous barrister whose wisdom was well known (albeit that he was intensely contemptuous of ignorance when it had no cause other than deceit) within the constricted legal community and the society at large, thought: *In a short span, the witness seems to be undergoing incarceration and liberation! Out of such transformative anguish—betrayed by shudders running through his broken body, ripples of intonation, and fault lines of sentiment—may yet emerge valor!* The counselor knew something, indeed much more, than others who had gathered in the inquest court.

Now soft again, reverting to a level barely above a whisper, Ish Aval's utterances splintered beneath machete blows of remembrance. Within him coals were heating the steam of angst, releasing the voices of poltergeists whose agitations he hosted and who moved feelings around in his mind as if they were physical objects possessed. Yet, since "the fall" their unassuageable sobbing and distraught howling had quieted somewhat. He willed them aside. *They are resting now*, he thought, *but for how long?*

It was not the magistrate's prerogative to comment on names. Nonetheless he could not restrain himself.

"Unusual forename. *Ne'*?" Magistrate Danie van Schalkwyk used the Afrikaans colloquialism to emphasize his sarcastic query. "What does it mean?" The witness did not have to wait before the stirrings recurred. *They are back again, flaunting their imperatives!*

"Man," he replied. "It derives from an ancient tongue."

Although Ish was a lover of literature and language, which afforded him temporary reprieve from his anxieties, he had no desire to alleviate the magistrate's distress—whether caused by bigotry, intolerance, or ignorance. *Any thinking person in this condemned place must be aware of the cronyism that installed him here.*

"Surname?" The question was posed by the magistrate with an air of hostility.

"Aval," he replied. Anticipating what was coming, he added, "Roughly translated, it means *doubt*."

The magistrate searched the limited repository of biblical sources that had been pumped into him by his childhood dominee, the priest of his Dutch Reformed Church in the small provincial town of Louis Trigaard. His hometown settlement straddled the Great North Road, stretching its way to the Rhodesian border at Beitbridge on the Limpopo River—which, during the dry season, is often more sand than water. In the spur of the moment, the magistrate could remember only that *the Old Testament was written in ancient languages . . . Hebrew, Aramaic . . . translated into Greek, Latin, and so on.* The allusion escaped him. His glasses rose on his itchy nose that bulged sideways. He drew a handkerchief from his robe. The display of blowing loudly was more of a trick to mask hesitation than it was to clear his red-rimmed nostrils and clogged sinuses.

"Identity number, as it appears in your book of life!" The magistrate plunged forth, his voice muddled. It was not a question, but rather an order, referring to the blue book given to whites in which driver's, firearm, marriage license, blood group, address, and identity information is imprinted on watermarked and thread-embossed paper specially manufactured by the government printer.

A propagandist tool to counter international abhorrence of apartheid and criticism of the infamous pass books *that the law requires black people to produce on demand*, Elijah Sweet, the only senior counsel in the room, thought in disgust. Saliva spurted under his tongue. It turned acidic. He recognized it as an omen of what was to come. *Better to meet one's enemy on the road than in the foxhole*, he thought, remembering what a man who had fought in a great war once told him before a trial that would sap even his irrepressible energy and test the limits of justice.

Upon being asked, actually told, to identify himself by a number, the witness recoiled. *My mother had her name stolen!* Like a bullfighter forced by injury from the ring of conflict, Ish Aval too had been gored by the horns of loss. It galled him deeply that he did not know his mother's numbers, tattooed crudely into the soft skin of her forearm, surrounded by snaking veins and unsightly protrusions caused by starvation and illness.

In their earnest perfection, even in the art of annihilation, the Nazis innovated with record keeping. Pull up a sleeve and the inmate's classification is revealed. A quick look. No contact. Contamination avoided. Tattoos dehumanize by numbers!

The witness felt his stomach lurch as he thought of the denigration of ancient traditions extending way beyond the Chiribaya mummies of Peru—even into the Ice Age. But he remembered also that the embalmed and wrapped bodies *were not only love ciphers, amulets, warders of omens, monograms, sentries at the gates of superstition—for they were symbols of punishment and degradation too. The Aryans knew this from their addiction to paganism!*

Just the vaguest memory of his mother's beauty remained intact as an obscure image described by the Crimean nurse. *Perhaps it is better that I never read her numbers*, he consoled himself. Reluctantly, bitten by the serpents of memory, he answered, and "for the record," he gave the year, month, and date in a monotonous string of eight digits.

The magistrate shot him a squinting stare. *He looks much older*, he thought. Noting observations on a yellow legal pad, he wrote, "Disabilities: A crooked arm, fingers distorted, a black patch covering a blind eye? Hard limp. Leans to one side, burn scars on face and hands. What else?" He felt irritated by the man in the witness box. However, despite his resentful feelings at having to preside over a hearing that he considered from reading the docket to be unworthy of his attention, he was duty-bound by law to proceed.

"Do you swear that the evidence that you shall give in this inquest shall be the whole truth and nothing but the truth?" Without waiting for a reply, the magistrate added, "Say, 'So help me God!'"

The witness was silent. His left arm, supporting the twisted hand that lay on the closed Bible, wavered. In vain he struggled to steady it with his other hand. As he was about to give up, it obeyed somewhat—the bone resisting, his impaired muscles bending the injured limb inward in a hug-like arc.

Sitting motionlessly at counsel's table, Elijah Sweet, the leading advocate, registered the omission of an affirmation required by law. *Like a poisoned arrow*, he thought as he put it in his figurative appellate quiver, just in case he needed to withdraw it later. Although he acted for clients pursuant to his brief, he nonetheless could not resist concluding: *My dedication is as much to a personally justifiable outcome as it is to the service of the cold and callous law.*

"Where were you born?"

The witness did not appreciate the relevance of the query. But, having been duly warned to answer "all questions," he uttered the reply that clamored to be spoken.

At that moment, Sweet, who expected a succinct response, was thinking, *If a long answer is coming, then a short inquest will follow. That suits my objectives here.* He noticed the look of growing anxiety on Ish Aval's face. *Strategy!* he reasserted to himself. *Tactics, not brawn!* He settled his silk robe, the cloth of "seniority," about him and determined that he would watch the play unfold.

"In a tank." The ceiling fan spun, slicing awkwardly through the overheated air. Winter still held sway. The appliance had been set to a date determined by government regulation. *On at certain hours. Off at others. Seasons be damned*, the magistrate thought, although he did appreciate the circulation of heat from raw elements exposed above the cracked Ionic crowns of the courtroom's columns.

Weeks had passed since the night that Yustus had gone to Figlands Park and hoped to attest to Mr. Aval's affidavit, while his strange slight wife stood by draped in a feathery coat that looked like a worn eiderdown. *There is no music, raucous or soothing, in the house of the law*, the attorney thought. Turning fan blades were the only sounds in an otherwise quiet courtroom that seemed to have hushed more so as a consequence of the last response.

"A what?" Magistrate Danie van Schalkwyk asked in a thick Afrikaans accent, scowling with unsuppressed frustration. He wanted to clear the docket quickly. Accentuating his incredulity, he said, "Sir, this is a serious hearing! Please do not be facetious or disrespectful to the bench. That will not be tolerated here! The question is asked in order to qualify you as a reliable witness. I need to know your background, starting with where you were born."

Ish Aval hesitated.

"Your Worship," he said slowly, pronouncing the magistrate's formal title clearly, "this requires some explanation. May I tell my story?"

The senior regional inquest magistrate looked impatient, fidgety, and somewhat baffled, but he held back. As he pulled himself straight in the upholstered green chair of the presiding officer, pigmented leather adhered to his gown.

Spiders spread their cobweb traps, Elijah Sweet thought, waiting, although patience was not his best virtue. Raising a quizzical eyebrow, the magistrate looked at the dapper advocate (always dressed impeccably), who nodded almost imperceptibly. The signal of consent thus granted by a far superior jurist, some measure of patience, even vague and hesitant sympathy, touched the magistrate. He took an audible breath of the heated air. It felt like prickly pears being swallowed, unpeeled. His lungs seemed to vibrate in protest.

The man is lame. His eye is patched. His arm is damaged.

When mounting the high steps of the witness box, he stumbled. What does he have to say? Tension rattled the sword loosely held in the hands of Blind Justice where she stood shakily in Doornkloof, her figurative presence fragile and timorous that day.

"Very well then. Continue."

Van Schalkwyk held the docket file in his lap, one elbow trying to relax with affected nonchalance on the armrest of his chair. *Are we all unsure of our way?* he wondered. The fear of affliction threatened him, just as the deacon of his youth had intended in sermons warning of the dire consequences that follow transgression and the insidiousness of wayward thought.

Many years before the events in the courtroom that day, a tragic event occurred at a place called Kikambala. There a sparkling white beach traverses the Kenyan shore, and the Indian Ocean's inestimable waters play with the strands of east Africa.

A small assemblage of thatched huts clustered together. Ostensibly drawing strength from one another, they seemed to struggle to remain upright. Beyond the huddle, coconut trees waved serrated branches in the sea breeze. Blanched shells glistened on the water's edge. It was one day before Christmas. Heat came down like burning particles in the aftermath of a distant volcano, its mountainous eruptions unseen and unheard, yet felt in the fiery air.

A heavy man, unusually tall with wide shoulders, strong arms, curly black hair, and a smile bent downward by the Havana cigar between his lips, sat with his two sons. They were ten and eight years old, respectively. In their shorts, the three were bare from the waist up and the knees down. Rubber thongs divided their big toes. They wore sandals made by native fishermen who found old tires floating amid the frothy flotsam, dumped carelessly in the ocean as if the sea could forever remain the limitless cistern of trash.

Their skin was red with sunburn. The father handed each son a blue tube of protective cream made of borax, menthol, thymol, and clove oil.

"This will ease the burn," he said, his baritone rumbling.

The boys squeezed out the silky substance. Sitting in the shade of the thatch overhang on the wide porch, they smoothed it onto their arms, legs, backs, feet, and chests.

"It will cool our skin," their father said. The boys listened. They tried not to complain. They bit their lips.

"Soon the sun will set behind us," he continued. "It will be cooler. Then we'll walk down to the lagoon and swim." The cigar end glowed brightly, its rim afire in a fuming ring. They waited as he told them stories of "the equatorial region," full of romantic mysteries and flamboyant heroes who stood with one foot in the southern hemisphere and the other in the northern.

"Pantheon Pirates! That's Greek. It means 'to every god.' But they had no deities except violence and greed!" their dad declared. "Swashbuckling plunderers, fearless swordsmen who roved the broadest circumference of earth's squandered oceans!"

"When they landed on hostile islands, the sun and the moon rose and fell together over mountains and valleys. They came for slaves in Africa, but turned and ran when the thunder of cannibals beating their shields with primitive spears filled the air!"

The father used the time with his sons well.

The boys forgot their burning skins. Their childish imaginations brimmed with the exciting promise of adventures—that day, the one to follow, and beyond.

Stars began to make their flickering appearances. Suddenly, a meteor shot overhead. It seemed to triumph briefly in celestial space. The man inhaled and removed the "Cuban," holding its fat shank between thumb and forefinger. When he exhaled, a full circle of bluish smoke twisted in flight from his lips. The youngest son, on his right, looked at the tendril looping and fading off, then at his father. Cicadas sang in stark harmony.

"Dad," he said longingly, "can I smoke?"

∞∞∞

Ish Aval had resumed speaking at the inquest.

"In 1944 the 'Austrian corporal' . . . may his name be obliterated forever . . . didn't like the Roman numeral *V*. So he had it removed from the old warhorse's predecessor when the new Panzerkampfwagen, 'Panther,' tank with the ordnance inventory designation Sd.Kfz.171 went into full production as an answer to Russian heavy mobile armor."

This preamble relating to a figure he admired seemed to unsettle Magistrate van Schalkwyk. He was certain that he would be criticized for permitting the witness to meander in testimony because Advocate Sweet had been known to vociferously resist irrelevancies. But Elijah Sweet remained silent and seated.

The magistrate's normally florid complexion grew paler, before reddening, color spreading down the sides and back of his neck. His faded brown moustache, stained by cheap tobacco, jerked sporadically. His teeth gnashed visibly. He was about to cut the witness off when, although due to his squint he could not be entirely sure, the magistrate thought that counsel winked, with almost a hint of conspiratorial intent.

"Continue," he said, the intended words of false rebuke drying on the tip of his moist tongue, which looked like it had been swirled robustly in red wine.

Ish Aval straightened slightly before lapsing into a stoop again. "That was after the losses of the Battle of Prokhorovka on the Eastern Front."

"I survived. I was an infant, lying beside my ill-fated mother and my still-born twin sister. We were inside 'the womb' of a German weapon. It was deserted by its five-man crew." His voice became bitter. "The Panther's ghosts are still fleeing through forests, whipped by branches, punished by cowardice, followed by indefatigable pursuers."

Magistrate van Schalkwyk felt as if the Achilles heel of his admiration had been pierced. Wincing at the reference to his heroes being described as perpetual fugitives, he asked in a taciturn tone, "Relevance?" hoping to appease counsel in case he had misinterpreted the wink. This time he avoided all eye contact, squint or otherwise.

Elijah Sweet, the Queen's Counsel, a small but intellectually powerful man, rose behind the advocates' desk and stared through his pince-nez, clipped with practiced confidence to the end of his aquiline nose. First he looked at the witness, delivering a dose of wearisome pity, then with utter contempt, at the magistrate. By force of habit and personality he impaled each on the barbed tips of condescension as he uttered a single word, sounding high and sharp like a Yorkshire terrier's bark.

"Truth!"

It was neither a question nor a comment. It was a command for revelation.

As the hearing transpired, that would be one of the few remarks he would make for the cost of his exorbitant retainer. Like a ball of string, the testimony had begun to unravel in the inquest court. *Such is the craftiness of narration*, Elijah Sweet thought, feeling satisfied now at the way things were going.

"You may proceed," the magistrate stated, trying to ignore the intimidation.

"Learned counsel," *asseblief*, Danie van Schalkwyk, the presiding officer, said in Afrikaans, "I'm sorry. Please, resume your seat for now."

Elijah was anything but charming. A brilliant, acerbic, seasoned barrister, he had no intention of being outgunned by any magistrate. *I qualified at the Inns of Court in London before this pompous individual was born*. Being a strategist, he knew when to fire and when to reload. *I will refrain this time. Later, if the need arises, I shall take aim.*

I was the confidant of royalty. It was true that a member of the royal household had been his friend at the Inner Temple when he was the top scholar. They had "eaten dinners" together, which the legal scholars are required to do as part of graduating privileges, according to old custom. Some rumors held that he was accorded "Q.C." (Queen's Counsel) status because of royal patronage. *Utter nonsense*, he scoffed as he recollected. *Such allegations of benefaction imply the stings of libel. They shall be met by the fire of retribution!*

During the punctuating silence, the Q.C. began his deliberately slow settling process. A large facial mole, ironically in the shape of Africa upside down, extended blackly from the skin of one cheek. Many made comments on it, but only behind his back. Although diminutive in size, he was a giant in legal stature. He went about the business of the law entirely fearlessly.

Elijah Sweet never missed a single remark and he never turned the other cheek, which he considered not to be an act of humility, but rather a demonstration of cowardice. Rumor percolated through the sieves of his amazing memory. It settled, although never permanently, alongside his prodigious knowledge of the law.

He could recall whole texts of judgments, opinions, journal articles, statutes, gazettes, and dissertations verbatim. Citing authors, dates, facts, and conclusions by heart came naturally to him, rendering his opposition awestruck. Everyone in the profession knew that he possessed unique and superb forensic ability. Thus he was dubbed the "Cerebrum"—Latin for *brain*.

Nobody dared ever call him by his first name, Elijah, except for his ninety-three-year-old mother, who had named her only child after her hero, the greatest of the Old Testament prophets.

On the day she finished reading the Book of Malachi, the name appealed to her. "Therein," she declared, "Elijah's return is prophesied. Before the coming of the great and terrible day of the Lord." At that time she was both heavily pregnant and deeply observant—"a formula for becoming susceptible to influence," she later said to him. Upon completing the book, she told her son (whose brilliance she recognized and fostered from an early age), "That morning, a postcard arrived from my only cousin, Dominique, in Paris" (which she pronounced "Paree"). On its reverse side, *Elijah Reviving the Son of the Widow of Zarephath*, a glossy photographic reproduction of Louis Hersent's masterwork, lay open to view. She described it as "a female exclamation of impulsive joy."

Young as he was, the future jurist understood. He remembered:

> The barefoot old prophet was depicted in a beautiful, simple flowing robe of apricot color, holding out a long-haired blond child whose enigmatic smile shone forth. It reached with both

tiny hands for the embrace of its grateful parent. The woman was dressed in purple. Not gazing at Elijah, the beckoning baby looked longingly at the source of its own life. Two of the three figures—the restorer and the receiver—were in right and left profile. However, at the center, the subject of adult attention was painted by the French artist in semi-full face.

"All were struck by a ray of heavenly light," Mrs. Sweet told her son. When she reread her relative's simple message, saved tenderly, Elijah was four years of age and already an academic protégé. It read, "With love, Your Cousin, forever, D." A telepathic wave overwhelmed her. Thus the boy who would emerge as a great Commonwealth advocate was told by his mother how he received his name, which means "My God is Jehovah."

As he completed his elaborate and demonstrative seating process in the inquest court, The "Cerebrum" managed to suppress the ironic expression that had begun traversing his face, transforming the big mole into a dark, infiltrating shadow. Elijah was contrarily proud of his disfigurement.

He who succumbs to the manipulative control that the law imposes at the hands of corrupt politicians shall not know tranquility. But he who admits the absurdity of the law may yet be appeased by its power and find solace in its influence! he reminded himself as he had often done during innumerable trials.

Elijah Sweet smiled his sardonic, rather rare and intuitive smile as the evidence continued to unfold.

"The tank had been rushed into service before it was ready. 'Because fuel is short and so is steel,' one of the generals risked his life in daring to tell the Führer." The witness, Ish Aval, suddenly hesitated, his voice disintegrating somewhat. He took a moment of recovery before continuing.

Let him proceed, Elijah thought. *It will serve my ultimate purpose! The secret is safe with me alone!* On the paper block lying on the desktop in front of him, he wrote compulsively: "I am anti-gas! In all of its forms!"

He turned slightly and handed the note to Yustus Toledano.

The Q.C.'s rather unusual and wounding humor was known to his instructing attorneys. Sitting behind, not beside, the Q.C., as Elijah insisted, Yustus read the perplexing words, without appreciating their true meaning. He had to think. Finally it came to him.

"Double entendre?" he asked, whispering to counsel as if in the intimacy of a secret. But Sweet did not like to be interrupted in thought, deed, or action. His head kept warm (even, some rumored, when he slept, which sometimes happened during boring trials) beneath the short-cropped wig of scratchy, gray, dyed horsehair, Elijah Sweet was known to have been deeply moved by his study of the Nuremburg Trials.

"Infamy unmasked. Justice almost served," he muttered, his face reddening. *The man is so dumb, I had better explain to him quickly*, he decided. Hissing through his clenched teeth, half turning to speak to the attorney, whose mediocrity he abhorred, Elijah said, "Otto Rasch . . . you have probably never heard of him . . . was a murderer with two doctorates! A killer of innocents, he was known as 'Doctor Doctor.' The Einsatzgruppen death squads in Eastern Europe used captured Russian tank engines to spew poisonous exhaust fumes into gas chambers. He was a *talented* professional."

The Q.C. had said what he wanted. He let the innuendo seep.

"Now," he added for good measure, "do not speak to me again until this is over!"

Yustus cowered like a chastised dog and obeyed.

After he had completed a course of lectures on the "A, B, C, & D groups," which he had been invited to deliver at the University of the Witwatersrand's sprawling campus in Johannesburg, he never called his office "chambers" again. Instead, the huge office of Elijah Sweet, Queen's Counsel, became "advocate's rooms"—and cursed be anyone who used the wrong wording or contradicted him, for the berating that would follow was not worth the risk of loose speech.

The silk lining of the senior barrister's robes rustled as Elijah gathered the folds around his small, now seated, frame. He flicked back the puffed sleeves, and looked up at the ceiling of the courtroom.

Yustus Toledano realised that he had better think again. The best he could produce with immediate effect was a compliment, albeit unexpressed: *He is the finest jurist at the bar.* Then feeling mortified, he lapsed backwards, duly chastened. He tried to shrink down as low as he could go. But he could not make his lanky frame shorter than that of the diminutive Q.C., for Elijah Sweet, even when standing, appeared to be seated.

As compensation for inadequacy, Yustus consoled himself. *That's why my father told me to brief him, as expensive as he is, for* "our important client and its negligent employee. The airline can afford it!"

Toledano had no inkling of what lay ahead in counsel's juristic ordnance. But, even if he had, there was no way he could have imagined the Q.C.'s tactical intentions.

"Respect . . ." the barrister had told him at the briefing in his rooms before the inquest, yelping in a higher-than-usual pitch, ". . . of self, is a prerequisite to respect by others."

"Judicial sovereignty is a myth," he added without waiting for a reply, as was his habit. "My duty is to carry ridicule to its illogical conclusions. No more, no less!"

The managing director of the airline had been present at the pre-hearing consultation. He gasped. Opening his mouth to utter protest at a perceived slight, a proverbial cat seemed to claw his tongue. Then, as the Q.C. stared unblinkingly into his eyes from behind his magnificently inlaid desk by André-Charles Boulle, it took a figurative bite, down hard. In the pain of screaming silence the managing director closed his mouth and thought about whether Advocate Sweet's outrageous fee was justified. Elijah seemed to read his mind.

"We shall see," he said. "This meeting is over."

He rose and walked out of his rooms for he knew enough to prepare for the day in court.

Elijah Sweet recollected a brief incident in the Supreme Court that had occurred a fortnight before the inquest. He had been appearing for a wealthy woman in "a rich divorce," as he termed it. She was obliged to take the stand to simply say to the judge presiding in the rotunda building, "My marriage has broken down irretrievably." That was all the evidence required for an uncontested decree of final divorce, preceded by a *rule nisi*, to qualify for grant a short while later.

But she did not make it easily to the witness stand. As she passed in front of the advocates' counter below the enthroned judge on his elevated bench, one high-heeled shoe caught on the hem of her full-length dress. She tripped and fell face forward. *Prostrate before justice*, as the advocate recalled. *A well-deserved cataclysm of confusion*, he concluded.

The judge recoiled. As the court orderly hurried to lift her, the Q.C., quick as a whip, asked rhetorically, "Madam, I trust you know the difference between 'a woman who has fallen' and 'a fallen woman?'"

Needless to say, she did not reply, he reminded himself. The judge tried to stifle a laugh. However he didn't quite manage to smother the humor, as a titter ran through the courtroom. Not very long thereafter, when nobody had come forward to "show cause to the contrary" as required by the rule of civil procedure, to her great delight the affluent woman was granted an accelerated decree of final divorce. The Q.C. recalled the inappropriate celebration.

Set in a sterling silver ice bucket, Dom Pérignon Brut Imperial champagne, named for the Benedictine monk who originated the marvelous drink, flowed. The impromptu party took place on the steps of the courthouse that opened onto Von Brandis Square, commemorating the "City of Gold's" early mining commissioner and "enforcer of speculators' justice."

Her victory was marred only by the persistent bruises on her knees. They spread in a profusion of purple rosettes. No matter how much she rubbed them with ointment, they refused to heal completely. *Analgesic indeed*, Elijah thought, *from the Greek, an* (without) *plus "algos"* (pain)! *Even ancient wisdom can be fallacious!*

"Daimler-Benz and the Maschinenfabrik Augsburg-Nürnberg Algemaine Gesellschaft designed the new thirty-five-ton mobile weapon of war."

"The Nazis were creative engineers. They kept the good engine of its predecessors. But they added a glacis plate, angled armor, and ridged coating that prevented magnetic mines from adhering to the steel hulls. Such Aryan arrogance it is to judge others by one's own standards for armaments, because none of the Allies used such weapons. Only the Germans themselves did!"

"Go on," the magistrate said, now keen to hear more about the tank, in which he was more interested than the inquest. Secretly he wished that he could own one and keep it in a shed on his small holding. *I would have the only key!* He thought excitedly.

He had heard somewhere that old German field tanks were available as relics, but at a price that he could not afford, even on his inflated and protected magisterial salary. So he was forced to compensate by frequent visits to the War Museum at the Zoo Lake where he could gaze at the contraptions of conflict lovingly housed in their Earlswold Way site in the classy suburb of Saxonwold.

"They retained a 7.5 cm Rheinmetall-Borsig KwK 42 high-muzzle-velocity cannon and two deadly MG34 machine guns. The crew stored spare shells as well as bandoliers of bullets in its sponson."

"That was not the finest plan." Ish Aval was going on while Elijah Sweet was getting somewhat impatient. The only reason for his remaining seated was that *this "war talk" suits my plans for the outcome of the hearing.*

"You see," Aval said, addressing everybody and nobody in particular, "that is where my dying mother gave birth to me, the first twin."

The witness's lips had begun curling, his good eye glaring, his bad arm shaking violently, and his spine distorting more than usual in his distress. Everyone present became aware of the stillness that followed those words. It intervened and stayed until he continued without regard for the magistrate's sudden and sporadic grunting.

"She only had enough energy left in her broken body to produce me. She died with the last effort to birth my twin sister!"

His voice grew dimmer, like a flickering flame on a bent

wick. "They killed her, those wicked, evil thugs!" He drew a handkerchief from his sleeve, wept silently, and blew his nose, which ran profusely in lieu of tears.

"Approximately six thousand such tanks were produced, but probably the side 'float' of the Panther in which I was born was the only one that ever served as a maternity unit! My tank bore the crooked black cross insignia with the number '666' on its flanks! Draw your own conclusion," he said, looking at all and at none, again. In that momentary gaze, unfocused distance turned into a flash of memory. "I was told the circumstances of my birth, the death of mother and of my twin, by the Crimean nurse."

"The side armor of the Panther was notoriously weak, vulnerable to Allied armor-piercing shells, although that part of the tank directly above the tracks included layers of hardened, supposedly bulletproof, materials to protect its occupants," he went on, having recovered his equilibrium. His chest still heaved.

"But it didn't work! A shell tore through it, ignited a fire within, and blew the turret off kilter, skewing and buckling its guns, leaving a smoking hole through which its crew, all wounded, must have climbed as their uniforms burned into their flesh in their rush to get away before being incinerated alive."

"The charred wreck was left, its tracks torn off," he continued. "It lay where it was when it was hit, hissing, cooling, stiffening into a steel hulk, broken, abandoned to rust in a field outside of . . ."

He never finished that sentence and never named the place.

The magistrate was all but drooling.

"Africa," on Elijah's face twitched. The courtroom seemed to have grown darker, blacker, and more ominous. He sensed what was coming.

"I was delivered inside the Panther by a nurse."

"How did your mother get into a German tank?" van Schalkwyk asked. He was caught up in the dramatic account. Saliva coated his lips, which looked like boiled sausages.

The Q.C. blinked, both hands tapping on the desk. *We all have a life story to tell. We are the products of fate*, he confirmed. Even a great mind can be nonplussed by the unexpected and startled by incidental truth, to which the Q.C. was fond of referring as "the mystery of legitimacy." *This is no ordinary witness and this is not a complacent enquiry by the state*, he had already decided in his "rooms" when studying his brief as he stressed the righteousness of his planned coup. He drew his short thorax upright and settled into a contrived pose of persistence—a condition that he loathed, *unless its purpose is optimistic and strong*. With a little bark, camouflaged as a cough, he concluded to himself: *The problem with patience is its insistence on endurance!*

At the back of the courtroom, where a few benches had been arrayed in the public gallery and a line separated "Europeans" from "non-Europeans" (although none of the latter were present), a large man with curly hair and an aura of charisma sat with his two sons. Inside his breast pocket he fingered a gold-plated cigar tube.

The audience of three, who had been invited by Elijah Sweet, Q.C., listened raptly. The barrister knew they were there, but he kept his acknowledgement of their presence secret. He had omitted their names from the witness list deliberately. *What can they contribute, except to explain the injuries of the primary witness?* He knew that the father wished their savior acts to remain in the vault of silence, and Elijah, of all people, understood the advantages of strategic discretion.

∞ ∞ ∞

The father recalled that the evening had come, and when the sun fell on the opposite side of the ocean—just as he predicted—the air cooled somewhat. Light faded, yet did not disappear completely. It clung tenaciously to the purple sky, glowing with eerie persistence on the mirrored waters of the lagoon, which was so placid that not even a ripple tarnished its surface.

The younger son still waited for his father to answer his question. As they gazed out toward the mango trees at the edge of the primitive Hammerhead Inn's perimeter, the last burn of a Romeo et Juliet Havana lit the tobacco wrapper's edges in fiery emanations, before turning to ashes.

"Yes, you may. But on one condition."

"What?" the boy asked. He hesitated. More light descended. It seemed to be chewed by the teeth of advancing dusk as it fell.

"That you smoke this whole thing." He held out a full cigar. "Nonstop, inhaling fully all the time."

"Sure," the eight-year-old answered, with the intemperate bravado of youth. His father went into the hut. He emerged with a clipper and cut the tip of the cigar, slicing two neat lines across. He flipped the excised piece with thumb and forefinger. It darted off the stairs. Then he lit the cigar and handed it to the boy.

"Go ahead!"

As his brother and father watched, the boy began to smoke. He coughed and then inhaled again. "More!" his father ordered. The boy was turning green in the face. He ran down the steps onto the scraggly lawn in front of the rondavel, leaned over at the waist, and began to retch.

Then it happened!

His older brother held a Kodak Brownie in his hands. The pictures he took with the box camera would one day be given to a man who had lost an eye and remained with deep aches from poorly set broken bones, burns, and scars to remind him of the evening on a beach in Kenya where he lay clinging to life in a place of flaming death.

The Beechcraft Super King Air swept over the indigo horizon, recently vacated by a tropical sun. As the aircraft left one dimension, so it occupied another. Its two turboprop Canadian Pratt & Whitney engines roared with fierce power, even at a distance. The noise grew louder, more insistent, as the father and his sons watched in bleak fascination.

Something was terribly wrong!

The sleek aircraft was very low, just skimming the crests of waves, coming straight toward Kikambala. Unexpectedly, as it reached the stretch of beach and overflew the lagoon, the aircraft banked sharply. One engine burst into flames. White plumes of smoke mixed with flashes of fire as it tried to level out, but yawed violently. Beneath each engine, the wheels were in a half-lowered position. At 169 miles per hour with an almost-empty tank weight of 7,000 pounds, the aircraft hit the shoreline.

One wheel bit into the soft sand declining onto the harder, wet, tide flats. It dug in as the other slipped and collapsed. Powered by the engine that was not yet burning, the port-side propeller caught the ground, tore into sand, and was ripped off. Like a live ghoul it spun into the coconut grove above the water, guillotining on its way, shredding leaves and scattering nuts before embedding itself in the pulp of surrounding papaya trees. The aircraft cartwheeled. Wing tanks exploded in balls of flame, spewing debris onto the undulating beach. As the fuselage veered, cutting deep ruts into the sand, it lurched violently then fell back, the tail partially shearing off in a scream of serrated metal.

Freed of one wing, an engine, and the scuttling superstructure of the tail, the aircraft began to roll into the onrushing waves of the Indian Ocean. Despite the surging seawater sucking it powerfully into the backwash, the flames were not doused on the starboard side, where the flap caught on the rim of a rock just below the surface, but part of the rudder remained stubbornly fast.

The tide was still coming in. Red flames hemorrhaged against the violet sky. In the commotion, the nose was detached from the body of the aircraft. Then the fuselage erupted, hurling fire, steam, avgas, and a single body that flew through shattered glass and somersaulted in the air. It landed with a loud plop on the wet beach just shy of the licking foam that edged the blackening waves.

At that moment, the boy who had smoked part of the "Havana" disgorged his stomach's contents profusely. His father and brother broke their stupor of disbelief and began to run toward the flaming wreckage.

The witness, Ish Aval, was answering.

"My mother was dying. I am sure she knew it, even in her feeble state."

"She must have been aware that to give birth in a place like that would kill her and her babies! After the war I met an ex-inmate whom the Nazis never succeeded in working to death. Don't ask me how or where, because I shall not tell you. On the last day of their imprisonment, the woman had been in my mother's dormitory. Though inmates were separated by numbers, she and my mother were bound together by theirs. Her numbers were the same as my mother's except for the last digit, for the reason that the woman had been standing behind my mother in the tattoo line when they arrived. This is what she told me":

Our heads had just been shaven by a muscular female. She was tall and broad as a man! When she cut our hair off, we lost the last of our identities. We were no longer people. All we had to keep us intact was the memory of who we had once been before God looked away! At the center of her starched collar was a small mother-of-pearl brooch inlaid with bright black enamel. As she lifted her arms to grab our hair violently and shave it off with an electric sheep-shearing instrument, her short sleeve lifted. I saw the *Blutgruppentätowierung* . . . the tatoos . . . two, distinct black-dot letters, "AB," imprinted into the skin of her left armpit. That was the blood typing, hardly ever done to Nazi females. But this one had it!

Waffen-SS!

We had been ordered not to stare into their eyes. "Look down, you dogs!" they commanded as they beat us. We obeyed, so that we could live! But I saw what I saw! I liked the shape and the warmth of your mother's head more than my own, which I could not see, only feel. And your mother's head I could only touch with my toes, in the dark, bitter cold when we lay in a filthy bunk, clinging head-to-toe.

Your mother had soft skin, even on her scalp. Surrounded by fetid smells, she would whisper in our most desperate stages. "God is not here. We think of Him but He left, because he could not bear to witness what He had created. To prove Him wrong, to bring Him back, we must try to beat Death. "In the hush of the night, do not rage, do not fight; think only of the spark of light." Thus she gave me hope.

On the last day, when the thunder of Allied tanks could be

heard, the Nazi female in charge of the women—the one who had shaved our heads on the first day—took her fate into her own hands. We were working inside that day in a storeroom filled with hair, clothes, shoes, and children's toys. She raised her short whip to strike us, but lowered it as if seized by a sudden realization. She reached for a simple dress on the pile, a pair of worn shoes, a threadbare brassiere more like a vest, and laddered stockings like socks. She turned away from us, undressed, and folded her uniform. Naked, from behind she looked like a man. She even stole a dead man's under garments. She said nothing. For the first and only time, we followed her. She headed for the crematoria. The furnaces still burned. With the braided handle of her whip, she eased open a steel door. Flames roared with the breath of incoming air that fired their licking tongues back into action. She hurled her Nazi clothes into the oven, turned around, looked at us, then cast her whip into the flames! Ash lay on the floor of the chamber. She stooped, took some of it in her hands, and smeared it onto her smock, begriming herself, to make her look more like a rural, nondescript peasant.

We saw her walk out of the camp, down the winding road, heading for the village below where people lived, worked, ate, played, and made love, all in the "Shadow of Death." She followed the path, kicking the stolen shoes, tearing the stolen clothes of dead people, shouting as if to warn the soldiers that something terrible awaited their arrival! That is how she escaped, acting like one crazed. Someone in the camp called after her, "Anmuttie." I think it is an affectionate name, like little Mommy . . . or perhaps "Gracie?"

"I had to believe that woman who told me these things," Ish Aval declared, "because she befriended my mother whom I would never get to meet, except in the forgotten moment of birth when all prior consciousness is swept clean from the infant with the first breath and an angel's touch on the philtrum to initiate a new beginning!"

"Your mother heard the silence before me," she explained further. "It was eerie. All movement seemed to have stopped. The guards were gone. The wires of the electric fences ceased their infernal buzzing. German shepherds had disappeared, taking their awful snarling, baiting, and barking with them. Smoke continued to rise above the brick chimneys. The camp looked like it was aflame, although, on that last day, the plumes were thinner and weaker than usual."

"My mother, whose name that woman told me was Eva—I am not sure if it was—had been 'given' as a 'reward' for 'good work' by the Kommandant to a young officer who wore a uniform as black as night. She told me that he nodded his assent and said, 'Take her!' After that, the Nazi officer raped her at will! She said, in a voice of torment, that what she hated most was his leather lanyard, which he never removed."

Despite his ordeal, the witness's voice grew stronger. Still no tears dared to run. But his nose persisted in leaking as he continued to narrate what he had been told.

> We looked through the window and then opened the door. The morning was prematurely gray. The usual mantillas of ash clouds had frayed but not disappeared. A weepy, sick haze hovered over the compound, covering it with a lacey disguise that was almost beautiful in its ugliness.
>
> Then we saw her: a woman wearing dark blue and red, the colors of a Crimean nurse with a white stripe bisecting her bosom and a cross on her immaculate headdress. She was fine and healthy, as a woman should be, not like we were, wretched and rat-like. She strode purposefully into the quadrangle. Then she stopped and waited. She was alone and glorious in our eyes!
>
> I pushed your mother forward, out of the door. It groaned. She struggled, hobbling barefoot, weak, sick, bug-ridden, and pregnant, until she reached the statuesque woman standing by herself there. She buckled before the Crimean nurse. The woman scooped her off the ground like a bundle of rags, lifted her, and carried her out of the camp as if she were a bloated puppet. I watched them move toward the blown-up tank. It seemed to be waiting for them. Then they disappeared inside it, through the hole where the shell had struck.

Ish Aval needed to proceed with his testimony. At last, tears ran down his scarred face from his one good eye and reached his lips.

"I was told that I lay on the metal floor surrounded by placenta. The Crimean nurse who, for reasons I shall never know because war hides its secrets, traveled with Eisenhower's forces. She listened for my faint cry, cut the umbilical cord, removed her coat, wrapped me in it, and walked a considerable distance to a regimental first aid station."

The walls of the courtroom seemed to buckle, then sigh. Even Elijah Sweet ceased tapping, as the witness added, "And so, in the German tank, a 'Sister of the Covenant' helped a dying young Jewish woman give birth to one living twin and one stillborn, who was left behind—rendered as much a victim of oppression and deprivation as her mother."

To this evidence, none of the lawyers present invoked the objection of "hearsay," and none interrupted a man who spoke distinctly, yet quietly, of such things that caused his eye and nose to leak in a stream, and his broken body to shudder relentlessly.

∞∞∞

When the elder son and his father reached the crash site, the intense heat drove them back. Behind them the younger boy was feeling wretched at the thought of having eaten mango while they waited for the sun to lose its heat. A sick patina suffusing his cheeks, his lips oozing emesis, he came running, trying to catch up. His face bore an expression of shock as he reached his father and brother, who had been forced back by the fire. The aircraft was burning ferociously as if gripped in the furious fists of hell itself.

Relegated to watching the conflagration, knowing that there must have been others inside the fuselage who were dying in a funeral pyre or were already dead, there was nothing they could do. So they turned away and rushed together to the body lying in a heap on the beach.

"Man alive!" the father shouted to his sons, over the noise of metal popping and bursting, giving way to such intense heat that glass, in pieces, had melted and aluminum had warped. He had seen the chest rise and fall, one eye openly staring at him, the other torn out. Ugly contusions surrounded the scorched flesh of the face. A runny discharge leaked from the socket like the yolk of a cracked egg. His legs lay trapped under him. The left arm folded back at an unnatural angle, extended from the elbow. Bloody shards of bone protruded through burnt skin. He smelled of aviation fuel and the sickly odor of a primal pyre. His age was indeterminable.

This man was thrown clear of the plane in the crash. He is "present" and "absent," the father thought looking at the wretched body, wanting to shield his boys from it but at the same time needing their assistance. *They must learn from the sight of human suffering,* he concluded as a quick compromise with the inevitable.

Together they began to pull the body farther up the beach to the rim of jetsam that a previous tide had deposited. Among the debris were green coconuts, bits of stringy sisal plants, a brown beer bottle, and the fin of a shark. Now surrounded by the wreckage, the barely living sole survivor of the destroyed Super King struggled to remain alive, tended by strangers.

They heard a noise, then turned to look at the seawater darkening in the fading light, lit now by fire, not sun, then dimmed by spewing oil and gas. The sheen covered the waves. It lubricated the remains of the aircraft's frame just as the last section of tail broke off finally amid the power of waves. It exploded and sank, in a matter of seconds.

The sun fell, losing its war with dusk. The moon rose presumptuously, followed by the glittering blue stars of a tropical night. A seagull late in flight squawked out a cry. The ocean answered with its wet, throaty, continuous gush, as if the metal beneath its surface deserved no epitaph for unwelcome invasion. Dad, who had a collection of glass ashtrays in vibrant colors throughout his home in Johannesburg, all grayed with the tipped ash of smoked cigars, thought of the Venetian doges of bygone eras, one of whose cardinal duties was to celebrate the "marriage" of the city to the sea by throwing a ring from a majestic barge. *But this sea has claimed a different nuptial rite and human "sacrifices" for its appeasement!* he decided.

Suddenly Kikambala grew intensely silent as if a great

force had tied a knot in the noose of infernal noise.

On the beach, surrounded by a halo of dying, artificial light cast by the flames of torches, the survivor struggled for breath. Blood gurgled in his throat. Coughs spluttered. His body jerked spasmodically, then curled up.

Far away in Kampala, the capital of Uganda, situated on Mengo Hill where she worked at the Buganda Court of Justice as an interpreter, a diffident petite lady felt a hard catch in her throat. Momentarily she lost track of the sentence she was translating from Swahili into English. As if something foreign obstructed her voice, she tried to eject whatever it was that plagued her. It felt like her blood had stopped circulating. Then an image struck her. In her mind's eye she saw the reflection of her husband. He looked shattered. Shadowy figures surrounded him—one large, two smaller. They leaned over him. Bile rose. She stood up, exclaimed a hoarse apology, swallowed visibly, and departed.

On the road from the airport to the city (just as one of the fairest views of the Duncan Docks at the foot of Table Mountain comes into sight when the boulevard takes a curve), a grand building liveried in white appears on the right. Groote Schuur (Dutch for "Big Barn"), the site of the world's first heart-transplant operation, *is a place for return of the living dead*, the father told his sons, using imagery from the stories he had related to the boys on the equator.

To that magnificent, sprawling hospital on the lower reaches of Devil's Peak the influential man had arranged for the sole survivor of the terrible air crash to be transported. The mercy flight took Ish Aval from Mombasa, where he had been stabilized, to Cape Town, with a refueling stop in Dar es Salaam and another in Salisbury. At "the Cape Dutch" as some of the staff called it, the broken man was reassembled as far as possible. One of the doctors said that when he was admitted, "he was more fluid than solid as if life had flowed out of him," adding, however facetiously, that "some tenacious weeds reroot themselves."

Thus after many surgeries and months of recuperation, a

burned man with skin like molten wax on three quarters of his body was discharged back into the world. As they moved slowly beneath the hospital's portico, his delicate wife, with whom he had been reunited at the behest of the philanthropic father of two sons—tried to apply her limited strength to ease him upright. They remained in South Africa, never returning to Uganda where he had also once worked since coming from Europe and where he had met "his canary," as he called her. Nor did he go back to Kenya—the excruciating memories of which even the salving gel on his burns and scars was never able to alleviate.

∞∞∞

"What happened that day?"

For two reasons the magistrate was urging a response. Earlier he had eaten a meal of pork pie. Perhaps the pig had been too old or the creamy sauce too rich, *but I cannot settle the meat, which is making me nauseated*, he thought, although he had been drawn into the story of war, cruelty, and what seemed like revenge in the making. The second, more compelling, reason was that Elijah Sweet, Q.C., had started drumming his fingers on counsel's desk . . . again.

Yustus Toledano was torn between sympathy and fascination, between patience and the drive for conclusion. As the Q.C. had predicted, he was too immature a jurist to know quite what to do, when or how to fence and thrust with the épée of jurisprudential skill. But Elijah did!

At last! the Queen's Counsel thought, having withdrawn his sympathy from the trap of compassion. Magistrate Danie van Schalkwyk was referring to an "incident" (as stated in the docket) that gave rise to the inquest being held in Doornkloof—"Thorn Ravine"—a town not far from Krugersdorp, named after the old president of the Transvaal Republiek. The hearing was located in the nearest magisterial jurisdiction to Jan Smuts International Airport, *in honor of the field marshall, who was one of the founders of the League of Nations and contributors to its charter,* Elijah reminded himself as he recollected recent political history.

Van Schalkwyk could have been confusing the day of the airplane crash with the day of the "incident of death" when a woman had fallen from an airliner and caused the beam of suspicion to be cast on an airport worker whose name and job description were underlined in the inquest docket lying open on the bench. However counsel Sweet was under no such illusion as he listened carefully.

Ish Aval went on with his story. He spoke as if in a trance, driven by an inner compulsion to relate the circumstances of his life.

"I survived death three times," he stated, frowning, the scars on his forehead creasing into patterns of pain.

"What?"

It seems to be the magistrate's favorite word, Elijah thought. *But he has the right to question from the bench because this is an enquiry, not a trial.* "Its aim is to get to the truth of a tragedy," the Q.C. had said when, as is customary pursuant to the rules of judicial etiquette, he visited the magistrate in his office to introduce himself before the inquest began. But he did not specify the nature of the "tragedy" written in the file. "Queen's Counsel, Elijah Sweet," he had said, without extending a hand of greeting. The magistrate had felt a small quake in the pit of his stomach. It rose through his coccyx, shivered through his solar plexus, crept up his spine, and erupted beneath his clavicles.

"*Dankie,*" he stammered in Afrikaans, "Thank you, I acknowledge you for the record as counsel for some of the parties," Magistrate van Schalkwyk said. He feared that under the relentless influence of the "Cerebrum" this inquest would go differently from what he had intended. The Q.C. did not correct the magistrate's generalization. "Let him puzzle over whom, or what, I represent," he thought.

"Once in the tank, when I was born," the witness related. "Once on the sucking sands of a place called Kikambala, near Mombasa in Kenya, and once at Jan Smuts Airport." Beneath the lip of his bench, below the line of sight of all others present in his courtroom, rubbing his hands with glee, the magistrate thought presumptuously: *Here it comes.* He assumed that

Ish Aval would relate the facts that would lead to self-incrimination, trial, and ultimate conviction of this witness for the death of the fallen woman. *The Afrikaaner airport worker will be exonerated of all or any wrongdoing! He will walk!* But van Schalkwyk had no way of knowing that the Q.C. planned a different outcome entirely—for reasons beyond the magistrate's unsophisticated assumptions.

Patience . . . again I shall allow it to prevail, Elijah Sweet concluded, controlling his reflexive aversion to verbosity. *He is neither our witness, nor theirs. He is the only significant witness.* The Q.C. could cut off or demolish anyone in evidentiary examination if he so desired. The intention not to do so had been formulated. He chose to listen further.

At 5,500 feet, forked lighting flashed through dark thunderheads. Captain Beau Bucker, "BB" as he was known, was not afraid. He had flown through many threatening storms. "Dark vacuums," he called them. Of all aircraft he liked the McDonnell Douglas DC-10 the best. "Safest plane ever built!"

He leaned to the right like a whisky vat tilting off its leveling shims. An aerated lumbar support, beneath the sheepskin cover of his leather seat, strained under the force of his body's weight. *Like my full bladder! No time to pee now! At least it reduces the pressure on my sacrum and my iliac!* he thought, copying his doctor's jargon, although he had glared a dire warning at the physician to keep his symptoms out of the "annual flight medical fitness report." The doctor got the message. BB was not a man with whom to tangle. In pilots' circles, and beyond, he was known as "Tarzan."

"Boy," he said, speaking to his copilot. "Don't worry, man!" BB always disregarded his own uttered contradictions. "The only way this baby comes down without my control is if we run out of fuel!" An American pilot in a Swiss passenger jet was unusual. But Captain Beau's reputation preceded him.

"An audaciously brilliant and capable pilot!" the specialist recruiter, himself a retired airline captain, had assured Swissair's board of executives. "Pay him whatever he asks. He's the best you'll ever get." Indeed Bucker was.

He pressed the intercom button. "Ladies and gentleman,"

he said, his voice a lazy, southern drawl that belied the sharp mind of the captain, "I trust y'all had a good night's sleep?" He grinned broadly at his copilot, exposing crooked, yellow-stained teeth. Captain Beau didn't hide "the grain of old chewing tobacco love." Nor did he care what others thought of his size, his Louisiana accent, dented cap, massively horned tawny moustache, and his unruly mops of red hair on scalp, arms, hands, and chest.

It had already grown dark outside when, at his interview in Kloten for the job of airline chief pilot, he banged a meaty freckled fist on the glossy boardroom table. In a brightly lit conference room of the main Swiss airport, partially located in the district of Bülach within the canton of Zürich surrounded by the Glatt Valley, such behavior was out of keeping. Neither aware nor concerned, he declared, "Take it or leave it!" His green eyes, flecked with gold spots, sparkled like exotic jewels as he pulled his sunglasses off the peak of his grubby cap and put them on to reduce the glare of fluorescent lights. He passed a note across the table to the immaculately dressed "gentleman" interviewers. A grimy, tobacco-speckled paper all crumpled up, usually used by Beau Bucker to roll his own cigarettes, moved reluctantly from hand to hand, down the row.

Pale lips grew tighter. Some of the "Severity Panelists" (as BB called them to their faces and behind their backs), used white paper napkins to dab their lips. Fine china coffee cups and superior cacao tablets from the *chocolaterie* of Maison Cailler, went untouched. A few present even used antibacterial wipes to rid their fingers of contamination by the note. Others adjusted their postures.

Their backs stiffened visibly. But, as Captain BB, whose floridness pulsed as if he absorbed heat during the day and emanated it at night, rose to leave their shocked presence before they answered, the board members accepted both the man and the outrageous salary—albeit with dual reluctance.

Alex, a humorless, intensely efficient graduate of the Swiss air force, kept his eyes on clouds that were full to bursting and shivered at the sight of forked lightning bolts below. Half expecting (as he always did) a small squadron of Swiss military jets to break through cover and zoom past the nose of the aircraft, which had occurred on many training flights that he had undergone around the Alps surrounding Geneva, he suppressed an intense fear of explosion.

To the left of the flight deck door there was another door. Behind it, a permanently mounted ladder ran up and down a rack of bunk beds. Company rules mandated periods of rest. BB was too large to use the top bunk, so he automatically reserved the lower one for himself, without request. That vexed his first officer whose manners suggested his birthplace. Alex had recently returned to the right-side seat, and sat at the copilot's controls. His rest had been disrupted, as always while in the air. He would fall asleep, only to be woken by a ghastly image flashing through his mind, accompanied by sounds so loud that they penetrated like holes in his head and poured unwanted noise intrusions into his brain. *Prokofiev's war sonatas! The sound of explosives!* he thought, being an admirer of military-style music despite his dedication to the national pacifism of his homeland.

He recalled that he had been on a routine single-jet patrol. The country was so small that acceleration of the supercharged plane required crossing over the border into France, briefly, with permission. On the return to Swiss airspace, he heard a squawk in his headset. He recognized it immediately, as Swiss air force pilots use their own tactical language for radio communication.

He swept the "Mirage" that he was flying, up from a low altitude close to the tapestry-like farmlands of the Swiss landscape and performed a high-velocity twisting, delta climb. G-force pushed back the skin of his cheeks, turning them a pale shade. He saw a small aircraft directly ahead of him! Applying the special muscle-tensing techniques he had learned in flight school to force blood back into his head and resist "gray-out," which even his pressurized suit could not prevent, sick to his stomach, the collision alarm blaring through the cockpit, he pulled sharply to the right. Thus he missed the little traveler by a wingtip-to-wingtip distance of less than half a meter. He gagged, spun, and dived back toward the shelter of ice and snow on dragon-like peaks where winter lingered and never departed.

The sickening specter of death gripped his mind, not just then, but at all times afterwards when he scanned the blinding blue, trusting his eyes more than the radar screen, looking for the plane that he missed but which still flew enough to haunt his corner of sky wherever he went.

BB had no such concerns. If something appeared where it shouldn't be, he would blast it out of existence, verbally and, if needs be, physically, as he had done above jungles in Asia.

Flying over Johannesburg, heading for the airport, he remarked casually to his copilot, "Too much vapor in the depleted wing tanks after nine hours of nonstop flight. If we get struck by millions of volts of concentrated electrical power, we are kaput." But BB did not sound too concerned. Alex thought of the long-haul route over which they had passed. *Italy, the Mediterranean, Tunisia, Libya, the Sahara wasteland, Chad, the skirts of Cameroon, the forests of Congo, the Kalahari desert of South-West Africa, and now over the ore-rich republic on our way in.*

Alex could not prevent himself from considering the severity of dangers that beset aircraft with updrafts as they sweep over the "kopjes" and "mine dumps" that surround the City of Gold in ringed mounds, their whiteness bleached by cyanide filtration, the hilltops fissured and guarded by the spoked wheels of headgear above old shafts sunk deep into gold reefs. From above they looked like monolithic crocodiles on enlarged rocks. The longer the journey, the more the 280 lives behind him tugged relentlessly at his Swiss conscience.

"Hail! I've seen this many times before in African summer storms," BB exclaimed with childlike excitement as the big aircraft entered heavy clouds. "The size of baseballs!" He deliberately used the American description. "Perilous stuff! We cannot go round this storm. It's too big. We cannot land at the next major airport; it's too far." He grinned wider, the half-moon expanse of his yellow smile reflecting the relish of challenges awaited. With a "Goldilocks" twinkle at the absurdity of the dilemma reflecting in his eyes, in mid-sentence, he scanned the instrument panel.

"Relax, Boy," he declared, his voice now thicker, harsher, a sure sign of impatience at Alex's stiffened back and white knuckles. Although he tried to hide it, BB heard the Swiss man's rapid breathing, being aware of everything in his *universe of flight*.

"I've landed empty crates on the decks of US aircraft carriers, in the middle of typhoons in the South China Sea! This ain't nuttin'."

He called all copilots "Boy," even though he had flown with female pilots too. There was only one exception, whom he named simply "The Man." That was because he survived a crash in the jungles of Vietnam and walked back to base with his skull showing through the back of his head, a broken femur, a fractured humerus, and a shattered ankle.

Alex gulped back his disdain for the habits, appearance, and speech of the captain with whom he had to share the flight deck. A product of rigid Swiss-German upbringing, he was galled to see Beau's flabby freckled face, his disheveled uniform, his black tie always askew and splattered with food stains, the top button of his shirt open, and his exposed russet chest hair that tufted outward. But he knew that this "Forest Bear" (which he would only think and never say for fear for being permanently damaged by a crushing "hug") was the best pilot of a DC-10, bar none!

The copilot looked out at the two big engines mounted under the wing pylons. He thought about what it would be like to try to glide a large passenger jet with the third engine at the base of the vertical stabilizer dead in the air. *Practice in a simulator is one thing. In-flight reality is quite another!*

Oblivious to the difficulty of landing the airliner in a powerful electric storm, the European businessman in the first-class cabin winced at the captain's accent as they ate nutbread spread with thick buttery cream from Alpine farms and Hero cherry jam. Coffee was served simultaneously—an excellent blend of finely brewed "Empire" beans from Ethiopia. The plane was descending. Its body began to shake as turbulence took hold. They would have to conclude breakfast soon, but the chief steward allowed leeway in an effort to banish anxiety over their predicament, of which he had an inkling.

BB had disabled the autopilot and taken over manual control. The lightning and thunder reminded him of air battles in which he had fought, killed enemies, and nearly died. "Nature is no match for me," he said impudently, grinning, his colors again flaring. Alex winced. He had noticed that the intercom light blinked on just before Captain Beau Bucker from Louisiana uttered those words for all to hear!

"Buckle up! Jan Smuts Airport here we come!" BB announced on the public address system, turned to Alex, and told him to pass the message to the crew that everything, including all food items, must be cleared immediately. He added, "All passengers are to be prepared in case of a hard landing." Looking across and down, treating the artifices of sky as he did the crosswords that he loved to challenge despite his oral inarticulateness, he found a "hole" in the cloud cover. Steering for it at a steeper than usual angle, like a surgeon searching for the ideal spot for incision, he swept the huge aircraft through it, banked in a stately wide turn, found his aim to be true, and guided the giant plane downwards on its glide path.

"Final approach requested," he said pressing the VHF transmit button. Air traffic control at Jan Smuts International Airport was calling. "FAJS here," the controller said in a thick accent. "Come in Swiss heavy." He had preempted BB who recognized the International Civil Aviation Organization call sign, named after the brilliant statesman and past prime minister of the Union of South Africa. *A bit late!* he thought, but was relieved to hear that he had been cleared for priority landing.

Captain Beau again ducked lightning and thunder, avoided the ammunition of hail, and relied on his forty years of seat-of-the-pants flying experience. He brought the passenger plane over the last rows of warehouses and factories surrounding the airport before settling into a smooth landing on the tarmac.

BB glanced perfunctorily at his copilot, whose face was white as a sheet, but whose hands were steady. *As befits a*

Swiss! BB thought, applying the reverse thrusters and acknowledging the control tower's "Welcome to South Africa DC, CH heavy."

Beau signed his logbook and wrote: "Landed through a hail storm in the southernmost country of Africa. All well! BB, Flight Swiss 666." With his tie still askew and shirt buttons popped open more than enough to exhibit his red chest hair, the eccentric captain joined Alex and the chief steward at the front exit. Behind them, the cockpit door was ajar. Beau wore his dented cap. At the back, on a coat hook where no one could see it, the ribbon and medal of the Distinguished Flying Cross hung under his spare cap. It had been pinned to his chest by General "Bill" Creech himself, commander of Tactical Air Command at headquarters in Langley, Virginia. The immaculate general smiled when he gave it to Beau, who remembered the general's pride in his courageous pilots, more than he relished the bestowal of honor upon himself.

The first-class passengers had disembarked. To the chagrin of the other two crew members, BB insisted on remaining "on station," so he said, until the last passenger passed them by on the way out of the front door. Those leaving through the other exits received farewells from stewardesses. The final three people, a couple and a single older woman, approached the front door. Captain Bucker smiled his unflagging, ugly, but affable smile.

The man hobbled with a severe limp. *His left arm is sticking out at the oddest angle I ever didn't saw!* Beau thought, assaulting the English language as usual and thinking back on his wartime days. Despite the patch over one eye and the bad arm, the man tried to assist the tiny woman next to him. He took her heavy handbag and strapped it with a camera over his right shoulder. She held his bad arm tightly around the bicep. On her birdlike face was a mixture of tolerant love, fatigue, and relief.

Ain't dat sometin'! BB thought in mangled words, but restrained himself out of deference for one whom he perceived to be an injured soldier. A steward moved to assist the disabled man. Beau gave the crewman a look of negation, so that he drew back. The unconventional captain watched the couple approach. As they passed him, he did something the others had never seen him do before. It was against company protocol. BB removed his cap and tilted his head forward. "Thank y'all for flying with us!" he said, saluting, his voice softly polite for a change.

In unison the peculiar couple nodded and smiled back, the woman's expression moist, almost leaky; the man's awkward and uneasy. Their visit to Switzerland had been undertaken for purposes of psychological recuperation. But it had had both positive and negative effects. The doctors in the private clinic and adjacent sanatorium in Zürich had been able to do very little to remedy the severe damage done to Ish Aval's body—still less for his moods and tormenting memories. But the scenery of the old city on the glimmering *Zürichsee*, downstream of the dam at Rapperswil with the shielding mountains so proximate as to be almost tangible, calmed and soothed—until the invasion of disquiet reasserted itself. He knew too well what dirty secrets lay hidden "in the basements of conscience," where the spooks of collaboration still lived "in airless chambers of shame so great that it could never be released." Toward the end of their visit there he had become uneasy, temperamental; disturbed that he should have sought curative intervention in a place of spectacular beauty, surpassed only by the supremacy of hypocrisy.

In a long silk dress with short sleeves, the older thick-set woman with a square face and a large masculine frame walked forward. *Ugly as hell*, Beau thought, refraining from smiling at her, his ebullient expression momentarily snatched away by confronting the woman's negative energy. Despite appearances and language to the contrary, BB was intensely sensitive to "auras," which he called his "radar homing device." *She is harmful*, he concluded.

Without looking at the men, she simply muttered, *"Ja."* Beefy arms (which Alex thought she should have covered) bulged. Her uneven gait made her tread heavy. In her left hand, clutched like a club, she gripped the handle of a large plastic shopping bag. Arthritically ailing, she grimaced and leaned on a glossy cane, bending to the right. Impudently, she pushed brusquely between the farewell party and the strange couple. The birdlike female gripped her husband's injured arm tighter. A piteous expression engaged her eyes. The corners of her small mouth moved as if she were about to issue a shrill call. But instead she whispered something into the disabled man's ear.

These last passengers—a one-eyed man clutched by a small bright-eyed woman with feathery hair, whose almond-shaped eyes met Beau's and held them for a solid moment of admiration (for she had a fear of storms), and a powerful woman whose advanced age had not reduced her bulky body—stepped through the doorway almost concurrently. Like acrobats about to perform aerial feats, they seemed motionless before the moment of irretrievable submission to the pull of gravity. At the top of the stairs that led to the concrete floor thirty feet below, they paused together on the platform in hesitant anticipation.

∞∞∞

Earlier that morning, a young Afrikaner, Pieter Terre'Blanche (a last name that means "white earth") parked his Toyota Bakkie, a small open-backed truck, in the staff lot behind a large hangar on the perimeter of the airport. He took his lunch pack and thermos flask from the passenger's seat. Then he headed into the cavernous building.

Pieter was late for work, which began at dawn and ended at dusk. He was tired, not having slept much as his wife tossed, turned, and snored all night for reasons he understood but did not wish to discuss. He was hungry, having left home in a suburb of the city of Benoni (which once he had been told was Hebraic for "son of my suffering" due to deadly illness there) without time for breakfast. Even if he had not been in hurry, he did not want to eat with his wife. He remembered the gouda cheese sandwiches and diced dried sausage that he had prepared for himself and left in the refrigerator the night before. *Coffee in the thermos will now only be warm, but it will still be black and sweet,* he thought.

"*Gooie more,*" Pieter said in Afrikaans before reverting to English, his superior's native language. "Good morning." As he entered, the boss was just leaving the hangar. At the airport both official languages were used interchangeably. However the Bantu language was taboo, even though all the heavy labor was done by black people. Having been raised on farms in the province of the Orange Free State—where he ate with his fingers, swam in above-ground cement dams beneath the slow, beating propellers of towering windmills surrounded by high maize plants, and pushed old bicycle wheels with wooden sticks as the little farm boys did, until he grew old enough to be told that it was forbidden to play with them—Pieter could speak the Sotho language. He had also picked up some Zulu and Xhosa dialects.

Walking over to the first set of stairs, he reached them, sat on the lowest one, unscrewed the thermos, and unwrapped his parcel of food. "Damn this work!" He took a bite, gulped, and cursed as he heard the high-toned engine whines of a big aircraft approaching. The rattle of vibration in the corrugated iron building was unmistakable. He looked out of a window in time to see the Swissair DC-10 dropping steeply through heavy storm clouds. *It's early*, he thought. Serpents of lightning bit the sky around the airport, sending their forked tongues down to the ground in splinters.

Pieter Terre'Blanche, great-great grandson of Dutch-born immigrants who had trekked through the hinterland and opened the interior to the white man, concentrated on his meal. He thought of his sullen cold wife tucked up in gray sheets, covered with coarse brown blankets, alone. Predatory birds of bitterness dug their talons into his skin, driving into his sinews. He could not beat them away as they advanced and began to peck inexorably at his heart.

"What my life has become!" If he could have mourned for what was most missing, he would have. But that too was denied him in his frosty matrimonial situation. Thus mired in self-pity, frustration, and anger, he forgot to check the sliding gate of the balustrade at the top of the mobile staircase, which it was his job to attach to the side of big aircraft. A simple hand lever had to be pulled from the vertical to the horizontal to lock the metal protective gate into place, so that the open space beneath the handrails would be closed off.

That omission would soon render its fatal consequence!

***

Attorney Yustus Toledano had briefed senior counsel on all the known facts, paperwork, and probable evidence, although he had not the slightest inkling of what Elijah Sweet had in mind to do. Only the wily Q.C. was privy to a result that none of the others could guess. *Ironically*, Sweet realized, *what is right is also wrong!*

Pieter Terre'Blanche, the airline, and the Department of Railways and Harbours (which paradoxically controls Jan Smuts Airport) will escape responsibility because I will let him and them! But they protect this Mr. White Earth at their peril! Cause and effect reach beyond a kangaroo court! When I write the truth of this matter, it will become known that the "ladder man" as good as killed the woman by his gross negligence. He will escape the fist of Justice, because the punishment of his miserable life will follow him for all of his remaining days. If I let him wriggle out of the net, Ish Aval, who is innocent of any wrongdoing, will swim free too!

The Q.C.'s expression grew grimmer with the realization that one man's liberty is another's imprisonment. Before the hearing began he had read the autopsy findings by the state pathologist. Now the report lay at the bottom of his worn-out briefcase. "A roll within a roll," he had remarked to Yustus Toledano as they walked into the court that morning.

"Pardon sir?" the attorney asked.

"Indeed," the Q.C replied with implicit meaning, adding, "Forget it," exuding his usual sardonic tension as he thought: *My attorney doesn't understand. He is too small-minded. He instructs me with the papers in a tight blue brief tied with a green string as is customary, and forgets that he put the report, the most important paper, inside the cardboard tube.* Elijah Sweet had a trick up his silk sleeve. *That is where it shall remain! A keepsake of one form of justice rendered and another denied!*

He remembered the question and answer session in the advocates' rooms, which were housed opposite the copper-domed rotunda of the Supreme Court's local division in the heart of the city. The Q.C. looked again at the one-eyed, lame man who stood at a dangerous angle on the witness stand and held the magistrate transfixed with his good eye as he related his story.

He speaks the truth of then and now, Elijah thought. He also knew that the "platform manager" would lie about his role in the death that formed the subject matter of the hearing so that he could escape liability. *Mr."White Earth" is an abysmal liar. He will come to the stand. He will state that he levered the lock into position when he knows that he didn't. There will be nobody to contradict him. Suspicion will turn to the disabled man, for it will have nowhere else to go! I need to liberate him from the confinement that could otherwise await him!*

The Q.C. felt sickened by the thought of Terre'Blanche's predictable perjury. But not for very long.

"We reached the platform at the top of the steps, all three of us at the same time. The big, rather elderly woman was on my right. My wife held onto my left arm. I shifted my weight to steady myself as best I could. I moved my belongings to my shoulder and freed up my right hand in case I needed it for balance."

Did she fall or was she pushed?

In Magistrate van Schalkwyk's mind the question reared like a mongoose about to deliver a lethal strike to the head of a poisonous snake. For the time being he suppressed it. The witness was speaking.

"As the captain and flight crew said farewell we stepped out together. The woman seemed to trip on the metal lip of the doorframe. She toppled, reached out with her right arm, flinging the cane away as if discarding it. It tumbled ahead of us, clattering down the aluminum steps."

"What happened next?" van Schalkwyk asked, feeling he had to take charge by interjecting questions from time to time.

"She didn't utter a sound, but I heard an intake of breath, followed by a sigh, much like a normal exhalation. As she reached for its support, the side rail gave way, retracting at the touch of her weight. She fell sideways, toward the fuselage, spun in the air head first, her feet and arms flailing, her floral dress deploying like a silk parachute, twisting and coiling but not opening."

"I saw the black soles of her shoes. Then I heard the hard thud as her body crashed into the squat camion below, with a splitting sound like a coconut being cracked open by an axe. I heard gasps from those who looked, in shock, as the body slid off the small truck and crumpled in a pool of blood onto the tarmac. The head was twisted all the way round. The neck was obviously broken. Her eyes were open. At the back of her splintered cranium, dark liquid oozed. A large stain spread through the fabric of her silk dress."

Magistrate Danie van Schalkwyk grimaced. Doubt flashed in his smirk. *But what motive could this disabled man have to push a big woman from the bridge of an aircraft's staircase? How would she not have been prevented from falling by a metal gate unless he had an accomplice ... an airport worker maybe? But that's farfetched, surely?* he reasoned, discarding the enquiry because it would open up too many avenues. *And I must clear my list so that I can get home early tonight.* He didn't feel too well. The early and not too appetizing lunch was exacting a price.

"Examination, Mr. Sweet?"

The Q.C. had heard enough. He simply moved his head from side-to-side once as he wondered, *Is it really possible to lie by omission?*

"You're excused," van Schalkwyk said, shrinking visibly on his throne. The witness looked at the magistrate, then at the lawyers. Finally, he hobbled away slowly and left the building. Outside, his wife waited to drive him back home. Her fingers ached with the stinging pain that besets a pianist.

"Call Pieter Terre'Blanche!"

The summons echoed in the foyer; it was repeated unnecessarily because only Pieter and some journalists who were waiting for salacious tidbits and a well-dressed man with two groomed young men beside him were there to hear it.

The Toledanos firm had to play a delicate game. If the finding was against the airline, the airport, and any employee, the adverse publicity would be highly damaging. If it was in their favor, a cloud of suspicion would still hang over them and could only be reduced by effective manipulation of the media. Public confidence and, consequently, revenue would be lost. Elijah Sweet, Q.C., however cared not about either outcome. *What lies buried in the roll of my brief, the state pathologist's report containing irrefutable evidence of who the fallen woman really was, and what Mr. Aval has so touchingly said in this court, renders the truth plain, although I already knew it! There are conse-*

quences to evidence, both good and bad! The law is man-made. A contrivance. An invention. So too, it can be unmade!

Mr. "White Earth" took the stand. He is the *epitome of the fatherland*, Elijah thought wryly. On the Bible that had motivated his ancestors to "civilize" the country, he swore that he would tell only the truth. Thus, the magistrate and all present heard that he locked and secured the sliding gate after he ate his cold sandwich and drank his tepid coffee. No one else would follow to contradict or confirm his evidence. He lied in court, crossing himself repeatedly as if to avoid the consequences of speciousness and the cosh-like blows of blunt fallacy.

"Any questions, Advocate Sweet?" van Schalkwyk asked. The Q.C. unfolded his tightly crossed legs. He leaned to one side, unclasped his leather bag, and reached in. As his undersized fingers found the strung brief and his hand closed over it, he stopped. Withdrawing, he straightened up, stiffening his spine. After suitable time for theatricality had passed, he replied, "None, Your Worship."

The exclamation took the magistrate aback. *How*, he wondered, *can the greatest counsel in the entire country remain silent at this inquest?* But he knew better than to ask why the advocate refrained from questioning either Ish Aval or Pieter Terre'Blanche. The Q.C.'s presence was intimidating in any courtroom. *Sometimes, his hush speaks very loudly, even yells*, the magistrate concluded, warning himself of its dire dangers, but feeling *oh so relieved!*

The state pathologist's report referenced the gross injuries on the corpse of the large woman. Under the heading "AGE," the number "70" appeared followed by a question mark. Under "SEX," the doctor had written, "Female(?)" and put an undulating line through the word "Male."

In the column "NAME (CHRISTIAN & SURNAME)," someone, not he, had written, "Grace." The handwriting appeared to be calculatingly harsh and sharp. It was not printed and seemed to be etched, as if scrawled on paper with a piece of broken glass dipped in Indian ink. There was no last name. *But it's none of my business*, he thought as he went about his macabre tasks. Under the heading "CONCLUSIONS," was written contradictorily, "Death may/may not have been caused naturally." In the column marked "MEDICAL FINDINGS," the pathologist, who was paid by the government to describe the medical cause of death stated: "Acute myocardial infarction suspected, but not certified, and multiple fractures of the cranium." A parenthetical gap followed. Then he added, "I cannot determine with any certainty if she was dead before she hit the truck or whether she died by fractures of the skull, consequently fatal brain damage, hemorrhage, and/or spinal cord severance after the fall." He signed the report. Then he printed his name and designation.

However, none of those findings that lay curled in the tube of the Q.C.'s brief had led him to remain silent in court and to release his tensed fingers inside his brief bag. Instead, it was a seemingly innocuous commentary on "BODILY FEATURES/IDENTIFYING MARKS" that had caught his eye before the hearing and now screamed so loudly as to deafen: "A tattoo, black dotted letters "AB," located in the unshaved left armpit, approximately eight (8) inches above the elbow," which might have attributed a false motive to Ish Aval.

Ish Aval is absolved of all suspicion, not that I had any at the outset, because he did not push her. He didn't know who she was, and he is disabled! By a warped irony of fate and good intention, he tried reflexively to save the woman who had brutalized victims in the camp! Elijah Sweet, Q.C., had known instinctively what question beleaguered the mind of van Schalkwyk when the disabled man gave his testimony. *Can justice prevail in the face of lies?* Learned counsel, prince of forensic science, did not answer his own penetrating question—until much later.

Having concluded a brief recess intended more to suppress his queasiness than to gather the spinning threads of reason, Magistrate Danie van Schalkwyk had returned to the courtroom at the magisterial seat of Doornkloof, and was again seated. He presided within a stone's throw of the farm where Jan Christiaan Smuts—who fought the British, although he was educated at Cambridge before becoming one of their great leaders—lived for over four decades. He died on a plain bed, in a simple house, on his land, in a beloved place of serenity.

The magistrate tried, in vain, to straighten the trenches ploughed deeply in his brow. Progeny of *Voortrekkers*, the senior inquest magistrate, educated in the Afrikaans medium at the University of Pretoria (known as *Tukkies*), tried to summon his voice consciously into firmness. At first his throat seemed to scratch with irritating hesitation. Then in false authority it arose. Opening his mouth, his moustache twitching unsteadily, he said: "The finding of this inquest court is that . . ." His body language revealed disquiet. Pausing before reading out loud the paragraph that had been typed onto government stationery through an inky ribbon on an old Royal typewriter, he gathered his judicial authority.

"No conclusion of blame or responsibility can be reached definitively. It is therefore the finding of this court that it is unknown or unproven who, if anybody, may have purposefully or inadvertently caused the death of 'the subject female' who fell approximately thirty feet from the top of the stairs of Flight SWS 79/666, in respect of which this enquiry was convened."

The reference was to the prefix year and flight number. Suddenly, he realized (which he hadn't before) that the number 666 was the same as that of the Panther tank in which the lame man said his mother had given birth. Forestalled by coincidence, confounded by brazen hints of menace oozing from Elijah Sweet, he added, "Accordingly, this court does not recommend the prosecution of any person or corporation, and renders formal "absolution from the instance." The court stands permanently adjourned without appeal. The docket is closed!"

"All rise!" the orderly commanded as van Schalkwyk inadvertently stamped his foot in a gesture of pugnacious regret. He rose and left the bench, nodding slightly to the lawyers, in compliance with etiquette. Behind him, in the vacated courtroom, the strains of hypocrisy blurted from an inquest that had been distorted by falsities. In a perverted twist of fulmination, the magistrate rushed to the "Gents" toilet and brought up his meal of pork pie, all pretences, including his penchant for preening and pouting, running down the exit hole of the toilet bowl together with his erstwhile sense of meritorious self-importance.

One year to the day after the inquest, at the conclusion of the most controversial murder trial of his long career, Elijah Sweet, Q.C., announced, "The defense rests, and so do I!" As was his habit, reaching for a block of paper on the leader's desk he wrote:

"Light in a Tunnel of Darkness." *This will be the title of my book, the memoirs of a commonwealth advocate.*

Then, in a clear voice, without caring who heard or did not hear, he recited:

> Deep in the man sits fast his fate
> To mould his fortunes, mean or great . . .
> He works, plots, fights, in rude affairs,
> With squires, lords, kings, his craft compares . . .
> Obeying time, the last to own
> The Genius from its cloudy throne.
> For the prevision is allied
> Unto the thing so signified;
> Or say, the foresight that awaits
> Is the same Genius that creates.

Extracts of Ralph Waldo Emerson's grand poem "Fate" seemed apt for a grand Q.C. who had chosen to lapse his professional endeavors, a vein in his temple thrumming in satisfaction to the recitation, which suited his mood and the finality of the occasion. Elijah Sweet swept from the courtroom without waiting for the verdict, for the last time, scenes of forensic battles replaying in his mind. *Perfection presents in different forms,* he thought. He did not wring his hands. He did not bark like a Yorkshire terrier. Instead, he adjusted his robe and wig, realigned his starched collar, and pulled his shoulders back. Consoling himself, he realized: *I have never crawled in the shadow of others.*

"Africa" twitched, contracted, and expanded before settling its inverted triangle on one side of his face as if the continent of bloodshed was itself temporarily at peace. He clenched his fists, then opened and relaxed his fingers. Silence followed his words like a trumpeting herald at the departure of royalty. All present knew that this meant he would retire to spend (as he had often been overheard to threaten) the rest of his illustrious career writing his memoirs in the quiet of his cavernous rooms, surrounded by the echoes of judicial victories—inspired, contrived, manipulated, and (as only he knew) also subject to chance.

∞ ∞ ∞

Pieter Terre'Blanche kept his job and still worked at the airport, at least for the time being. He brought his cold lunch pack and barely warm coffee in a thermos each day. It seemed to taste colder every time. He sat at the bottom of the high stairs that could reach the sides of the biggest aircraft. He thought of his miserable wife who did not love him, because she was incapable of loving anyone. For the first time in his artificially privileged adult life wherein his job was secured by laws that favored whites such as himself, he thought, *Perhaps I am unlovable?*

When he finished his breakfast, he climbed to the top of the staircase. Just as he reached the platform, he heard the high-pitched engine whines of a large aircraft approaching. It was a familiar sound, a call to work. Applying thuggish force, he pushed the lever from the vertical to the horizontal positions. He heard the loud click of the lock. It sounded resistant. It punctured his thoughts. But he thrust the memory of falsehood away, relegating it to the dark corners of mind where a famine of conscience had not yet wrought its full havoc amid thieves of hope and plunderers of luck.

When Elijah Sweet's memoirs were released, Terre'Blanche would not be the only casualty of that writing! "Idioms of Idiots," the talented wordsmith called the chapter dealing with the inquest and all that led to that day in Doornkloof. How the Q.C. knew what really happened when the DC-10 unloaded its passengers nobody but he had any inkling, for with deliberate guile, he left his readers guessing that facts and truth can be strangers passing on the same road to destiny, with barely a greeting or glance between them.

***

In the shallows of the Indian Ocean—beyond a moonlit lagoon, off the coast of Kikambala on the shore of Kenya, not too far from Mombasa—a reef of organism coral had continued its tenacious growth amid long barbed sea urchins, deadly stonefish, and waving kelp around the sunken fuselage, one twisted propeller, and the severed tail section of a King Air.

Close to the village on the edge of the beach, where forested areas abound and rural habitations nestle amid burgeoning foliage, a rainstorm broke suddenly over the trees. Impertinent wind drove it in slanting sheets over the canopy. Its waters became the tears of sustenance to those who lived there. The sound of rain was like liquid music played behind veils of condensation. In striking glory it beat out the noise of the ocean's breaking waves. Before the tropical sun could suck up the excess in a thirsty gulp when evaporation would quickly lay claim to errant puddles, growth would be renewed. Simple farmers and tribal hunters dependent on the bounty of nature would benefit by the prospects restored to vegetation.

The father and his two sons would not see it because they were not there, but the rain of salvation had come to Kikambala. It had spread its nourishment. Like a grave dancer sent by an abstruse power to encourage the spirit of optimism and elicit the thrill of revival, its work had been done.

A young man who had once watched his father smoke a long, noxiously redolent Romeo y Julieta cigar imported especially from Havana, feeling his heart beat harder and faster in his chest, never asked again if he could copy that malodorous habit.

Long before the inquest, he, his brother, and his father had returned to the scene of the crash. One evening before it grew completely dark, they swam through the waves and reached the spot. Taking deep breaths through snorkels poking like miniature poles into the twilight, they dived. It was not yet illegal to break coral. But even it if had been, the father would have made an exception, this once.

With a rubber-headed mallet in hand, he knocked off a piece that had rooted around a spar of jagged metal with a shard of glass protruding through it. Handling it very gingerly, to avoid cuts that would send biting organisms into his bloodstream and inflame the lymph glands in his armpits, he surfaced and called his boys. He dropped the tool. It rotated down through the cobalt water and settled on the shattered glass that never seemed entirely destructible, its claw turned upward like an accusatory finger pointing at rocks that floated in the purple mist.

On returning to Johannesburg, the father delivered a box to Hofmeyer Chambers. At the Q.C.'s rooms a junior counsel (the same one who received crumbs of wisdom from his leader, whenever the senior counsel felt the impulse to cast them about) took the delivery. Later that day, when he arrived at his office, Elijah Sweet, Q.C., found the box. He opened the envelope taped to the top. Inside it he read the note from his friend. The father asked that it be taken to Figlands Park and given to Mr. Ish Aval, anonymously. *A worthwhile task for Toledano. "It may motivate 'Yustus' to strive for 'Justus.'"* The Queen's Counsel never cared if that was the real name of his "errand boy."

The barrister smiled sarcastically.

He almost barked, but refrained.

Ish Aval ("Mr. Doubt"), who had once taken a death-defying flight from Uganda to Kikambala to advise coffee growers on the feasibility of clearing land to cultivate Kenyan beans away from the highlands, did not know what had occurred in the mind of a great advocate that day in the inquest court. He only knew what was written by the Q.C. on court stationery handed to him by Attorney Yustus Toledano at the end, as he passed by on his way out. "We are all sick, you know. Only some of us haven't yet been diagnosed, and none is ever entirely healed."

He kept it in a shoebox under his bed with some fading Brownie photographs that had arrived after the hearing, together with a recording on a cassette. He had played it several times before secreting it. The voice was distinct, like a barking "Yorkie."

"Ish Aval," it said, "this is Advocate Elijah Sweet speaking to you alone." A long blank followed as if the speaker had fallen asleep or wished to deepen the anodynic value of the message to follow by using a pause.

"I have something of value to tell you. My research, through means known to me, reveals on good authority that when the

Allies entered 'the camp,' a crazed inmate rushed a soldier, grabbed his rifle, ran down the path that led to the 'village of innocents' (or so they all alleged, having seen and heard and smelled naught!) and shot three men in the back. One was a young officer who had been given a woman as a 'pet,' but had discarded her when her pregnancy revealed itself. He died with a leaking hole in his heart on the border of the community that 'knew nothing.'"

Another intercalation of silence followed.

The words were spoken with calamitous accuracy, the high intonation and precise articulation of the grand Q.C. present in each syllable. A few full minutes passed, before the voice continued. "I hope this helps to allay the restless ghosts that inhabit the Ghetto of Gehenom." Elijah Sweet referred to the Jewish concept of hell. He used it in the sense of a second chance, not a final destination, because he knew that within the terrible wounds and scars from Ish Aval's birth to the crash on a deserted beach near the equator, unappeased anguish must have pursued its ghoulish purpose for too long.

There was a bark, like a yelp of tribulation, followed only by the sibilant hissing of tape running through sprockets. Along with the tape came Elijah's personal letterhead with his title and the address of his rooms boldly embossed thereon. In his unique script the master of enigma had rendered:

Justice is served when Justice is deserved.

Yours, Elijah Sweet, Q.C., Guardian of Truth.

The seasons changed, seemingly taking some pain with them. At the end of spring, the influence of summer suggested itself. A garden arose in the grounds. Dead vines were removed, even from the chimney. The house was painted. Turpentine was brushed over the gazebo, its rotten wood having been replaced. Although a pungent smell entered the house through the open windows on a warm breeze, it did not bother the occupants. The shutters had been repaired and fastened back to let in light, warmth, and encouragement. Even an air of hospitality hovered hesitantly over the house.

As if motivated by a mysterious force, the lesions on the

face of Ish Aval had started to heal. It occurred soon after the arrival of the tape and the brief letter. The "Ghetto of Gehenom" to which the Q.C. had referred in his remarks by his oblique references to an elevated purpose and an honorable vocation, was deserted—laid bare of all inhabitants.

At the entrance to the house a stopper made of natural coral, metal, and glass stabbing through its top like a dorsal fin, held the door ajar to admit balmy air. On the doorpost, the mezuzah's wooden surface of polished driftwood shone from frequent touching. It reflected the rays of sun and moon. Ish Aval had never forgotten its meaning.

Each night when the sun had settled down in depleted fashion, his wife drummed out Bartok's "Nocturne of Insects." Aqueducts of tears flowed no longer. Now her playing occurred with less tumultuous thumping and gentler lyricism. Her Steinway seemed stirred by joy. Her fingers, which felt better, silhouetted by electric light, fluttered lambently across the keyboard. The sounds and companionship were quite enough to give Ish Aval the rest that his troubled mind and his damaged body so intensely craved.

Thus, peace enveloped the residents of Figlands Park—at last.

∞ ∞ ∞

Hester's Folly

> How still the night is.
> The queen surely sleeps, protected by a lady
> keeping a faithful, loving watch there
>
> **Libretto from** *Il Trovatore*

I t shot out of the sky.
Like a cannon ball, the *thing* plummeted to earth. It trailed a red and white plume that looked like something being peeled, perhaps ripped, off something else. It had rained the night before. Water pooled in troughs. Just beyond the cowshed, where on clear days outdoor milking was once a joy, the ground it struck was moist. At great speed it whistled down, hissing as it went, like an angry witch.

The impact made a loud plunking sound.

It reminded the girl of cows' hooves emerging from mud. Instantly, air rushed in, trying to fill the hole, for Nature abhors a vacuum. But the object was not freed. It went in deeper, entering the yielding earth with great force.

Although the girl did not yet realize it, the deadly power of gravity was spurred by conflict.

"Secret, yes. Disguise, no," Frau Anneke Gluckel, the girl's foster mother decided on the day that Hester was "given" to her.

When Anneka and her husband lived in the village, before moving to the farmlands, she loved her neighbor, the beautiful Jewish woman with dark eyes and black hair who had only one child, little Hester. Frau Gluckel had no children of her own.

She was my best friend. We shared the delight of confidences . . . love beyond love . . . loneliness . . . longing. . . . Things that women tell each other and nobody else, without fear of betrayal.

"I will save her."

Those last words passed from one woman to another as a declaration of the deepest reciprocal affection.

Days later, without time for farewell, Hester's mother disappeared, and her father too. They were put in a cattle car heading "east." An only child, small and extremely quiet, Hester had become an orphan, even before her parents were exterminated, although mercifully she was too young to know it.

The girl wanted to walk around the small farm before full daylight emerged. Without conscious reason, Hester always liked the half-light, a dappled time of solitude and serenity. The earth seemed fresh. Life felt abundant. No veils of rain had covered the face of a new day. Only a fragile mist hung in the shadowy air, like a celestial smile.

"It's dangerous," Frau Anneke told Hester.

"Why?" the child asked, her lips puckering.

"The war rages on and on! We see no end!" Frau Anneke replied, sighing fearfully.

"Not here," the girl insisted with childish conviction.

"Yes, even here," Anneke said, her blue eyes brimming with transparent tears. "We may not see it. But it is all around us. If you must go outside, be careful, *Liebschen*," she added, her voice trailing off.

Before she came to the farmlands, her husband, a rough-handed but sincere man, kissed her goodbye as usual. Herr Werner Gluckel headed to work in the railway station near their old town. It was there that a stray aerial bomb fell. The explosion decapitated him, leaving his dismembered body smoking and unrecognizable to rescuers. Frau Anneke identified him by the ring on his finger. As she removed it, a part of her died too.

She kept to herself. The other farmers' wives were infrequent visitors to the solitary widow. Contact seemed to have withered, like shrunken grapes left unpicked on a vine.

People are afraid. Neighbors are suspicious. This was not always so, she thought, remembering better times.

However because of the girl, Anneke was thankful for her solitary life. *I can keep her safe with me!*

The widow had let word leak out that her niece had come from Hamburg, *after my sister died*, she said. Anneke had never mentioned a sibling before. Nor did she say how her "only relative" had passed away. Nobody asked. They just assumed that the war took her. Residents of the small town near her farm nodded at the news. Death in families was common. When greetings were exchanged, sympathy did not stray into speech. Lips were tight.

"One never knows who is listening to what," the inhabitants had learned, fear having taught them well.

Frau Gluckel had a plan for wartime survival. She determined to be as self-sufficient as the yield of her small plot and three farm animals made possible. *I cannot hope for more. Not now.*

She knew that the animals were her last resort for meat.

If it comes to that!

Hester breathed in the fresh air.

The distant hills were brushed by strokes of lavender. Early morning held the promise of excitement as it painted the farmlands and swept across the fertile land before it.

Something good will happen, the child thought as she walked past the shed.

She noticed a creeper. As always, it insisted on stalking up the side of the barn, its many suction cups gripping tenaciously.

Drops of heavy dew clung to tall stalks of grass. *Diamonds for a princess's crown*, the girl imagined. It was a happy, childish thought.

In one corner of the otherwise clear blue summer sky, a

host of cumulus clouds clustered, as if seeking the protection of a crowd. They hovered, still and silent in the distance.

Unbeknownst to the girl, they hid a terrible truth.

Hester was a quiet, introverted girl. She did not notice the whine or the spitting metallic clatter of conflict between flying war machines. Somewhere in a field a dog barked. It wasn't theirs, although Hester longed for one. Anneke Gluckel was afraid of dogs.

"They bite," she said, ending the request as it began.

But a cow, a pig, and an old horse seemed to trust her, and she them.

High above, the remote vapor floated persistently. It hid the remnants of night rain and something else.

The aerial engagement was brief and brutal.

Bullets spat. Cockpit windows shattered. Airframes tore. Blood splattered against glass.

Men died in the sky that day. Those who lived flew off to fight another day. War went on, just as Frau Anneke had said. Only this time, proof came to Hester in a way that would change her life.

She heard a thud.

As soon as she saw it, she realized that the head had no identifying features. It was just an object that flew out of the sky with others, as she watched the squadron scatter like angry bees and head in disarray for temporary sanctuary beyond distant horizons.

Hester approached the thing lying in a hollowed little grave, carved by the force of its impact.

It lay backward. All skin was gone. Everything that made a face was obliterated by shock, speed, and the rip and claw of violence. Mud filled the eye and nose sockets. Toothless jaws locked fast. Charred bone smoked. On one temple a neat hole had been drilled roundly. On the other, bone splinters fragmented where a machine gun bullet had exited.

The girl looked down. She stared awhile, standing as still as a silhouette.

"Who was he?" she asked in a voice of softly whispered secrets.

It was one of the few things she ever said, then or later, and the question was posed to herself alone.

A wooden box once housed fodder for the farmyard animals. When Werner Gluckel was killed, Frau Anneke put his tools away in that box.

Slowly Hester walked back to the shed, her galoshes sloshing in mud pools. She opened the container. Its rusty hinges groaned reluctantly.

With a wood-handled shovel in her pink hands, the girl returned to the hole in the field. Mud around lay splattered thickly, like treacle. She shoveled it in. Then she dug up lucerne stalks and placed them in a thatched pattern over the spot.

Hester's work was done.

The child had always been quiet. But after the head fell from the sky that day, she enveloped herself in profound silence that grew and grew. Frau Anneke did not know what to do.

I have no idea how long the war will last. If Hester dies, I will burn in the eternal hellfire of a broken promise, because I pledged to her mother that I would keep her alive!

Sometimes, her dead friend appeared in her dreams.

"Send her away, to safety," she pleaded. Then each time she disappeared impetuously into the haze from which she had emerged for those short hallucinatory visits.

One day, shaking with the effects of her heartrending decision, Anneke dressed the girl in the only nice clothing that she possessed, the smock she had worn on the day she had come. Anneke stuffed the pockets with coins wrapped in rags. It was all the money that Frau Anneke then possessed. She took the girl and left her at a convent not far from her farm. On the note that she pinned to Hester's pinafore she wrote, "God save this child. She does not speak!"

As she turned away from the girl's astonished stare, Anneke's heart broke. She had redeemed herself from everlasting damnation. *But I have hurled my soul away!* she declared to her sickened self.

Never again in her life would Anneke feel whole.

She returned to her small farm.

That night she lay down on her bed and waited for sleep to enfold her. It did not come in the way she wished for it. When she awoke the next morning, she rose and washed the tear marks off her face. Looking in the mirror, she noticed an ashen expression. Her hair seemed to have grown white during the hours of darkness. The color almost matched the paleness of her cheeks.

Werner loved their rosiness. He said they made me look like a pretty Gypsy flower seller!

Previously her hair had been speckled blonde and those roses had still bloomed, albeit hesitantly in her cheeks. But now and for the rest of her days, color never returned to Frau Gluckel's face.

The German sisters had heard of the "Kindertransport."

"Surely," they reasoned, "this child will be sent to safety? So she will live!"

Their optimism derived from their own principled order.

"When fear plunges, hope rises. In Jesus, the Child of the Immaculate Conception, we trust!" they told one another frequently in those times, and especially when they turned the girl over to the Red Cross to join a children's transport into the care of unknown people.

Their duty thus done, they went home to the convent, where prayer and praise awaited. When they recited the Nocturn, the young nun who had been the last to lay a palm on the child whispered the Absolution, reciting the words with fervor burning like a fever on her lips:

> *A vínculis peccatórum nostrórum absólvat nos omnípotens et miséricors Dóminus* May the Lord Almighty and merciful break the bonds of our sins and set us free. Amen!

∞∞∞

Hester arrived with other children in England. She never said to anyone how that came to be.

As time passed, her elective mutism turned into intense inhibition. On the brink of womanhood, her silence solidified around her like a protective shield. Within its hushed epicenter she found a haven, a place where none but she could dwell in the concord of silence. At the "Children's Home" where she lived—though she had already then emerged from childhood—she learned to sew. Her hands became the tools of livelihood. From simple materials, she made beautiful clothing for women.

One Sunday, she passed a millinery shop in war-ravaged London. Explosions had torn away an entire building, save for a single structure that remained largely undamaged. Even the thin glass windows of the small shop, called Milano's, had been left miraculously intact.

She went inside. Summoning her greatest strength in an effort that threatened to invade her refuge, Hester spoke.

"Sir," she said to the shopkeeper, "teach me, please." She stammered, uncertain whether she had spoken correctly, or at all, for she did not recognize her own voice.

The rather round, friendly owner stared at her. His heart stirred. She was young and strikingly beautiful. Samuel Rubin, well trained to observe ladies' accoutrements, immediately noticed that her dress was handmade. It was purple and full length.

Utterly perfect in fit and design! This, in wartime? His eyes widened.

"Did you make the dress you are wearing?"

"Yes," she replied, the strain of speaking pressing upon her like hundredweights. Mr. Rubin motioned for her to sit. She obeyed. He went to the back of the small store and returned with a lady's extravagantly styled hat in his hand.

"Do you think you could make this?" he asked, the sound of his voice benevolent, but nervous in anticipation of her refusal.

She nodded.

"Good," he said, feeling relief wash over him. "Let's see what you can do."

Samuel Rubin led her to his own sewing bench. Materials were in short supply. His curiosity soared to new heights as he looked more closely at her and made sure she had all that was needed for the experiment.

Indeed she is beautiful. In demeanor and movement. In finesse and grace. And, what's more, something profoundly attractive emanates from within. She simply radiates, he thought. *I am lucky beyond words! Thank you, God, for this angel whom you have sent down to me!*

I shall restrain myself from looking until she is finished, he decided, as he placed the model hat on a round head-shaped stand. His heart beat faster than usual.

It did not take very long, although it seemed as though the millennium was grinding slowly through its mid-point as Samuel Rubin waited.

Unhurriedly, Hester tidied ribbons, stiffening materials, cotton, and utensils. He heard the sounds, which he knew so well from his own work. She rose and walked to the counter where the portly avuncular man busied himself over his limited stock of items and wondered, as he looked dejectedly at a brick wall from which bits of plaster continued to fall: *Will this millinery survive in more ways than one?* Although he was never sure of the answer, the milliner remained ever hopeful.

Hester extended her elegant arms and delicate hands, offering the product of her labor. Mr. Rubin gasped. In all his years as a hatmaker, he had never seen a more spellbinding lady's bonnet. It abounded in feathers. It showered ribbons and filaments of cloth that waved in luxurious splendor.

"My dear," he said. For a moment he was rendered speechless. Regaining composure, he continued, "You were born to do this. There is nothing I can teach you!"

Compliments caught in his throat. *I am blessed to have this exquisite young woman enter my world. The famed couturiers of Milan who gave both my profession and my enterprise its names could never have been more fortunate!*

He paid her as handsomely as his small income allowed.

Samuel Rubin bowed low and beamed with pleasure as money passed from his plump hand to Hester's supple fingertips. Then he reached into a drawer of his bureau.

"Forgive me, I do not have much money, but please take

these to enjoy," he said, blushing vividly, stammering his joy, as he handed her a fistful of chocolate bonbons, each individually wrapped in red cellophane, which he had saved as if they were precious heirlooms.

So Hester obtained a job in the East End of London, a place battered and broken but not beaten by a reign of terror from the skies. The Nazi warmongers had not bargained for the resilience of its hardy inhabitants—particularly a beautiful, hushed refugee with skilled hands and the superbly creative eyes of an artist.

The Curzon Crown Residential was a neat hotel, not prepossessing or ostentatious, just clean and properly managed. It suited Hester well, as talking was not essential to being a resident there. When the need arose, she could simply write a note of explanation or request and hand it in at the reception.

Her room was simple. Red velveteen wallpaper in hypnotically repetitive swirling patterns aided her imagination. Whenever she looked intensely at them, numerous stylish shapes came to mind. Some ultimately manifested themselves in modish creations that she assembled for her grateful employer.

Samuel Rubin always spoke kindly to her. He never asked her questions about her past, present, or future. To him she was simply a "Godsend."

The war boomed its last, or so Mr. Rubin thought in his naively contented way. Normality seemed to return, although many had forgotten its attributes. The tight tourniquet that had stifled, but not destroyed, London began to loosen.

Business had improved from the first time that a stunning hat had appeared, alone on display, in the window of Milano's.

Now it is really good, Mr. Rubin thought, smiling through the prism of candid optimism, which colored his observation of the world and everything in it.

The building around his little shop was being rebuilt.

Proprietors of adjacent establishments welcomed Samuel Rubin's shift of fortune. They considered it an excellent omen, especially because his business had remained intact, despite the haphazard obliteration caused by flying bombs. If anyone felt jealous of his survival, he did not hear of it, for he relegated rumor to oblivion.

That I can do quite easily, he thought, *because I have my own protective hearing aid that I can switch on or off at will!*

Mr. Rubin never placed another hat beside a "Hessie." He considered that to do so would be disrespectful to Hester's unique style, and the delightful femininity of her extraordinary handiwork.

"Works of fabulous opulence!" he called them, extravagantly describing hats that "adorn and compliment the loveliness of ladies!"

They became highly prized collector's pieces, especially after the royal couple visited the East End. As luck would have it, the sovereign's wife had seen one of Hester's works of art in the window. On orders, an equerry bought it—for British monarchs dare not be contaminated by the commonness of money. Samuel Rubin was thrilled when, just once, he saw a picture of the hat adorning the head of royalty.

The reconstruction of the area had a frightful consequence. It seemed long after V-Day, but it really wasn't, when the explosion occurred. Some said it was gas main that ignited. Others, especially the milliner, knew better.

He had been at home in his small flat when a worker's pick blade struck a hitherto unexploded bomb that had fallen nearby. It sparked into massive detonation. The heavy shockwave set the building aquiver, though it did not topple.

Hester was in the shop when the bomb went off.

Her head was bowed over her work, her hands skipping, her eyes darting from a charcoal sketch she had made to the emerging "cappello," as Mr. Rubin liked to call it, using the only Italian word he knew, aside from lines memorized from his favorite operas.

Until then she had ignored the noise generated by the workmen.

The humming sewing machine, clicking thimbles, snapping scissors, and sighing pedal pumps were welcome friends. So also were the divine voices (her employer's description) that flowed from "His Master's Voice" gramophone whenever Mr. Rubin was in his place of business. Samuel, a single man, had a generous heart, notwithstanding that its stirring was sometimes borrowed from tragic melodrama set to music.

"Singer and Song," he loved to remark, his eyes twinkling with delight.

"One gave me my livelihood. The other gave me bliss."

"Ah, and you, my silent, beautiful, dearest one. You are everything!" Hester's smile lay trapped within. But sublime warmth spread through her each time he paid her one of his patriarchal compliments, color flushing her cheeks.

Surrounded by the safety of her private cocoon, in the absence of Mr. Rubin, she did not put on a record that day, although he always encouraged her to do so. Nimble as she was, her fear of shattering the means of his listening pleasure was only surpassed by her terror of losing the work she loved.

The crash of bricks and the smashing of glass destroyed her tranquil world.

Her slim body was hurled against a wall. It went limp. She slumped to the floor and lay still, like a rag doll discarded by a bored child.

A few days later, when she was released from the hospital—Mr. Rubin, fussing attentively and declaring that he was her only "relative"—she went into a deeper state of silence. This time it was complete—save for her last utterances, which occurred the day after she had a terrible vision.

Since that time in the field, she had experienced the brutal nightmare only once. Strangely, it occurred long after the bomb went off—dispelling the elements of mental peace and security that working and sharing space in the millinery with her kindly employer had given her. To these she clung as much for the love of her work as for the maintenance of her fragile sanity.

After a full day's work at Milano's she returned to her bedsitter at the Curzon Crown Residential. In tunnels beneath the damaged city, trains were running. She could feel the vibrations when they passed under the hotel. The day before, seemingly at random, Mr. Rubin had said, "Rats, cockroaches and the Underground are indestructible, even by the Luftwaffe!"

The walls of the station nearest to the hotel on Baker Street were covered with cream-colored tiles. Slippery surfaces discouraged but didn't eliminate graffiti. Below the red circle bisected by a blue line with the station name lettered in white, in an act of defiant freedom of speech, an anonymous artist had sprayed, "Evil," then reversed it to "Live." For good measure the painter had left black spatters underscoring the insignia of the London Underground.

She stared unblinkingly at the words, then at the hands that bracketed them, wondering which was being shoved out and which in, by the stenciled finger commands.

"So soon after the war, and who can tell the difference?" someone near her commented aloud, as if reading her mind. Hester did not respond, remaining trapped in silence.

In her room she undressed, bathed, put on her nightclothes, and got into bed. The clean sheets felt cool and crisply comforting. Vaguely, within a hazy nimbus of isolated memory, she could sense her mother tucking her into bed, whispering sweet blessings in her ears, stroking her hair as gently as a weaver touches cloth, and smelling of lavender.

She fell asleep. Oddly, she hardly ever felt really tired. No matter how hard she willed herself to be weary, some compulsive energy seemed to intervene, especially at night when her impudent subconscious exerted its controlling influences. Normally, when she awakened Hester could not remember her dreams.

However this time was different. She woke before her bedside clock raised its shrill alarm, even on Sunday. It was still dark outside.

Every sight and sound of her nightmare, in which not just one but many skulls fell out of blue skies filled with terrible noises, remained hotly etched in her mind. Her body was wet, her hair in disarray despite having been combed and pinned up at bedtime. Dampness clung to the nape of her neck. She had been crying in her sleep. Her pillow felt moist.

Was it only a dream?

She rose and bathed again, washed her hair, then dried and plaited it. In the open closet, she found the purple dress. It was still the best she one that she owned. Above it, on a shelf, the first "Hessie" waited. It was the original that Mr. Rubin insisted she should keep.

"It is too beautiful to sell!" he declared. "Take it. *You* wear it," he urged.

Following many refusals, one afternoon when tea was over, she found the bonnet. It was on her chair beside the workbench. She took it home. But she had never worn it. Not until this day.

Hester left the room, ignoring the breakfast offerings in the dining room that had been set up the night before. Coffee boiled in the urn. It smelled foul. Nobody was there at the dawn hour. White columns in the lobby shone, bathed in weak artificial light. Although she had not eaten anything since the previous day, she was not hungry.

Back in the station, she saw the graffiti still on the wall.

A train rumbled to a halt. She got out at an entirely different location than usual and took the stairs to street level. A busker's trumpet calls echoed through the subterranean tubes where people streamed like ants, even so early. Someone must have paid him to play "The Last Post."

What a bold bugler, she thought. Once she read that the call had been played every day at Ypres, to commemorate the fallen in the Great War, except when the Germans occupied Belgium.

Notes struck thunderously on her eardrums like discarded cans clattering in an alley. She had always been sensitive to loud sounds. The trumpeter was getting his piece in, before eviction. A Bobby was coming down the stairs as she was going up, for some always complained when others made or tried to make music.

I must tell the Queen! It was an inner command that could not be denied. Not on this Sunday when she felt so strange after her nightmare.

On the sidewalk beside the street, she saw that a gate was slightly open. A gardener had wheeled a barrow through it. He was visible, far back in the garden, but had not returned to close and lock it. The heavy chain dangled like a gutted snake, shining in the clarity of a new day.

Hester opened the metal door and closed it behind her. In the lovely dress of her own making, her hips swayed as she walked the grounds in flat shoes, heading toward the grand palace. As if wishing to suggest nonchalance, she used the pathway that meandered through the grounds.

The gardens are splendid, she thought.

Hester passed an artificial lake. It was entirely surrounded by festooning flowers, grand trees, and exotic shrubs. The benches beside a little pergola were empty in the sun. Variety and perfection preceded and followed her like persistent, but suddenly disarranged, shadows.

She was close to the side entrance of the magnificent building when a voice boomed out.

"Halt!"

She ignored the order, even though she recognized its meaning and menace. She had heard it spat out at innocent men, women, and children . . . like she had been . . . when too young to understand the degradation that would befall them. It seemed so distant.

Another place. Perhaps even another life? The young Queen is my age. Her beloved father died recently. She mourns. I know she will understand!

∞∞∞

Chris Jones was new to the duty of patrolling the grounds in disguise. He was not wearing the red and black uniform of the immaculate guardsmen at the front gates. Instead of shiny patent leather shoes, he wore the rubber boots and the cloth coveralls of a gardener. But in his wheelbarrow under clumps of peat moss a well-oiled Lee Enfield No. IV, MK1 bolt-action rifle lay beside a shovel.

Inside the tunic under the coveralls, at his waist a blade pressed against his right thigh. It was held snugly in place by an olive-colored canvas scabbard, cutting edges and socket brazed together into a singly forged, extremely sharp weapon. The cold handle reminded him of its presence and of its lethal purpose.

"You! Stop!" he yelled.

Hester continued on. Now she was near a side portico. She heard him, but did not care. *Only a few more steps to go and I will be there.*

"State your business here!"

The voice was increasingly threatening, rising in pitch. But Hester would not speak. Silence had always gripped her tongue, holding it prisoner to her palate.

I must speak only to Elizabeth the Second, Regina, Queen of the Realm! Hester screamed in shrill silence. Then she began to run.

Jones reached into the wheelbarrow. He pulled the rifle to his shoulder. "Halt or I shoot!"

She ran even faster. *A gardener cannot kill me!*

His heart beating thunderously, goaded by training, Chris Jones, member of the Queen's secret guard, squeezed the trigger. The bullet jammed in the breach. "By God!" he yelled.

He had not seen her face. From behind he thought she might be a young woman. But he had been taught not to make assumptions in the heat of an emergency.

"Don't be fooled," his commander had taught him. "Killers come in all disguises." The warning had been uttered so often that it was branded into his brain. It compelled his reflexes. He reached under his coveralls and pulled the weapon from its scabbard. With a swift movement he locked it into place beneath the Enfield's muzzle.

"Assassin!"

The word lunged. And so did he! The steel bayonet manufactured by Singer caught Hester between her shoulders. It plunged into her beating heart and exited her chest between her breasts.

The bonnet burst from her head. It fell to the stone path and lay in a crimson pool of blood. She tried to reach for it, but her fingers numbed, then stopped in mid motion. Faster than her brain, her heart was dying.

Deep within her mind's closing eye, she saw the images of her nightmare, those she wanted to share with the young Queen so that she—Sovereign of the Empire, Defender of the Faith, possessor of majestic power and influence—would stop the many skulls raining down like bizarre balls of flaming bone from the sky where darkening storm clouds never ceased to gather!

She saw the patch of earth in the farmland. The hole was

filled with mud. Above it, lucerne grew, ever greener, the stalks more translucent than when she was a child on a German farm with Frau Anneke, her mother's friend who loved her so much that she sent her away.

Jones knelt beside her, staring unblinkingly into her face.

It is him! she thought, startled by onrushing recognition. *The young man, who once had a nice face. A pilot whose skull fell in Frau Anneke's field.* She felt no pain or fear of any kind. *He barely has hair on his rosy cheeks. A boy, only a handsome boy!*

"Stay alive!" He was ordering her, again, his voice shocked and strident. Her beauty and youth were screaming at him as he raised her forehead from a cushion of stone.

I am not "hidden" any more . . . no longer "alone" . . . not "taken" . . . not "given" . . . I was small . . . so much has happened! She tried, but failed to speak. She could only hear her own words echoing in a chamber somewhere far off, as her shuddering body grew colder and colder, despite the warmth of summer. She began to drift, as if borne by wind.

I remember my mother's name. Her inner voice rattled. *Esther!*

And my father. Moses!

The Queen's guard in the mufti of a gardener leaned closer to hear her words, hoping against hope for a confession to save him. But none came.

Tears fell onto the sleeve of his coveralls. The gurgling in her soft throat ceased. As life left her at the entrance to the palace, her eyes remained open as if with the inner knowledge of fading consciousness.

Later that same morning, seated on the back bench at Milano's, Samuel Rubin was intensely worried. Since that first day when Hester entered his world, he had moved to the rear of his own shop.

Why is she late? She's never late! Even on a Sunday. She must have had some pressing business of her own . . . or, God forbid, something happened!

His double chins wobbled. His lips trembled. In an effort to suppress rising anxiety, he put on his favorite record. The black disc spun dutifully.

Ah! se l'error t'ingombra.
>If the chains of error,
>Daughter of Eve, have bound you . . .

Presso a morir, vedrai
Che un'ombra, un sogno fu . . .
>Know when you come to Death's door,
>God offers you His grace,
>And when Life's dream is over
>You will come to see Him, face to face . . .

Vieni, e t'asconda il velo
Ad ogni sguardo umano . . .
>Come then and let this veil
>Shroud you from earthly eyes.
>Free you from earth's dark jail,
>Win for you Heaven's prize . . .

The haunting refrain of the hidden "Nuns' Chorus," stirring in its magnificence, filled the small millinery. Tears fell from the hatmaker's eyes, as always when (with his hearing aid turned up to highest volume) he heard Verdi's tragic masterpiece and he cried in time to the music.

Only, this time, overcome by the power of telepathic grief, he wept for the loss that his benevolent heart told him would never be assuaged.

∞ ∞ ∞

A House Too Small

> Here at our sea-washed, sunset gates shall stand
> A mighty woman with a torch, whose flame
> Is the imprisoned lightning, and her name, Mother of Exiles.
>
> **"The New Colossus" by Emma Lazarus**

Beside the infant's crib in which she lay, a small replica of the Statue of Liberty, like a toy, settled in a spreading pool of blood.

It had seeped through creamy sheets. Now it dripped, in uncongealed drops, onto the suicide note.

> In an infant's bed I lie
> Barren
> here, at last, to die!
> Childless present,
> the kindergarten
> begging this, seeking pardon.
> Shall I always so remain
> Captive

in a frost of pain?
Trampled wishes . . . broken hearts
Who from such deathly trap departs?

Edna lay curled in a fetal position, breathing in shallow bursts. Both hands fell limply between lacquered slats. Touching her neck, his fingertips felt for her carotid artery. There was no pulse. There was only a mild flutter. Her face had drained to deathly white. Her lips pulled into a weak, faintly aborted smile. On her wrists, veins were flayed open in brazen surrender, and razor blades had carved herringbone patterns of glistening crimson despair.

The note was unfinished, blotched. The childlike script seemed to contradict her obsessive neatness; it appeared to be the writing of a stranger. *This sad and lonely rhyme must have been written in sporadic moments of lucidity*, the professor thought when he found her, with the poem and the little statue replica. *She had wished to end her life, but she did not succeed*, he realized, feeling strangely calm in spite of the grave situation. *She hadn't the strength, railing harshly and abusively at herself, her anguish spiraling uncontrollably.*

Beneath the aborted lines he could still see the outlines of a simple picture. It was of a house and a path and, down in the garden, a tree with a swing dangling from a branch. All were soiled by her blood.

He did not yet know it, but this, the final time, a live oak would save her!

Grabbing the cordless telephone off the pedestal, he dialed 911.

"What's your emergency?"

There was no sympathy. No commentary. Just a quick question asked monotonously. His mind spun like the moving parts of a machine in perpetual motion. He breathed deeply, trying to still rampant annoyance.

How can this woman understand?

As if declaring an oral conclusion to a tragic play, mastering the demands of brevity he replied simply, "Finis!" thus ending a call that he was certain meant nothing of great importance to the person on the other end of the line. Then, realizing the error of such terseness, with a note of resignation infiltrating his voice, he gave his name: "Professor Adam Sherman."

When he awoke earlier that morning he had sensed his wife's absence from the bed next to his.

A bad omen, he thought.

They slept in the same room, but separately. Physical contact, no matter how superficial, had become risky because of her unpredictability, and thus eventually ceased entirely. A sense of duty supplanted it, though ripples of love moved through him when least expected.

Sentimental ambushes, he called them.

Perhaps such reactions are the unintended consequences of awakening when at first I do not wish to think, but prefer to remain wrapped in dream. He could not stop the flow of thought. *Some things defy true understanding, ruin logic, exile judgment. How can she be reached? How can I alleviate her suffering? She cannot have gone far*, he thought, knowing that she seldom wandered out of the house and had never learned to drive.

Logic was the professor's usual approach to life. He was not ready to abandon it now. Based on her prior "attempts," he was accustomed to a regimen of rapid investigation. He quickly found her in one of the spare bedrooms of their cavernous house. Each bedroom was filled with children's playthings. Each had a crib. Often she held parties for children who were invisible to all but her. *She sees them with spectral clarity and speaks to each in infantile words, jumbled, but gentle.*

∞∞∞

Many years before when Edna was an adolescent, she had been "selected" by a Polish doctor, in a "camp," which was the worst euphemism for a place of torture. Forever after, the word had become a thorn festering in the tissue of her mental anguish.

He wore a spotless coat. In the chest pocket directly above his heart, a pen and stethoscope glinted.

A manic look pierced his eyes, but his bearing remained composed; his face serene, his deathly white hands as steady as insensate utensils.

On his orders a group of pubescent girls had been brought into the room. They entered in a ragged march. They were lined up and displayed. All wore baggy garments, like soiled sacks, over their naked bodies.

Experimentation is justified! Medical science demands it! He checked himself, damming up the pressing flood of anticipation.

That winter was particularly cruel. Outside, snow fell like frozen tears of floating grief.

None of the adolescents wore shoes. He looked closely at each of them, stopping before their shivering emaciated shapes. He stared unblinkingly, his, eyes raking from bottom to top, then down again. Flicking a finger he dismissed each, except for one. He stopped, and took a sharp breath.

She may survive the procedure!

He decided to use her.

The girl looked down, her delicate lashes hiding dark eyes. She concentrated on her blue toes, trying to still her trembling. With a rubber-gloved hand the doctor touched her beneath the chin. Gently, almost with the subtlety of a caress, he raised her face toward his. She saw him clearly. Within her, a storm of violent abhorrence raged. Panic gripped her. Then her mind began to close like a fan, and within its tender folds she found secret refuge.

"I must study a young woman's ability to endure pain to the point of death!"

She lay on the table. Leather straps held her legs apart. Cuffs pinned her down. Without applying any anesthetic, first he probed the soft skin. Then, he swabbed an area of her abdomen and made a small incision. Finally, bending forward to add force to his own weight, he pressed hard with a scalpel, down and across.

"Blood wine!" He spoke to the female collaborator who followed his movements, holding the girl's head over to one side where he could watch her contract and vomit in the throes of pain. In his other hand he gripped a stopwatch. She hemorrhaged. Her eyes rolled back. Her frail body went slack.

His high-pitched, strident call of victory rang through the white room.

As she retreated into darkness with a mental crash, the girl understood his words, spoken in German. They came to her from a place of fundamental awareness, beyond the senses. That voice of irrational conquest would remain with her for the rest of her life.

He had stood so close—with the familiarity of a lover—that she could see a furry coating on his tongue and smell his horrible breath. White fetid flecks of spittle congregated in the corners of his mouth. His lips curled. A rosy hue spread across his cheeks. Like a satiated lothario, a blush tinged his skin.

She fainted.

The doctor shocked her back using an adrenaline-like substance so that he could observe her intimately, and she could see him again, in the bare room. To the sound of her screams, he ripped out her fundamental means of reproduction. Then silence trumpeted its triumph. Contemptuously tossing the excised organs into a metal bowl, he timed the girl's recession into unconsciousness and began to count down the minutes toward her death.

Calm now, he made notes of his observations in a leather-bound book. He added statistics, followed by cryptic commentary. All were written correctly in a precise and refined script.

But she did not die!

While studying subatomic particles in the Philadelphia laboratory of the university where he had held tenure, the professor discovered an unusual and, until then, unobserved phenomenon.

"It was," he told reporters, "a split off a split." They did not appreciate his laconic description. One described his manner of speech as "reticence, bordering on arrogance." The journalist was entirely mistaken, for Adam Sherman was a calm, kind, almost shy man not given to hyperbole. In keeping with his traditional prerogative as a scientist, he gave his discovery a name and confided it to his trusted assistant.

"Pardon?"

Puzzled, his assistant felt compelled to ask what it meant. A long silence followed before the professor replied.

"I feel like the impulsive boy who asked his father, Helios, for the ultimate favor in order to prove the father's divinity."

"'Let me drive your sun chariot, just for a day,' the youth

pleaded precociously," the professor quoted, thinking of the dangerous power of his discovery if used inappropriately.

The lab assistant still failed to comprehend the riddle, which was what his teacher intended.

"Message in myth," he added cryptically. Then, regretting that he had placed the burden of mystery upon a student who was always eager to learn, he explained, "Zeus had to stop his son, the aberrant driver whose recklessness played havoc with Nature and soured the sweetness of Creation! He was left with no choice. He had to strike the runaway with a lightning bolt because it was his duty to arrest the ultimate ruination of all!"

"I am a physicist," said the professor. "I study the microcosm in order to understand the macrocosm."

His investigations into the puzzling realm of physics had made him a thoughtful man. "Matter, matters," he added, thinking that the quest for knowledge must be approached with humility.

"Ours is the wearisome art of trying to prove the 'unlikely' whilst confronting the futility of the 'plausible,'" he concluded, smiling as he ended his soliloquy.

Notwithstanding his soaring intelligence, Adam was unable to sound the depths of his wife's illness. *It dwells in a pestilential location . . . beyond the reach of love . . . distant from the shores of order*, he realized.

With all his heart, the professor wished he could set her free.

His sincerest efforts to help his wife by all the means at his disposal most often ended in failure, each more damaging and deepening than alleviating, no matter how hard he tried. As resignation clutched his heart, he concluded: *My liberty comes at the expense of her imprisonment because I feel so guilty about being "normal" when she is so deeply troubled.* The very thought of that discrepancy was an appalling condemnation of his marriage.

The King himself awarded the prize.

Filled with dignitaries, the ballroom of "The Majestic" glittered. Chandeliers dangled from the lavishly frescoed ceiling.

In keeping with the occasion, the invited guests, dressed in tuxedoes and gowns of exotic materials, had gathered to witness a noble ceremony.

On the rooftop of the magnificent building, in a stiff marine wind, seven flags flew on angled staffs. Below, spotless windows sloped to render fine views of the quayside. Ferries were berthed and tied up, side by side. Nearby, a greenly coppered dome reflected light off its curvature. The rays seemed to travel and return, boomeranging over the closely placed buildings competing for pride of place on the waterfront. Lapping waves held cold blue tints in their curling arcs. Above the Swedish flag, a single seagull winged lazily, its shape set in stark contrast against the pale sky of the northern latitudes.

The recipient was not so young any more. Neither was the King.

On the tenth of December over one million dollars passed into Adam Sherman's hands. But far more than the grand prize, he was instantly catapulted into the bonfire of fame. Research grants followed. He was rich, sought after. But he was terribly alone in a disintegrated marriage that was doomed before it began, although he had not known it then.

Paradoxically, the man who had access to arcane knowledge could not understand his spouse. She never told him what had befallen her. Nor did she disclose which organs had been cut from her youthful body in a place of utter bleakness. The violence that had been wrought upon her went beyond her own comprehension. It existed in a realm of distorted and repulsive fantasy. There, only mocking phantoms chuckled and danced sadistically to the music of her escalating lunacy.

As requested by his institutional sponsor, in his acceptance speech the laureate revealed the name of his discovery.

"Phaëton," he called it, with deliberately mysterious intent.

Some in the audience nodded, pretending to know the meaning. Others looked puzzled, but tried to hide their ignorance. His assistant, whom he had brought to the ceremony, smiled knowingly.

Before he left the podium Adam felt compelled to comment on what he called "chemical concoctions of the guilty."

"Beware," he announced unexpectedly, shocking the polite elite, "lest those who seek to ignite the explosive wick of condemned knowledge succeed in their dastardly endeavors!"

Adam had met his wife through the vicissitudes of misfortune.

When the ship that brought her to America steamed past Coney Island, a beautiful young woman named Edna, who was born in Hamburg, looked into the morning mist. Off the starboard beam she saw an amorphous shape. Tinged with an olivine patina, it was distorted into ethereal grandeur by the combined effects of distance and fog. But the torch, held in an enormous hand, dispelled the settled gloom.

A tiny glow lit in Edna's heart, which until then had seemed petrified like a fossil. Its unfamiliar flash threatened to flare. Frightened, she quelled it until it disappeared just as the lantern faded from sight.

The next time she felt a flicker in her heart was at Emily's Social Club. Because of an unexpected desire to dance, she met the man who became her husband.

Adam had one aunt.

She was elderly, astute, and especially fond of reminding him that she "came *von Deutschland*." Her long life had taught her many things, not least of which was what her only surviving nephew needed "most in life."

"You are a flat foot!" she declared on one of his visits to her apartment. It was filled with the clutter of memories. Not having learned English properly, the old lady, who liked to be called "Oma," often used malapropisms without embarrassment. Not waiting for any protestation, she ordered, "Go to Emily's!"

Oma's expression may have been literal, but her intention was figurative, Adam thought many times thereafter.

"At home," she said, "we learned to move with music."

Now as slow in thought as she was careworn in movement, she took a while before adding in conclusion, "The couples' dance, partners holding each other, began there you know . . ." Her voice trailed off.

Her brief speech had emerged more coherently than usual.

But it ended abruptly, as if the stress of a foreign language were too burdensome. Adam knew better than to argue with his aunt. He also knew that he would never master synchronous steps or rhythm, no matter how hard he tried. Nonetheless, such emphatic advice weighed persuasively on the single man. Already by then he was middle-aged and bald, save for an unruly shoot of reddish hair near the middle of his pate. He was tall and slightly stooped. His well-cut features were those of a handsome man. Having a good but not very well paying job, Adam could be called "eligible," at least in the opinion of his Oma, which he dared not dispute.

"Perseverance is the mother of success," said Luis, the effeminate dance teacher from "somewhere in Latin America" (he was never precise about the country), who had a habit of distorting expressions to suit his purposes.

Whether he had borrowed the phrase from another source or simply created it to soothe his inept students, Adam neither inquired nor cared. His concern lay with his own disobedient feet.

Luis was not the "Emily" of the Social Club and never would be—perhaps to his chagrin.

"Close enough," Luis once responded when someone asked him where Emily was. So the secret of the founder's whereabouts remained intact.

At a moment when Adam felt sure he had inadvertently injured an excessively patient and hugely obese partner whose gaze rested on him more intensely than was good for his comfort, a beautiful young woman close to the mirrored wall suddenly clutched her stomach and fell to the shiny floor.

Writhing in pain, she did not utter a sound. Adam saw it all, as if in slow motion, for his lack of poise was compensated by keen powers of observation. Deserting his clingy partner, Adam reached the stricken woman in a few open strides.

He did not lift her.

Her slender fingers, which were the finest he had ever seen, dug into her abdomen, clawing in an attempt to induce some relief.

A pink telephone hung on an ornate hook just above the spot where she had fallen. Adam lifted the receiver. That was the first time he dialed the emergency number for Edna. Sadly, it was not the last.

The teaching hospital in New York City was renowned for its pioneering excellence in surgery. Edna was admitted to a gynecology ward. At first the medical staff thought she was in the throes of an early miscarriage, until closer examination revealed an entirely different diagnosis.

"Get her to the operating room! Now!" The admitting surgeon's voice was sharply authoritarian.

Adam knew what it was like to have only one relative. He wondered who Edna's family, if any, might be. He had no way of knowing that there was no one.

That night, the professor was restless. Insomnia plagued him, sticking its malicious tongue out, provoking him to stay awake.

In the morning he drained a cup of bitter cold coffee left over from dinnertime. Feeling somewhat refreshed, he followed his routine of fastidious ablutions, shaving more closely than usual, applying pomade to his carrot curl until it shone and obeyed his comb by remaining upright. From the few that he possessed, he chose his best suit. Then he left his bachelor's apartment and rode on two buses to "The Place." It was an abbreviated name for one of the finest hospitals in the country. On the way, between stops, he made a spur-of-the-moment decision to visit a florist.

When he reached the ward, despite his best intentions, his carefully crafted, well-rehearsed words of sympathy froze, with him, at the door. Looking through the vertical pane of glass, he saw her.

She lay in an iron bed, the first of that kind he had ever seen. It was slightly raised. Her head was cushioned by pristine white pillows. Her long hair tumbled in dark ringlets around her strikingly beautiful and youthful alabaster face. Her forehead was high. Thin brows above dark eyes arched as if in permanent inquiry. The nose had a slight upturn. Her lips were full. The chin blossomed like a budding rose. He could not see her teeth, but imagined them to be arranged in white rows. *Like Pennsylvania corn on the cob*, he thought.

Pain seemed to become her. He noticed that she wore a

half-smile, as if she were tracing an invisible line between the ache of suffering and the emancipation of love.

The florist had chosen for him half a dozen Flora Dora roses. Around them sprigs of baby's breath floated, adding white dots to a fragile spray of green. Immobilized by the ache of pity, he did not enter the room. Instead he returned to the nurses' station, which he had passed on the way in.

On a piece of scrap paper he wrote, "May these flowers hasten your return to good health. Courteously, Adam Sherman, PhD, Emily's." Hastily, he appended a postscript with his home telephone number. Empathy washed over Adam, threatening to drown him. He wished that he could soak up her pain and make it his own.

One week later (he remembered the date and day), his telephone rang. Normally, he would not have answered an unexpected call on a Saturday. However, this time he did, some intuitive impulse motivating him.

"Adam?"

"Speaking."

"Thank you for the lovely roses." Her emphasis was obvious.

The voice was supple, delicate, refined. With its faint tinkle of European timbre, it sounded gentle. He thought of colors at the beginning of spring . . . something he never did. His heart skipped a beat.

Three months later, they were married by an elderly orthodox rabbi whom they both admired—not because he had walked halfway across Europe with a Bible in his hand, but in spite of it. To that old man who lived what he preached, courage was not a badge. "Survival," he said "is neither shame nor guilt. All that maketh Man are gifts bestowed upon us from the Supernal Being." Those words, Adam remembered, derived from one of the rabbi's own inspirational sermons.

On the first day of their modest honeymoon (spent like many couples before them, at a motel in Buffalo advertised as being "near to Niagara Falls"), he discovered that her collapse on the dance floor in full view of the adult class had been caused by complications from acute appendicitis.

"Triggered," the hospital's discharge report said, "by extreme trauma suffered by the patient pursuant to a crude hysterectomy, excision of the ovaries and fallopian tubes estimated to have occurred in her adolescence."

Edna had left the report behind, like a deliberately rejected message from a source of tyranny.

That night, despite her extraordinary beauty and the flowering passion that he expected, they did not consummate their marriage.

∞∞∞

"A house too small!"

It was the first complaint that Adam heard from Edna. She said it with such passion and at such a volume that he should have paused to analyze it.

He liked his little house located across the river in the suburbs of New Jersey. It had a garden.

"We have all the comforts of home," he often told her compassionately. But she persisted, until the recitation became a mantra.

"I need a bigger house for all the children!" she shouted.

That strident voice was what confronted Professor Sherman each morning and each night in the house on the water's edge. Edna followed it with another, even more vociferous, command.

"Adam," she cried, "You must go to your rabbi. Ask him for my miracle! I have waited long enough."

He obeyed the second command before the first.

One day during the festival of Passover, after prayers, he asked the rabbi for an audience. The old man nodded his agreement, his silver beard flapping like a banner of wisdom. His study seemed as old as its occupant. From floor to ceiling, heavy books filled sagging shelves. He had never put a single one there that he had not read.

The rabbi waited. He knew that something heavy troubled the supplicant's heart. After silent minutes had passed, he turned his wrinkled hands over, the palms facing upwards. That was permission enough.

Adam Sherman unburdened himself rapidly, the outpouring having been suppressed for so long. After listening intently, the rabbi rose from behind the antique desk, pressing his gnarled knuckles onto its top to raise himself to a standing position. He left the room. Adam remained, alone, surrounded by The Written Word. When the rabbi returned, he held out a paper plate. On it was a single piece of unleavened bread, baked to golden crispness. The simplicity of the offering emphasized its appeal. Its stark symbolism was not lost on the professor.

"Keep this," the rabbi said in his steady voice. "Place it in a kosher container. Look closely and profoundly at it. Do not stare. Just see it! Understand its meaning by applying the cardinal skill of meditation. Think of it as the 'bread of affliction.' One day, it will bring you solace."

His voice personified assurance. His demeanor warranted truth to be revealed.

Almost to the anniversary of that meeting, Edna was not pregnant and never would be, as the rabbi had known intuitively. That morning, Adam found her in the main bathroom of the new, large house that he had bought with his prize money. She was naked.

A vegetable paring knife had sunk to the bottom of the ceramic tub.

In harsh clarity, he saw the wood handle worked finely onto the steel blade, its nails smoothed to perfection. Ripples in the water distorted the honed edges. Like dissolving permanganate crystals, her blood formed liquid tendrils.

Edna's chin (that delicate apostrophe of her face which had so quickened his pulse when first they courted and still worked its magic on him) was almost below the water line. Under the surface, the small cut in her neck, just shy of her jugular, bled.

The wound was subtle, but its effects profound, providing a strangely beautiful sight that prevented Adam from turning away. Then, reality tore through his trance.

He gave the address of their house and its name.

"Relativity Point," he said.

It is, after all, what she wanted. Big, with spacious, brightly lit rooms for unborn children!

It sat on a promontory jutting out into a small lake that trickled to the intracoastal waterway along the eastern seaboard from a sliver of land before the ocean took all. Adam Sherman—who understood the depths of Einstein's genius and named his home after a formula that changed the world, winner of a supremely prestigious prize, physicist-at-large, freed from the laboratory—was now imprisoned in a house that seemed to echo with chaotic screams of conscience.

He felt robbed of options.

Thus, his brain addled and distraught by his wife's unrelenting derangement, the professor temporarily conceded defeat.

Adam was listening to an uncommon recording of *Faust*.

At flea markets and garage sales, he spent time rummaging for unusual musical pieces and horological heirlooms. In such places nobody recognized him. That suited him well.

My reluctant celebrity is best confined to the rarified atmosphere of academia, he thought. *Even there,* he realized with a tickle of patient amusement and a wriggle of instinctive sarcasm, *the air is becoming thinner now that I have retired.*

When he found the old eight-track tape for which he still had a player in an antique automobile, he was thrilled.

All five acts by Charles Gounod to the French libretto by Barbier and Carré, tracing its storyline back to Goethe. Indeed I am a lucky man!

The thought itself had the barb of a lampoon, because in his heart, he knew that he was a visitor to a palace of splendor amid the squalor of Edna's anguish.

The professor had come to terms with his wife's uncontainable anger, the kind that so often accompanies depression. While he collected relics of the past to be catalogued in his luxurious though cluttered hobby room, he knew that Edna was, as he described it, often *absent*. Since the earliest of her many "attempts," her behavior had become increasingly erratic and bizarre. Only two things seemed to soothe her when she "traveled," as one of her psychiatrists said, using an annoying euphemism.

Adam knew what they were: *roses with baby's breath, like the very first time . . . and mementos of things, both visible and invisible.*

***

Adam and Edna went to The Oasis treatment center.

The entrance was a hoax, designed to provide the appearance of a spa, whereas what the building really housed was a sanatorium.

Medical offices were discreetly located to one side, accessible only via a lobby of colored glass, ornamented with a floor to ceiling aquarium. Inside, strikingly alien fish swam in languid brilliance.

As if continual roaming will liberate them from their luxurious detention . . . like me! Adam Sherman thought on seeing it.

In the morning newspaper, with idle curiosity he had read his horoscope. "Pisces, the Fish," it stated in clichéd presumptuousness, "has a surprise in store for you. The alignment of Jupiter and Mars with the Moon and the Sun is auspicious." He had stopped to consider what might follow.

"Tragedy may occur. But, the future is certain."

Wondering who writes such simplistic platitudes for a living, with a gentle hand Adam guided his wife into the doctor's office. The specialist was said to be the best in his field.

Indeed, Dr. Wo had heard of the professor. The first time they met, he greeted Adam as if he were the only one present, ignoring the spouse at his side. With a wry smile accompanied by some puzzlement on his lunar face, he made a laconic, though complimentary remark. "It's my pleasure to serve a distinguished laureate."

Adam interpreted the deep bow that followed as dubious sincerity.

I am not the patient, he thought, then revised his thought. *Perhaps I am. Maybe we all are.*

The news that Wo rendered, like a final judgment handed down from a court of appeals, came in two parts, oral and written, as Dr. Wo (*aptly named*, thought the professor) looked at Adam quizzically and spoke sotto voce. One was explanatory, devoid of encouragement; the other an unapologetically and crassly delivered bill in an extravagant amount. As if tendering his resignation, Dr. Wo handed Adam the note containing his diagnosis, as he said, "Sorry." It was written in stylistically miniaturized calligraphy of Asian origin which seemed to complement the diminutive apology.

Dear Professor Sherman:

My tests are complete. Your wife's condition is atypical of patients suffering from trauma that occurred in their lives at some point. So, I am driven to my own conclusion. I believe that she is engaged in an unusual form of "infantile regression." In other words, she is withdrawing as if by some peculiar intention she wishes to return to the womb!

Some possible, unorthodox treatment suggestions are appended. I do not guarantee that they will work.

Sincerely,
Wo B., MD

The note confirmed what Adam already knew.

The drive home was quiet.

Edna lay curled up on the back seat. She never wore a seat belt. She did not sit upright like a normal passenger. Once again silence, the familiar adversary, gripped his heart implacably. Adam glanced at Edna in the rearview mirror. Her face was ruthlessly and deceivingly beautiful.

If only . . .

The words remained unexpressed, concealed within a throbbing ache of wistfulness.

Large, masterfully set windows looked out onto the open areas surrounding the gracious house, rendering a constant visual gift. When Edna did look upon the garden beyond the room, she seemed blind to its splendorous beauty. To her husband, Edna's innate sense of appreciation appeared to have long since crumpled and fallen to the ground, like the disappointing note from Dr. Wo.

She imagined herself embalmed, an ancient hollowed-out being; disemboweled, shrunken, bandaged, and plastered into oblivion. Thus a brand of seemingly endless damnation occupied her. She never walked in the garden. Nor did she tread on the small paved path that led to a bricked-in circle nearest to the high panes.

***

In her deranged state, Edna had no way of knowing that in a distant place a centenarian half lay, half sat, strapped and bound tightly into a wheelchair. The headrest was padded to prevent him from jerking backward in spasmodic fits. He drooled onto the metal wristbands that held his hands fast to the armrests. His legs jutted out at odd angles. The eyes were sunken, the head emaciated like a prehistoric skull with errant strands of matted hair. His nails were long, his fingers curled. His clothing was soiled and yellowed by stains that appeared to be indelible.

"The pain of an emerging young woman is purity," he mumbled so incoherently and spuriously in dialectic German mixed with hybrid Argentinean Spanish that the bored aide ignored her charge's utterance.

He spat up the bolus of his last meal. The jerking resumed, so powerfully as to penetrate the worn padding, sending his head crashing into the hard brace of the restraint.

"Be still!" the helper ordered, impatiently. But the camp doctor was beyond all receptivity, for he had retreated into the abyss of senility.

By a quirk of fate, when the terrible incident of Edna's attempted suicide in the baby's room occurred and Adam rescued her, she had seen the tree. In the house that replaced the "too-small one," from within the void of perceived loneliness and worthlessness in which she dwelled, she noticed it, as if it had never before existed.

The sole live oak within its ring of brick stood alone and majestic. Its armored trunk seemed to split into boldly defined branches tipped with delicately embroidered leaves of emerald green. A shaft of light struck the trunk, igniting it into a blaze of glory. A child's swing, handcrafted from chipboard and white rope, hung from a branch, empty.

Alone it swayed. Beyond, water rippled under the touch of wind, which also caused the swing to gently bounce and turn. Unlike Edna, it seemed to delight in itself.

On that morning when Adam found Edna lying pathetically in the crib, the small plastic Statue of Liberty rested in a pool of her blood.

The object, a remnant of her arrival in the United States as a girl years before, was the one to which she had clung until the souvenir, together with her message, fell from her weakening grasp.

Just one day before, Adam had strolled repeatedly around the tree. His mind was set on the quest for his wife's emancipation from psychosis. He felt like Don Quixote tilting at windmills.

Adam had barely noticed the oak when suddenly a breeze ruffled its leaves and seemed to whisper to him. The insistent rustling sounded like a troop of pipers calling him to duty. In a burst of clarity, Adam's mission defined itself.

He tinkered with an old watch that he had unearthed from a pile of eclectic objects at an antique store. With a flat knife he opened the rear clam-like plate, then oiled its rusted springs and sprockets. He wound it. He held it up, listening to its ticking return to life. As he reset the fine hands, a frisson passed through him. He remembered a strange but true story:

> In the latter part of the eighteenth century, Marie Antoinette commissioned a watch to be made for her alone. It would be the most extravagant watch in all of *le monde*. However, it was never produced during her lifetime, but only many years after the queen was beheaded.
>
> The masterpiece was inexplicably lost. It disappeared from a museum in the Holy Land, only to reappear in puzzling circumstances. The legend of the vanished timepiece inspired a celebrated watchmaker to make a new one before the original resurfaced.
>
> The case would be made of wood—not any wood, but only that from the doomed queen's favorite tree in the garden of the Palais de Versailles, where he imagined her to have gazed upon it with an awful yearning for loveliness itself. For such was she . . .
>
> He offered to purchase the lone tree, to no avail. It was simply given to him before he could pay for it. Filled with gratitude, he felt compelled to make an extravagant donation to *The Petit Trianon Château* that the spoiled queen loved.
>
> Thus the task of recreating The Marie Antoinette commenced.

When Adam Sherman read the story it was not the romantic lavishness of the project that bore upon him. Rather it was the devotion to the return of perfection that impressed him so.

Walking the tree, as he described it rhetorically, suddenly cast the tale's moral upon him. "Yes, indeed!" he declared out loud, like Archimedes discovering what had always been there, but had not yet been defined. Inspired, he rushed back into the house on Relativity Point, determined to tell Edna that he would make her a watch with his own hands.

All out of wood, except for the cogs and springs!

He flew into the room, filled with anticipation that she would be thrilled at the idea, if only he could explain it as one would tell a magical tale to a child. When he saw her curled up, pale and withdrawn, he knew that the chasm that separated her from him was unbridgeable.

A wave of disappointment crashed over Adam. He felt forlorn, deserted, hopeless.

The next morning when he found Edna, he made the emergency call, convinced that she would be lost forever.

Even skilled surgeons may not succeed in bringing her back this time!

But he was wrong, for she had seen the tree—brandishing its life for all to witness.

As she had began to faint, a tiny spark—an unaccustomed, almost rejected seed of comprehension that her barrenness was not her fault, not the embodiment of her pain, guilt, and remorse for surviving and marrying—entered her like an uninvited guest. Not through the portal of logic did it come, but through a soulful gateway.

It glimmered like the torch of the grand welcoming Lady, as she had seen her in the mist of optimism on that first day of arrival.

Before passing into the relief of coma, like on the deathly winter's day when she had lain on a cold iron plinth protected only by the silken folds of an imaginary fan, Edna did not feel obstructed. A door was opening, and she was reaching beyond—to something higher, better, fuller.

Her strength waning, she smiled at Adam. He saw it, understood it, felt redeemed by it. He smiled back at Edna, his wife, and joy leapt in his heart like a wild animal freed from a trap.

In that fleeting moment, the whisperer of secrets gave them a new awareness. No longer in turmoil, they saw each other truly, unified and liberated. They felt the proximity of the Maker, the Redeemer, the Taker, the Giver—perhaps as the old rabbi intended when he gave Adam the "bread of affliction."

Adam reached for Edna, wishing to embrace her in tolerance and acceptance. So they rejoiced, alone, and for the briefest instant together, as it was meant to be.

∞∞∞

Lady Dorothy's Dilemma

Hope has returned to the hearts of scores of millions of men and women, and with that hope there burns the flame of anger against the brutal, corrupt invader. And still more fiercely burn the fires of hatred and contempt for the filthy Quislings whom he has suborned.

Prime Minister of the United Kingdom Sir Winston Churchill, delivering an address to both Houses of Congress in the United States of America on December 26, 1941

Oh yes, she had thought many times, in her ever-diminishing interludes of sobriety, *my husband certainly spared no expense to allow his eye to fall more commonly on beauty than on ugliness.* But that only applied to her immediate gentrified surroundings. *Knight Commander of the British Empire . . . who disappeared from my life in England and beyond for long periods! That double-dealing, chauvinistic, racist bastard was "autochthonous" (a word he loved to use, to confound me and blare his "superior education." But, he did not know that I bested him during his restless bouts of drunken sleep when I learned of his "clandestine activities." Yes, his "conscience" (if he had one?), his hateful out-*

pouring of demonic fantasies came to my knowledge between snores, when he spoke in the language of devils!

The columned house stood high on the suburban hill of Durban, South Africa, known as the Berea, not far from the university campus. In its white-painted luster, it topped the manicured terraces of the garden like the cardinal jewel in an emerald crown.

Where she stood the woman had a splendid view overlooking the downtown buildings, the harbor, and the great mound structures of the sugar terminal in the port.

"Carillon of the damned!"

She muttered the words under her breath as the sound of bells came welling up from somewhere within the city that spread in irregular patches below her home. The church was lost to sight, absorbed within the urban sprawl.

Lady Dorothy of Somerset, the childless widow of Sir Roland Gaylord, felt as if she were a mammal trying to breathe underwater, dragging cylinders of oxygen on her back along a road paved with coral. It led, she was certain, to an amorphous statue deep beneath the sea. Muffled and indistinct, her speech emerged as though in a cloud of bubbles. She wished that the utterances of her anguish would burst forth into the ether of significance.

But it did not work that way.

Instead, the slur of words tumbled in disarray as shards of partially chewed ice fell from her mouth. She raised her veiny hands to her lips, besmeared with waxy lipstick applied by shaky fingers. Then she plunged her fingers feebly into each ear as she tried to shut out the drifting, yet insistent, clangor.

"Be gone!" she cried. Nobody heard the spluttered maledictions of a wasted dowager whose youth was but a distant memory, and whose titled status and aristocratic wealth had become the relics of a shrunken empire.

Lady Dorothy preferred night to day, which seemed to lie in wait ready, to press-gang her into the idiocy of routine. She had not slept well last night. Nor the one preceding that. Indeed, she had not experienced true rest for a very long time.

The lady was certainly in no mood for the insistent calls of the church. They served only to emphasize the chill of loneliness. Her companion had become the square bottle filled with a fermented extract of juniper berries, her music the tinkling indifference of ice cubes.

Trying hard to focus properly through the netting of a severe headache, she stared down upon the rambling city below her vantage point on the wide verandah. The incongruity of her appearance, dressed in a flowing chiffon frock, alone and drunk before noon on the Lord's Day, did not bother her. She began to sway as if to the vagaries of the warm and wet wind. On its way up from sea to sky laden with dense humidity, it brushed past the posh suburb straddling the hillside, dampening the stone floor as it went by.

By force of habit she had positioned herself between the neat sections of light and shadow marked by the smooth support columns. They stood firmly, shining in sparkling white below the iron filigree of the roof eaves. A high front door led into the round parlor. It, too, was the same creamy white.

The color of impurity, she thought. The entrance was set in a tall frame that her late husband had chosen deliberately to accommodate his height. From the street, the house looked more like a Masonic temple than the grand, private residence of a titled aristocrat.

Her deceased husband, Sir Roland Gaylord, had possessed an ego that matched his great size. Ever the man of "imperial authority," he had instructed the builders and carpenters of his home to ensure that no portal touched the top of his head, or hindered his long strides when he marched through his rooms. Such exits had a way of coinciding with the slightest enthusiasm that his wife ever exhibited, albeit diffidently so as to avoid his strident outbursts.

When sober enough to make the effort, Lady Dorothy remembered her husband's resentment at having to pay for the construction of his home.

"Grand Britannia" he named it, in honor of the British colonial system that he pretended to so greatly admire, although he was no more than a traitorous exponent of its influence. "Cecil John Rhodes," he was fond of remarking (although she did not not listen, which caused his moustache to twitch); "now there's a man who understood our rightful claim to Africa. That's why he ensured that the width of the railway gauge would be identical from the Cape of Good Hope to the Nile delta." He used any device he could to deceive, even when talking to his wife.

"I served royalty," he remarked to her, more often than was good for their sorry relationship. "You know that my lineage is traceable to the sovereign's family." *Another lie.*

Sir Roland deliberately omitted mentioning that the line was attenuated by many a mishap or, if the rumors could be believed, even deliberately concealed miscegenation along the way. When he said such things his cheeks glowed and his forehead glistened. She was never quite sure if these animated expressions were the results of arrogance or, as she suspected, if they derived from a deeper, more shameful core. *Like bad roots that sour soil, rob it of nourishment, strangle its essential fertility*, she decided.

"Why then do I not qualify for a 'Grace and Favor' home?" he would inquire with a sharp glint of resentment and a flicker of sinister jealousy in his eye. He was of course referring to free homes given by the royal family to "deserving relatives" (usually indigent ones) like tidbits thrown to ravenous dogs. Lady Dorothy knew that his expectation was perfidious. She also knew that it would be pointless to pander to her husband's misplaced pretensions. So she said nothing.

Let him pay, she thought, *as wretched and unreasonable a thing as it may be for him.*

Glancing over at the door, she saw a shriveled Christmas wreath. In and out of focus it floated, turning alternately gray and brown as she watched the object convert from a circle to an oblong. Try as she might, Lady Dorothy could not remember who put it there or how long it had remained pinned to the entrance of Grand Britannia.

"Who cares?" she said in a rasping voice. "It is withered and waiting for one day, just like me."

The shaking that assailed her frail body was not induced by

a drop in temperature, but rather by delirium tremens. She wanted to stand still, but her knees rattled.

Her mind filled to overflowing with the fear of being forgotten by all, including herself. Then it shrank like a squeezed out sponge, robbed of fluid.

The lady had once been quite attractive, though haughty, the perception of superiority being as natural to her as indifference to the plight of the unfortunate masses. Too much gin (though diluted with tannin-laced tonic water) had worn away her once-untainted face. She had spent excessive time in the company of horses with colored masks, their sweaty bodies supporting small jockeys in fluttering silk livery, their high riding boots heeled with silver spurs. Too much sun had filtered through her expensive broad-brimmed hats. Now her head was topped by thinning hair.

How many interminable cricket and croquet matches, fetes, and club galas without a partner on my arm have I attended in the name of social nicety and the pursuit of sycophantic glamour?

Time had become her punishment. The more she had of it, the more it injured her. Along the latitudinal line of the Tropic of Capricorn, indolence and affluence had coalesced. With malice they had imposed their peculiar wreckage upon her. She was alone, as she had been for many wretched years.

Always so utterly, so sorely, alone am I!

The realization made her cry.

Already she was onto her fourth drink, each of increasing concentration. Her indifference to everything and everyone grew in direct proportion to her consumption of the insalubrious mixture of melting ice, sour gin, and tannin.

Before her, the scene was indeed splendid. Through watery eyes, meshed with red vessels, she did not see the sordid poverty brushed away into the frayed corners of the city where lower-caste people were crowded. She had forgotten the discarded wreckage of humanity drawn from their homeland as "a labor force."

Sea, sky, city, slum-dwellers had become one.

One had become all.

***

A sordid dagger of depression punctured the remains of Lady Dorothy's trembling normality. She had become neither afraid of life nor drawn to death. Both seemed unworthy of consideration any longer.

The familiar heaviness was upon her again.

Like Homer's Scylla and Charybdis, the terrible gaping jaws of competing fates opened before her. Had Dorothy been sober, she would have understood that, like Scylla, her existence had hardened into rock as punishment for destroying the softness of life.

She looked in the direction of the fishpond settled into its depression on the terrace below the house, giving it a false impression of endurance.

That damned man would not build me a swimming pool, she reminded herself. In her intoxicated state she barely achieved the clarity of recollection.

I was young and beautiful then, and I wanted it! That is why he would not give it to me! Her inner voice raged, but did not reach her lips. *The bastard insisted on having the British coat of arms inlaid with mosaic stones into the cement floor of the pond so that he could gaze upon its shimmering image! But I knew the real reason: It was part of his elaborate disguise.* Her mind had cleared enough to allow her that conclusion.

There was the shield underlaid by rose, thistle, and shamrock; the three lions, the harp, and the garter bearing the motto *Honi soit qui mal y pense* (Evil to him who evil thinks). *How appropriate*, Lady Dorothy thought. The unicorn and surmounting crown with the sovereign's maxim: *Dieu et mon droit* (God and my right) lay below it.

As if that privilege had been his too!

She perceived herself as a discarded woman. At its core such a description was merciless. *How many times have I thought of drowning myself in the shallow pond?* Lady Dorothy wondered.

Yet, strangely, her salvation lay in a contradiction. Because she had never been taught to swim as a child, she was so afraid of water that she stayed away from the very substance that she had wished to use to end her life.

***

The telephone rang. Lady Dorothy's life was at very low ebb. She moved to the door and peered inside the house. Through rheumy eyes with her pupils slothfully dilated, she could dimly perceive the stark contrast of the dark interior. It looked like the draconian cave of her social isolation and self-inflicted incarceration. A chill gripped her by the shoulders. Cold shivers chased up and down her spine.

Inside cannibals wait, ready to devour me!

The trains were running again. *Maybe they never stop? Or is it the phone?* she wondered in confusion, as the monotonous noise bored into her skull and set the few remaining original teeth in her receded gums on exquisite edge. She struggled to find the telephone, although she knew where it was kept.

The telephone sat on a little Queen Anne table that looked like a miniature ironing board. Next to it, tea cups and saucers were permanently set and waiting for ladies of her "class" whom she was sure she had invited. *But they never come to join me!* It was a futile exclamation. *How I hate the way they refuse me the basic companionship and common charity of their presence!*

The chinaware and spoons were rattling in accompaniment to distant vibrations. *The cursed trains?*

"Stupid people!" she uttered, before adding without regard to conscience or self awareness, "The rich, the vain, the pious, and the drunk!"

The ringing continued.

She tried to walk in a straight line. But that required her body to make demands on her brain and vice versa, tasks that neither seemed willing to undertake. Her motive was not so much to answer the summons of the adamant telephone as it was to shut it up.

"Hallo! Hallo!" she said, indignantly, mispronouncing the words of greeting, some of her loose false teeth colliding with her implants. But it was a hollow gesture, because she had not reached the instrument. In any case she did not realize that she was merely rehearsing the words that she would say if and when she did get there.

At last she found it, just as it stopped its infernal noise. For no apparent reason, other than her internal emotional disarray, she slumped to the floor. Her frail body slid down the wall beside the Queen Anne table. It came to a rumpled rest on the red carpet. Its woolen pile was thick. *My dead husband brought this home from an interminable tour of duty in India! From that day forth he refused to walk on it. I, however, never cared for such silly foibles. Perhaps I wished he was dead when he was alive, but not that he is alive since he is dead?*

Occasionally, if sober enough to feel anything, Dorothy experienced a keen thrill of pleasure while trampling on that rug with the spikes of stiletto-heeled shoes. Despite the havoc that this uncomfortable footwear wrought on her feet, she wore the pair in deliberate defiance. They enabled her to hack at one of Sir Roland's favorite *objets d'art*.

"You despicable man!" she wailed, as if his ghost could hear her voice echoing through the halls.

Lady Dorothy did not realize that she was weeping, as she passed the last signpost on the road of regret and entered a shameless zone of self-abnegation. The ringing began again. Only then did she wipe her eyes with the backs of her hands, trying to clear them enough to see the telephone.

She reached for it.

Fumbling, she knocked the table. The black receiver spun from its Bakelite cradle. It came to rest beside her shaking hand.

"Dorothy . . . Dorothy . . . is that you?"

The weight was back, the water heavy again, above, around, and beneath her.

Only this time there was something else present. It was dark, gross, and sinister, like some gigantic coiled beast. Its sinuous limbs were reaching from the recesses of rocky submerged grottoes. She struggled to avoid them, but her wriggling only rendered her more desirable to the repulsive creature of her own creation. Tentacles reached her, pinching, worming toward a place deep inside her. Now an amorphous cloud of Delphian ink surrounded her.

She was not certain whether the words were real. She could not identify to whom the voice belonged. She failed to understand why the person on the other end of the line was being so stubborn in not responding to her answers, which she gave over and over in her head, her lips moving silently.

"Are you okay?" the voice asked, this time more firmly.

"Yes," she replied, very loudly it seemed. Then she screamed out, "No!" in a display of futile anger. But the line had gone dead, and she never discovered who had called her.

Her servant came into the lounge, having heard her scream.

"Go away!" she yelled at him. He did not reply and just stood directly in front of her, staring unblinkingly.

"Why don't you obey me?" she cried, her fury exacerbated by despair. "Don't you hear me?"

The little black man, whose improbable name was "Future," simply ignored her as much as possible when, as he described it in his own language, she was in one of those *dakiweyo* drunken states. The Zulu understood that it was the liquor speaking. But his considerate disregard sent paroxysms of futile anger through Lady Dorothy. When she stopped pounding her fists into dead air, small as he was, he merely lifted her from the floor and carried her frail body into the large bedroom. There he lowered her gently onto the vacant bed.

How I hate it with its rolled head and foot boards! They shine by day and night! They never grow dull. Damn their beauty! She detested everything that the bulky bed represented—its emptiness, its tight-grained beauty, its rarity and perfection. All of it evoked haunting loneliness.

The end of the week had come, and the Lady was again no more than a shambling bundle of wreckage. By the ingestion of alcohol in toxic dosages, she had sabotaged her coherence. It was time for Future to attempt to draw the exact amount of the wages that he had last agreed upon with Sir Roland many years earlier. As always, whenever he found it, he poured her liquor down the drain of the kitchen sink. But he did not always discover where it was.

When he had made the lady comfortable and finished all of his chores for the day, his hand entered her handbag, as it did each month. He would take the precise amount from her purse, never a penny more, although no increase had ever come his way by offer or request. Future would carefully fold the paper money and place it in his pocket. Only this time, as on many prior occasions, she did not have the money.

So he took nothing at all.

Lady Dorothy slept. For once it seemed like a good rest because when she awoke it was afternoon. An unfamiliar sense of refreshment filled her. She rose from the bed and walked to the expansive bay windows. Pulling the heavy brocade curtains aside by their sash cords, she let the afternoon light spill in. Slowly, her eyes adjusted, but she did not appreciate the curved view of the garden, extending in the direction of the bay, and the city overhung by the hill of the Berea.

A Sunday newspaper lay on her dressing table. Future had left it there for her to read. He was the last and the only servant whom she had kept on. Like an imperishable heirloom, Future was a remnant of the past.

My "Future" is small, she thought.

When her husband died and took with him the final vestiges of her belief in her own diminished worth, she would have gotten rid of Future too. Sometimes she wished she had. But she needed someone to attend to her needs, as much as she hated the admission and despised the requirement. Loathing, the inbred and unwarranted reaction of aristocrats, ate away at her insides, not least because of her intense dislike of the small Zulu's nickname, which, once allotted to him by a well-meaning missionary, had stuck to him like the coal blackness of his skin.

Future did not reciprocate her sentiments. Despite the intolerance of the society that surrounded him, he recognized that he was a visitor in the white man's world. Thus, he accepted his condition and remained intensely loyal to his deceased employer. Outwardly the little "houseboy" ignored the abominable bigotry that Sir Roland cast like stones at his servants. On the day of Gaylord's funeral, Future transferred his misplaced allegiance to the lady, ever grateful for the means of survival that her anomalous patronage bestowed on him.

So he served the widow well, tending to the garden, keeping the house in good order, fixing all manner of things. And when she collapsed in a broken heap under the influence of alcohol, he, a simple black man who had no expectation of ever being fully freed from servitude, carried his employer gently to the bedstead that belonged to her deceased husband and now to her fractionally living self.

Although her hands shook with the task, Lady Dorothy put on her reading glasses and slowly stretched a pair of white gloves with lacey wrist frills over her hands, working them into place with concentrated effort. She began to leaf through the newspaper, barely attending to the articles, until a single headline caught her attention:

CIRCUS IN TOWN TODAY! ONE DAY ONLY! DON'T MISS IT!

In a spontaneous burst of determined will such that she had not experienced for a long time, Lady Dorothy made a decision. She walked, with difficulty, to her bathroom across the dividing hallway of the old house.

She ran the water into the free-standing cast-iron tub. Reaching into a glass jar she withdrew a fistful of bath salts, then threw them into the swirling liquid.

With her gloves still on, she tugged at her dress, until she pulled it off. For the first time that day she noticed the stains of alcohol, the marks of spittle, and blotches of tears on the material. In abject disgust at her own excretions, she flung the dress and her undergarments into the corner where she knew Future would find them. Without demur, he would make sure they were properly laundered, ironed, and put away in her sandalwood closet which, like most of the furniture in the house, came from India—a convenient "retreat" for Sir Roland Gaylord. *Whatever Roland thought was right, was usually wrong because, to me, the motive was guilt and the expense an undesirable sacrifice*, she realized, yet again.

In her fumbling and groping manner, Lady Dorothy understood that there was something vile and detestable about possessing articles the acquisition of which she had not exerted any of her own taste or control.

She was about to step over the tall side of the bathtub when she caught sight of herself in the full-length dress mirror fastened to the wall. She stopped, stunned into immobility by her own reflection.

The naked, old body was emaciated; the skin wrinkled and folded in upon itself. From her bony feet tipped with gnarled toes, up the ladders of her legs, bluish varicose veins rose like clinging ivy. The fronts of her shins protruded, in contrast to the loose bulbs of her calves and the atrophied muscles of her thighs. The flesh on her belly was milky white. From her thin chest, her dried breasts hung down like brown bags. Reaching to the navel, the nipples dropped like wrinkled purple prunes.

Her breath caught in her throat. She took a step backward as if by moving away she could discard the reflected image.

How I wish I could reverse the ugliness that age and neglect have wrought upon me! Her own body had become a stranger, indeed an enemy to her. In her deepest recesses Lady Dorothy had developed her own private understanding of pain.

"It has a voracious appetite," she muttered, "but it likes to devour in small bites."

She needed to bathe, recognizing that the bad odor assailing her nostrils derived from none other than herself.

Blood, mucus, tears, she thought. *The liquids of my suffering!*

Tearing away from her likeness she stepped carefully into the bath. There was nobody there to assist her because Future respected her privacy—at least until, as quite frequently occurred, his natural reticence was overtaken by her need.

Lady Dorothy held onto the handles embedded into the walls of the tub. She steadied herself as best she could and sat down. The hot water felt good on her old skin. She reached for a natural sponge that her servant had acquired (without her asking) at the Indian market in downtown Durban. There, everything from skeletal remains of vertebrates to the choicest of oriental silks were sold to anyone who wished to brave the hustle and bustle of narrow streets, teeming bazaars, and audacious odors.

She held the oblong object in one hand. Only then did she realize that she still had her gloves on. She removed them slowly and placed them in the washing box. She began to scrub away the traces of corporal disgrace.

When Lady Dorothy finished, she felt that the water and activity had temporarily muted her anger and cleansed her spirit. She rose from her seated position in the bath and dried herself with a large terry towel. It had become hard through many manual washings by Future, who did not use a fabric softener. He habitually forgot, being so busy with the other jobs that fell solely upon him as manager of the Grand Britannia homestead. Usually she hated the roughness of the coarse cotton, *like the substance of ridicule*. However, this time the towel felt surprisingly good.

She stood in front of the mirror again.

Her skin glowed pink under the soft, almost secretive, light descending from the bathroom ceiling. She was not wearing her glasses. That allowed her to fool herself into imagining a youthful blush on her cheeks. It appeared to be spreading across the top of her chest, down to her buttocks, even into her groin.

There was something expectant about the color. She could not quite define it.

Instead of analyzing how she felt, she became absorbed in the more mundane activities of ablution. A large bottle of eau de cologne stood on a glass shelf next to the basin. She inserted the plug into the drain hole. After pouring copious quantities of perfumed liquid into the sink, she laid her hands in it, at first one at a time, then together. She left them to soak there, in the sweetened water.

This cologne comes from a polluted industrial city in Germany. It is derived from bergamot and other citrus oils that were believed to have the power to ward off bubonic plague! It had better work for my affliction too! she thought, remembering something she had read.

Subliminally she knew that she was trying to have the substance enter her bloodstream, and so replace the sluggish liquid of life that flowed through her veins.

Draped in a robe, she returned to her bedroom and withdrew fresh clothing from her wardrobe: underwear, shoes (nicely polished by Future) with dangerously pointed high heels, and an excellently tailored suit. Many years before, she had had it secretly designed and made exclusively for her by a black dressmaker. The excitement of doing something audacious for herself, going to a seamstress outside of her "circle," was palpable at that time, muted only by the disappointment of not being able to wear the garment in public. All she could do was to hide it, and remove it and gaze on it when Sir Roland was out of town or roaming the terraces of Grand Britannia. He would stop suddenly to gaze longingly into his fishpond, thinking of his unfair deprivation by the royals. Very occasionally she would wear *the* suit when her husband was not around. "Off on some 'external duty,'" he called it.

She knew better. *To hell with him and his lies . . . he is a liar's liar. He hasn't changed his true loyalties despite the intervention of time and the fall of the Reich!*

She had to be careful that nobody would remark to Roland about her attire, or casually mention it during a conversation that could be easily overheard. Lady Dorothy had not worn that particular outfit for more years than she cared to remember.

That day, however, in a surge of revenge against a society that had betrayed her, and a husband who had abandoned his country's principles, along with her desires, aspirations, and affections, she determined to recoup her loss by emerging in public.

Thus, she dressed as purposefully as her frangible condition would allow. She was about to leave her bedroom, when she remembered something.

Returning to her dressing table, she found what she sought. The miniature ballerina was frozen in motion, the folds of her porcelain clothes arrested at the moment of manufacture. The doll would only pirouette when the music box that housed her was wound. *Oh how I envy her!* Lady Dorothy thought.

The legs of the fine ceramic doll were clothed in white stockings, the feet tipped with black pointed shoes almost touching the mirrored surface of the ingrained willow wood box. Above her head, the dancer's tapered arms in elbow-length gloves culminated in delicate hands. They arched gracefully into an apex. On her head she wore an intricate diadem, which reminded Lady Dorothy of a tiara that her husband had once brought her as a sop for his absence and his unconfessed, yet scarcely disguised, promiscuity. At first sight, she had hated it because she was sure he had not purchased it for her and probably had received it as a gift for a favor procured on behalf of a maharajah.

"They always sought some special treatment from the imperial authority," he had let slip, more often than was wise for such a duplicitous gentleman.

However, Lady Dorothy had sense and foresight enough to accept the tiara. *For my financial security*, she remembered, notwithstanding that she had never worn it. She did not fail to notice that after Sir Roland handed over the gift, not once had he ever asked her to wear it. Nor had he concerned himself over its whereabouts. *Thus behaves one who has stolen a heart, only to turn it to stone*, she thought.

Strangely, her husband had admired the music box doll, commenting, "It was made by people who have a great history of artistry." Dorothy wondered about that, knowing that it was made in Germany. Once in a sarcastic riposte to that opinionated, ramrod man who professed publicly to be the epitome of domestic husbandry, she said, softly but firmly, "I thought they were the fascist enemies of Great Britain?" Sir Roland's color changed, growing dark, before receding somewhat. *Like the rise and fall of the empire*, she thought, but remained quiet rather than test his mercurial temper, usually directed most harshly at her, but only in private.

Lady Dorothy loved the dancer doll for its delicate femininity. She pulled a small drawer by its diminutive handles at the front of the box. A spring mechanism triggered the tiny ballerina into spinning action, so that she pirouetted across the glass in little circles as a Strauss waltz played in tinkling tones.

"A scene designed to delight a child," she cried, wondering if she had once really been one herself. The doll came to a stop when the drawer was fully extended. Inside, at its center, she found a white satin bag. She untied its thin drawstring.

The magnificent necklace slid out slowly. Twelve Mikimoto pearls, pure white, set perfectly apart on opposite sides of a segmented platinum chain, fluoresced like illuminated balls.

Languorously, she drew them across her perfumed palms and trailed them between her arthritic fingers. She thought of the women divers of the Orient who risked bursting their lungs to pull the shells from the Sea of Japan so that the fine results of molluscular irritatation could be removed, sorted, and sold as adornments to the rich.

"Futile female courage," she whispered, the words tumbling out of her dry mouth. "From Ginza in Tokyo to Durban in South Africa . . . quite a journey for jewelry of my misfortune!"

She laughed out loud. Immediately she reacted, alone, to the self-contagious, cackling sound of her voice. "That stupid, stupid man! He thought he could purchase my favors without earning my love."

She grimaced at the pain of reminiscence.

Lady Dorothy could not remember the last time she had worn the precious necklace. Her mind was much clearer now, perhaps as a result of seeing the beautiful piece again, after so long an absence.

It has been there, available all this time, she realized, with a start. *It is I who have been absent from it . . . as from my former life!*

For a moment she digressed into thinking about love.

Love is realizing that it cannot be defined, she thought. She refined it. *Love is to be found hiding in optimism. It emerges by doing what is right in every way possible, even if nobody notices.*

That felt gratifying, even though she knew that she had failed miserably. *At least I have thought of it,* she concluded, knowing that she had paraphrased sayings of her mother. As the superlative piece glided back into its satin bag, it wriggled.

"It has a life of its own," she said, imagining it to be a seductive serpent, paradoxically afraid that its allure would be the cause of its own demise when exposed to the hostility of light.

Since the bath, she had been thinking, indeed speaking, quite articulately. The alcohol had left a burning hole and deep thirst in her midriff. But her mind was lucid. "Oh so horribly clear!" she observed.

Dorothy looked at the palm of her left hand, which, like the other one, was remarkably devoid of lines, the skin unblemished and smooth. The dramatic contrast with the reverse sides, where twisting lines and speckled dark liver spots had taken hold, was unavoidable. Lady Dorothy hung the string of the bag on a glass ring tree that stood on the top of her dressing table next to an engraved sterling silver brush and comb set. It had been a birthday present from her parents, long ago. She had cherished the set as a young girl when she used it to tease and shape her long blonde hair.

In the ancestral family home on the Severn Estuary, her mother had often repeated to her as if to drill it into the core of her character: "Remember, always be a lady. No matter what, never give in to the barbarism of triviality." It had seemed so wise, so enticingly aristocratic and plausible—yet so far removed from the reality that later confronted her. *My parents had offers for me*, she recalled, thinking blankly of how pretty she had once been—and of how arranged marriages can destroy the heart of a woman.

My title became a hangman's noose! Now the brush served merely to straighten the thin and sparse strands that only partially covered the patches of pink skin on her dehydrated scalp.

Lady Dorothy thought broodingly of her lost marriage. It was not its passing that she mourned, but rather its doomed value. *Marriage is fake emancipation, a tear in the fabric of independence*, she reflected. *When we are a part of it we think that we know its meaning, its disguised liberation. But we do not. It is spatial, limitless in potential, yet fathomless in failure, a temple without a roof, a well with no bottom.*

"Venom can be unleashed in different ways," she declared. "He had his. I have mine!"

She glanced, perfunctorily, in the direction of a burled wooden urn. It stood on its four-clawed stand in the corner of the bay window.

"Macabre," she uttered in distaste.

Wrapped up in her reverie she failed to notice the crystal vase or its contents: premium roses resplendent in cinnabar, surrounded by delicate white sprigs of dogwood blossoms.

Dorothy had not put them there. Future had.

***

When cleaning the lady's bedroom Future noticed the dried flowers that he had placed previously. He removed them and cleaned the vase until it sparkled. Then he dipped the newly cut blooms from the splendid garden into the clear water.

Around the purposes of his life a certain layer of happiness settled. Although modest and quiet in demeanor, Future was a man who remained unabashedly in touch with his own values. With all of his guileless heart he hoped that the deep color of the fresh blooms had the power to revive Lady Dorothy's weary soul.

Somehow, he wished that the tincture and perfume of such flowering perfection would lift her from the depressed state into which she had sunk. Steadfastly, Future clung to such favorable intentions, day after deteriorating day.

Lady Dorothy had a cat. She barely remembered that it existed, let alone that it lived in her house. It was a Persian that she herself, when sober and not mired in discontent, had named Aryenis.

Once (it seemed so long ago), she had been a devout student of ancient relationships, subconsciously hoping to gather insights into her own failed state of matrimony. Discovering through her reading that Aryenis was the maternal grandmother of Cyrus the Great of Persia, she felt obliged to honor the cat with a fittingly royal name. Obese (through overfeeding by Future, who gave it thick maize porridge with sugar, salt, and milk several times a day), indolent, spayed, and no longer of any comfort to her owner, Princess Aryenis nonetheless continued to prowl through the hollow rooms of Grand Britannia unhindered. Her droopy stomach dragged across carpets, leaving trails of hair.

The cursed cat has overstayed its welcome. It gets in the way! Lady Dorothy thought perniciously as she shoved the cat off the chair in her bedroom where it had settled comfortably and harmlessly.

"Scat, you ridiculous cat!" she declared. "Renunciation of the crown—a suitable abdication for Persian royalty!"

Lady Dorothy had long ago abandoned the company of others, whether human or animal. *Or they forsook me!* she concluded. Just being herself created difficulties that were hard enough to bear. Oblivious to the niceties of perception, she never realized that the cat seemed to have a permanent expression of discontent on its pale face that remarkably resembled her own.

"Help me put this on."

Fully dressed, wearing her white gloves, which she had deliberately retrieved from the laundry box before Future could wash them, Lady Dorothy was struggling with the clasp of the splendid pearl necklace once again removed from its silken bag. Her achy hands shook with uncontrollable tremors. She needed help!.

Other houseboys might have quailed at such a request, but not Future. He had done many intimate things for his lady employer without her even knowing or remembering such favors. On those occasions the stress of just remaining alive was almost too great a burden for her to bear, without aid and comfort from a source that nobody else in her social class could imagine—let alone tolerate. In such times, Future understood her torment and accepted her helplessness as a natural outgrowth of the sadness that he had observed so often.

Future stepped up behind her.

He was ready to do as asked. Taking the necklace in his steady hands, he deftly mated one end to the other. It was a simple task for him. Nothing compared to having seen his "missus" naked, drunk, and gagging on her own regurgitation more times than he could count. Whether by word, deed, or gift, she had never thanked him, although without his intervention, she would have dehydrated to the point of madness, fallen, drowned, or simply wasted away. As for Future, he had expected neither gratitude nor recognition.

All he wanted was a place, simply to be.

"I don't want to go to the *isekisi*. Please Madam, no *sirkus*." Future was emphatic in his pleas, lapsing into Zulu colloquialisms, shaking his head vigorously as if in the grip of a pitiless premonition, when she put the invitation to him.

Lady Dorothy had nobody else with whom to go. There would only be one show as the newspaper advertisement made clear. She was determined to see it, having made up her mind that watching wild animals perform to commands would somehow render her own pathetic inadequacies insignificant. She also had a childhood fear of spastic clowns, falling acrobats, and mauling jungle creatures to overcome, lest it increase its invasiveness as it had a habit of doing when she least expected, after a few tots!

Allowing herself to imagine having the power to control rebellious instincts, she concluded, would make her feel better. *Is that possible?* she wondered, having a bout of second thoughts.

The outing would serve another purpose as well. Life in a strictly segregated society did not offer many opportunities for multiracial entertainment. Just this once she felt that kindness, even her tarnished brand of philanthropy to Future who didn't want to go, could not be delegated or postponed; for, if it was, she would be pulled irretrievably into the deep, dank prolapses where the devils and demons of Sir Roland Gaylord's fanatic prejudice dwelled.

Future's reaction to Lady Dorothy's invitation was as puzzling to her as his refusal was unacceptable. Considering it more carefully, she realized that she was not all that thrilled about going herself. Ever since she was a little girl, Dorothy had not really liked the circus. The sights and sounds had upset her. The thought of entering a tent with a sawdust floor where frothing animals pranced to the sting of flicking whips, acrobats somersaulted high above, and deformed people cavorted to the mocking hysterical laughter of children produced conflicting emotions in her.

Her adult recollections of her childhood reactions made her realize that it was not magic that had motivated applause in those distant days, but rather the expectation of imminent tragedy. Now, as the antique that she perceived herself to be, life itself had become a theatrical farce clouded by distorted memories and warped by the bitterness of her old age,

Notwithstanding such feelings, she made up her mind finally and would not be badgered into altering a decision that had consumed so much of her energy.

"Future," she said, "we are going whether you like it or

not!" She hoped that her voice carried more emphasis than her frailty portrayed.

"Get dressed nicely, in your white clothes. Don't keep me waiting!"

The manservant's normally bright face seemed to crumble in disappointment. Some years earlier, when the circus had come to town, he had gone, only to return filled with fear generated by superstition and aversion. For days after he had felt sick, although he was not sure why.

Future wished that he could maintain his refusal. But he could not. So, he nodded reluctantly. Then he left for his spartan room in the servants' quarters to retrieve his starched whites from the rickety cupboard that housed his few possessions, gathered during a lifetime of work for his master and his missus.

∞ ∞ ∞

Lady Dorothy was in no condition to drive.

That would have been true whether she had been drunk or, as on this occasion, only partially sober. Nonetheless she did, and she had the foresight to retrieve some money from a shoebox under her bed. Unsteadily, she steered her brown and cream Bentley with its wavy sides that looked like unmixed chocolate rolling horizontally. Future was pleased, although only slightly, to see that she wore her gloves because they allowed her to grip the wheel. On the running board, the spare tire encased in shiny metal seemed to be afloat like a life raft beside a vessel on the verge of sinking.

She was alone on the front seat. Future sat at the back, in the middle.

He was torn by the competing discomforts of impropriety and luxury. Beneath his buttocks and at his back, the material was soft and pliable. However he did not feel at all comfortable. His fear of being seen in the automobile or in public with his white employer hit him hard every time he lifted his head and looked out of the clean windows. The passing splendor of white suburbia drifted by. On countless weekends he had cleaned the vehicle, inside and out. At the seats he lingered, massaging them with saddle soap, refining them to suppleness. He polished the bodywork until it gleamed. But the stately vehicle remained confined to its garage, unused and unseen.

Instinctively Future knew, without having to say it, that those who would observe them thus would reduce the spectacle to murmured scandal. Their positions should have been reversed. Future should have been driving and Lady Dorothy should have been at the back, being driven in the comfortable elegance of her expensive automobile. But he had not learned to drive and, he feared, as a shudder of foreboding thrust him inadvertently deeper into the layers of soft leather, neither had she.

Future looked smart in his whites, usually reserved for special occasions at Grand Britannia that had become very scarce as the years passed. He was wearing the tennis shoes given to him by Sir Roland in an unusual moment of generosity when he discovered that the toecaps were working loose after a game at his private lawn club.

"Take these," he had said. "They are worn out."

In giving the discards to his servant he spoke like a rich man saying to a poor man, "Get over your poverty!" However, Future, being pragmatic, tolerant, and frugal by nature, took the old shoes of his master to whom he had given his promise of fealty.

So, Future repaired the pair of used tennis shoes with glue. Then he washed them thoroughly, inside and out. Finally he added layers of white paste on the canvas uppers and smiled when they emerged into new service. They looked bright, and even he had to admit with satisfaction that the shoes seemed better than when his boss had worn them.

Lady Dorothy drove the Bentley, a look of studied determination on her face. "Godless people," she announced, just wanting to be heard. Whether the remark was intended as an insult or a compliment and for whom, she neither considered nor cared.

The huge marquee was pitched on a grassy field of Mitchell Park, adjacent to the waterway through which ships of all shapes and sizes passed on their way into and out of the bustling harbor. Beyond the jetties and buoys where green and red lights warned of entry to the open ocean past the calm of the wharf, a summer rainstorm was dying amid the rolling waves.

After a frightfully disjointed journey, the grand motor car came to a rough and uncertain halt at a gate that blocked off the parking lot. Lady Dorothy withdrew paper money from her handbag. She passed it in her gloved hand to the Indian attendant. She did not wait for change, despite overpaying by a considerable amount. Her attitude to money had altered over the years. It had lost all of its allure.

It is the stuff of which comfortable loneliness is made, she thought.

The heavy automobile lurched forward before the attendant could place the ticket under a wiper. An open spot, next to a broken down three-wheeler rickshaw, presented itself. Dorothy steered in too hard and too fast. The Bentley's heavy tires ripped up grass, spinning away masses of green. As Lady Dorothy yanked the handbrake while still accelerating, the car groaned in protest. When the Bentley stilled, she shut off the engine, but left the car in gear. Before exiting, Lady Dorothy placed her gloves in the "cubbyhole" compartment. Thus finally parked, they dismounted. She forgot to lock the doors.

In her high-heeled shoes with Future in his white livery beside her, she lurched unevenly to the tent. Across the brim of her straw hat, ostentatious ostrich feathers fanned forward and backward as if in awkward salutation. It did not concern Lady Dorothy that her attire was entirely out of keeping with the occasion. The grand fashion of the "Ostrich age" had long since gone. So the "Barons of Oudtshoorn" in the Cape of Good Hope, who had lived in palatial houses surrounded by sandy plains filled with large roaming birds, became the lost vestiges of European taste.

"Dissolved amid the fickleness of pretension and the triviality of faddishness," one of her fellow expatriates had said with a wistful look of longing for unattainable bygones. Future's decorated missus reminded him of a strange bird that could not fly which he had once seen in the zoo. He didn't remember what the white people called it, and could not ask any of them as it was "blacks only visiting day" that day at the zoo.

***

At the two-sided ticket booth, one for "Europeans," the other for "Non-Europeans," on this show day, which was, unusually, not for whites only, the girl behind the cashier's bar smiled, suppressing a gasp as she saw the pearls strung across Lady Dorothy's thin neck with its mottled crepe skin.

The girl had difficulty drawing her attention away. "*Necklace*, indeed! Whoever invented such a description?" Dorothy exclaimed. She took the tickets, then moved off on her unsteady heels. There was nobody behind her. *Surprising*, she thought. *They must all be inside already.*

She expected to find Future right next to her, but he stood near the back of the long line for the black and colored people, not wanting to embarrass his employer. When he saw her, he moved out of line and followed behind as she made for the entrance to the big top. There again they separated at a sign that pointed the way around to the back.

"We shall meet after the show," she said.

"Yes, Madam," Future replied, lowering his head. He considered hiding until it was over, but realized that she would probably ask him about what he enjoyed most. So he held onto the ticket Lady Dorothy had given him. An Indian boy stood just inside the flap door.

"Ticket please. Please ticket," he said politely to Future, who showed him the pink paper with the row and seat number printed on it.

"This way please, please," the boy beckoned, bowing politely in time to the repetition. Future followed. They mounted broad plywood steps laid out on the iron scaffolding bleachers and reached a roped-off area high up in the far recesses of the tent. It was smaller than the rest of the seating sections. The boy unclipped a cord that closed off the area. He shone the beam of his flashlight to illuminate a single empty seat on a row occupied by black people only. They sat so close to one another that their hips touched and their elbows collided.

Future excused himself as he struggled through the narrow gaps between rough shoes, homemade sandals, and bare feet until he reached his assigned seat. Promptly, he sat down, hoping that nobody would be angry with him for disturbing them or for wearing his white tennis shoes which some, he feared, might consider to be the ostentatious symbols of a privileged "domestic."

On entering the circus marquee, Lady Dorothy was blinded, not by light, but by darkness. In her fragile state her senses were seriously disturbed. Loud circus music blared from instruments that she could not see but which she imagined to be playing at a funeral for the blind and the deaf in an obscure location. Noise crashed about her eardrums. The smell of sawdust, greasepaint, and animal dung assailed her, sending her head reeling. In her vicinity she did not see any other white people. She tried to walk backward toward the tent flap that she noticed vaguely somewhere behind her. Filled with trepidation and claustrophobia, she wanted to get out. But suddenly the attendant closed the flap. The show was about to commence.

I am trapped!

Powerful percussions slammed inside her head. Without realizing it, she had moved forward into the deeper darkness, not backward away from it. A white usherette was standing at the end of what seemed like a long corridor with tiered seats and benches pitched at steep angles leading to the ringside below. She led the way to one of the better seats in the marquee.

"I am being strangled!"

"Help me! Please help me!" Dorothy was quite sure that she was shouting.

"Do you hear me?" She dropped her handbag. Her hand flew up to her neck then began to flail at the unseen strangler.

"Get away!" she cried.

"You dare not choke me, you dirty fiend. I am a titled lady!"
"Don't you know who I am? Let go of me!"

But with each of her frantic cries, the grip encircling her throat became stronger. Her fingers found the rope that her assailant had thrown around her, ready to garrote her.

"I am strong!" she yelled, trying to intimidate her attacker. She tore at the strands of pearls decorating her neck, sending the pearls rolling. She had no idea where. Wooden floorboards scraped her knees. Her skirt rode up. She tipped forward. Hands reached under her hollow armpits. Voices filled the space near her.

"Give her a glass of water," someone said.

"Get the *shmelling* salts," another ordered, his voice thick with authority. She thought the accent was German. Her head tilted back. She felt like she was floating.

I am being carried away . . . She wondered where she was going.

"She'll be fine," the guttural voice proclaimed. Nobody argued. The others fell quiet. "Put her in the vacant VIP reserved seat. Stay with her until she feels better!"

"Yes, sir." This time the voice was that of the young white attendant.

Something very sharp and highly astringent hit her. It struck like a lance to her forehead. Suddenly she felt almost revived. The light was bright. The band was playing. She could see horses' heads bunched together closely as if held by a single bridle.

"How are you feeling?"

It was the young woman again. This time Lady Dorothy was comfortably seated in an upholstered single chair, far better than the original one, and the closest of all to the ring itself. She could see the speaker more clearly.

"Would you like to leave?"

"Leave now? Is the show over?" she asked, confused.

"No, it's just begun," came the reply.

The few white patrons nearby were looking at her. She noticed them for the first time. She hated the fuss.

"Why on earth would I leave if the show is starting?"

"You were feeling faint."

"I'm fine!" Lady Dorothy declared. "You can leave me alone. I am used to that!" Her voice sounded more confident to herself than it did to the usherette. But the arrogant man in khaki jodhpurs (whom she now saw clearly with one booted foot casually displayed on the ring step nearest to her), simply nodded. Then he gestured with the handle of a whip. The girl left. The lights dimmed. She felt as if she were participating in a nightmare with all of its lurid clarity. He moved closer still and leaned right over her.

> *Esto mihi in Deum protectorem, et in locum refugii, ut salvum me facias: quoniam firmamentum meum, et refugium meum es tu.* (Be Thou unto me a God, a Protector, and a place of refuge, to save me.)

How utterly odd, she thought, as she recognized the verse. The Austrian master of ceremonies was whispering the Introit into her ear, usually reserved as the antiphon from the Psalms for the introduction of Shrove Tuesday. Although neither chronological in rendition, nor his liturgical privilege to declare, the words nonetheless contained a profound message. He moved off.

Then there was a change. An announcement boomed out.

"Hear Ye! Hear Ye! Ladies *und* Gentlemen. Gather round! Welcome to the circus!"

The voice of authority and enticement expanded. He stood in the center of the ring now, a microphone jutting forward. In her eyes, which had cleared, although not entirely, Lady Dorothy thought he looked like a miscreant, some ogre-like creature with a single horn growing from the center of its head. *Why does he have to shout so?*

Lady Dorothy clutched the side of her chair. She opened her handbag to retrieve some tissues. A small tray table had been propped up beside the chair. A single glass of cold water caught the sweeping beam of a stage light. She looked at it, then dipped the tissue into the sparkling liquid. Slowly she rubbed the wet paper across her eyes before wiping her knees. She had expected pain, but there was none, as if the fall had not hurt her.

Strange, she thought, wishing it were a glass of gin, not water. The craving became stronger. She tried to remember whether she had put a small flask in her handbag. But she dared not look. *Not now*, she cautioned herself, trying to evade the thirst by concentrating on the team of dappled horses whose backsides touched as closely as their heads.

A pair of giant cymbals crashed in the band. She looked in the direction of the sound. It was quite dark, but she could make out black faces and many eyes staring down at the ring below. The prancing animals had formed up in a precise row, flank to flank. They rose, standing as one on their hind legs, obedient to the crack of a long whip. She thought she had returned to childhood.

The disgusting memory of the circus. She tried to banish the recollection. But it was too unrelenting.

Lady Dorothy placed her hands around her neck. It felt so much better, now that the choking had stopped. The show proceeded to its conclusion when a clown fell on his face, kicked his feet up behind him to show off the long leather soles of his flapping shoes and striped stockings, and a rumble of kettle drums accompanied a banner that unfurled downward from the big top with the words "The End" emblazoned in red right across it.

When the show was over, concern for her welfare was conspicuous by its absence. She had been left to her own devices and the helping hands of Future. Not one of the well-to-do whites who had witnessed her being carried to a "special" chair and fussed over came to ask if she was all right. Their aloof selfishness reminded her of the abortive telephone calls that plagued her when she was drunk and the ladies who never came to tea, although fine china had awaited them for years. The conclusion was obvious, even to her addled mind. She did not care if they saw a black servant assisting her.

Such people, even when nearby, are not really present!

When Lady Dorothy and Future reached the Bentley, she suddenly remembered her white gloves, which she hoped still held residual eau de cologne in which she had bathed her hands. She opened the cubby hole and reached in, shakily. It was empty!

Who in their right mind would steal my gloves and not my automobile? she wondered in confusion. *They take that which I love and leave behind that which I hate!*

∞∞∞

The drive back to Grand Britannia was a silent affair. Lady

Dorothy never asked Future if he enjoyed the performance, and he never volunteered his opinion.

She felt as though invisible apparitions of privation were observing her, but it mattered not. The big car did what it had to do, even under her unsteady guidance. It brought them back to the Victorian house on the hill of the Berea where the wealthy lived in secluded grandeur. She did not remember how she parked the Bentley or how she limped into her home, with her knees hurting for the first time since she fell.

It was dark inside the empty house.

She did not care to switch on the lights as she made straight for her bedroom, stumbling uncertainly through the somber entrance hall and down the unlit corridor. Lady Dorothy was about to enter her bedroom when she changed her mind. As quickly as she could, she headed back to the dining room, remembering that she had hidden a bottle at the back of the sideboard where the fine dinnerware and silver lay wrapped in velvet. It was a hiding place for liquor that she was sure Future had not discovered.

He has that damn knack of finding my stuff everywhere, she muttered, using one of her favorite euphemisms. *But I have beaten him this time!*

She smiled wryly at the thought that she still had the cunning to outsmart her manservant. It was a wicked expression of putative victory, because in her embittered heart she knew that he did for her what she was incapable of doing for herself.

Again she was on her knees, this time voluntarily. The carpet was soft, not like the abrasive boards that had torn her skin at the circus. It felt good, *like a dressing*. The key was in the lock of the heavy mahogany cabinet. She turned it only to find that it was unlocked already. Immediately a sense of foreboding struck her.

In the dark she fumbled, feeling behind a pile of blue Spode crockery, seeking the space where the square bottle should have been lying on its side. However, only emptiness revealed itself to her fingers as they crawled like insects over the hiding place.

Then, unintentionally, she touched something wrapped in an

oily rag. *There must have been a reason for me to cover it like that.* However, she could not remember why.

Dorothy withdrew the object. Her eyes were watery, her vision hazy, but she recognized what it was even though it had been hidden for so long. She had put it away, casting it aside as a painful relic of shame and disgrace.

Her desire for liquor reared, more challengingly, like an untamed beast. In no mood to read what was inside the cloth, she thrust it into a fold of her garment. Despite the intervening years, she almost knew its words by heart. The corners, she remembered, were curled and dingy with soot.

Roland had tried to burn it, but didn't have the courage!

"Damn!" Her voice grew weak and croaky, as if she had a bad cold. Her body began to shake. She cried soundlessly, only her shoulders shaking. She raised herself up, using the front panel of the sideboard as her support. Lady Dorothy stumbled back down the passage and pushed open the door of her bedroom. To her surprise, one of the bedside lamps was lit.

She hadn't left it on. But Future had. He did not want her to come back into an entirely dark house, despite the fact that she always scolded him for wasting electricity. Then, collapsing into a petit point chair in her bedroom, in spite of herself, she unwrapped the cloth and read the letter once more. It confirmed what she already knew from Sir Roland Gaylord's nocturnal mumblings: ". . . Aryan ancestry . . . eradicate the vermin . . . code machines . . . gas . . . boats . . . submarines . . . long reign . . . a thousand years or more . . ." and so it went on.

>Vidkun Abraham Lauritz Jonssøn Quisling
>Minister President of Norway
>Bygdøy Palace, Oslo
>Your Excellency:

>Greetings! I trust that your health is good and that of your wife, Maria Vasilijevna? I admire you. Under your leadership and that of Johan Bernhard Hjort, the Nasjonal Samling Party has grown in strength since you formed it together on 17th May 1933 and became its Führerprinzip. You have overcome your setbacks. The Reichskommissariat Norwegen is imple-

menting its tasks according to plan. Your reinstatement as Head of State sometime ago is most laudable.

We hear that the deportations of the "aliens" are proceeding well. During the Second Boer War in South Africa from 1899 to 1902, my father was one of the Senior Officers who ensured that the Afrikaner guerillas were properly interned in the camps so that our British victory over the insurgent "Dutch" farmers could be gained, and Great Britain could annex the rebellious Orange Free State and Transvaal Republieks. Some say the two hundred million pounds spent on the last imperial war was too much; that the Boer families who died of starvation, disease, malnutrition and desperation all deserved their fate. But your Excellency, I implore you to remember the outcome! The Treaty of Vereeniging secured Imperial dominion. You too can achieve such greatness when victory comes to you and to your followers. Rid your country, indeed all of Europe and the world, of the "strangers in our midst." Let those working in Häftingslager camps complete their worthy tasks.

Our sources bring us news, with pride of what is happening in Natzweiler-Struthof in the Vosges Mountains of Alsace. Josef Kramer is supplying August Hirt with the bodies of dead Jews and Gypsies gassed or shot, so that those anatomical specimens can be used at the medical school of the University of Strasbourg. This will advance the Purity of the Race! It will bring new discoveries! You can be proud of this work. Amongst those of us who admire him, gratitude abounds to Wilhelm Keitel, Generalfeldmarschall, hero of the Reich. May he have a long and good life!

The Norwegian King and his Parliamentarians who "escaped" to Britain are traitors. Do not concern yourself with such defectors. They are under our watchful eye.

This letter will be dispatched to you in secret. There are sources for such communications that are safe. A fisherman named Peter will deliver this to you. He is authorised to return with your awaited reply.

I remain, yours in profound admiration,
Roland Gaylord

Her late husband's penmanship was neat. *As exact as his barbered moustache*, she thought, scoffing.

The date had been eradicated by flames. *I remember it was during the war, closer to the end.* The letter bore a red wax seal. Despite her attempt at flattening it, the aged paper insisted on turning up at the corners. The edges were burned severely on one side, as if a candle had been set to it. *Or perhaps,* she thought, *it had been cast into the fireplace, then whipped out before it could be consumed.*

The handwriting was uniquely recognizable. And so too was the signature of a Knight Commander of the Order of the British Empire!

Morose, sad, frustrated, and angry, she threw her handbag onto the bed that she hated so much; she felt as though it had incised a such deep hole in her innards that she could almost thrust her hand through.

It will come out the other side without hindrance.

Lady Dorothy could only be certain that he had betrayed her. For her old country she could neither be an apologist nor an accuser. She lacked the energy. Now a serious dilemma confronted her.

Shall I keep this letter, reacquired by my husband after the war, I know not how? Should I perhaps even publish it? Or should I destroy it?

For a while she pondered. Then she reached for the pull string of the bell.

Wires of woe, she thought. Future had deftly rigged it, almost invisibly and most discreetly through ceilings and wall space to the junction at the front porch. There the brass bell hung in its plastered housing. When she yanked on the string, the bell clanged. By day or night, wherever he was on the grounds of Grand Britannia, the little man heard the summons. He came immediately, as always.

He is so reliable, it's disgusting!

Although the night was hot, she ordered Future to make a fire in the bedroom grate. Puzzled why the widow should be cold on such a warm night, nonetheless he did as he was told. When the flames rose high, she said, "Go back to the servants' quarters now." She always used the plural when referring to his room, although he was the only servant left. He obeyed without demur.

In the beginning, Roland expected a servant to be present to attend to all of his whims in every room, when he strode around during daytime. But he never acknowledged a single one!

The fire roared upward, leaping *stupidly*, she thought, into the chimney, *the quicker to be consumed!*

She pulled the drawer of her jewelry box. The little dancer leapt into motion, immediately coming to life and spinning on her delicate porcelain toes. Only then did Lady Dorothy remember that her pearl necklace was gone.

She looked into the fire. It was indigo blue now.

The color of burning carbon, the stuff of matter, she thought. Only a slight hesitation halted her. Recovering from its mesmerizing influence, she shoved the letter back into its oily rag, then threw it into the flames. It burst into bright orange before withering as she watched it. A bizarre thought struck her.

Was he a traitor? Or was he engaged in counter-intelligence? The truth shall never be publicly known, but it will in my heart!

She smiled, a cynical sober smile, and turned away from the flames. Near Grand Britannia, a garbage truck banged its way down the hill of the Berea. She could hear the rattle of its mudguards.

They are collecting rubbish at night. They never do that!

The lights beyond the bay window were man-made. Coming from the vast sweep of the city below, they looked like incandescent layers piled upon each other up the hill. Once there, they spilled aimlessly over the gates, across the manicured lawns and along the walls of the houses that had been erected like ramparts on a fortress of prerogative.

At long last she was ready, willing, and finally able to do it.

Lady Dorothy limped over to the alcove near the bay window. In her shaky hands, she lifted the burled walnut urn from its resting place. Holding it with one hand at its base, the other pushing down on the lid, she moved it slowly aside. The wooden container, hand-cut on a lathe, sanded, stained, and polished to perfection, felt as smooth as a baby's skin to her touch.

Clutching it to her chest, she stumbled to the window. She lowered the container onto the curved bench that hugged the concave shape of the wall. The window's handle turned easily, the spindle moving obediently. When it had retracted fully, she stuck one hand outside to feel for the breeze.

At first she detected none.

Then, to her surprise and joy, she felt a light ruffle on her hand. The wind from the seaport below grew stronger and began to sweep over the tiered terraces. As soon as it was blowing steadily outside the walls of Grand Britannia toward the garden, the street, and down the hill where the harbor led out to the open sea, she made her move.

It was easier than she thought it would be.

She simply turned the urn upside down and tapped its base with her skeletal fingers. In a smooth flow the ashes, no more than a few handfuls, came out. They caught on the breeze that took them, greedy to bear them away.

"Good riddance at last!" she proclaimed, as if her enraged exclamation could be heard by the ashes themselves and all that they represented.

Lady Dorothy watched the gray particles disappear with the wind against the backdrop of the muesli-colored sky. She closed the window and lay down, fully dressed on her bed. Once again, she was entirely alone. Her head rested on a tearstained pillow. She wrapped her arms around her shivering body in a childlike hug as there was nobody there to comfort her but herself.

On the floor beside the big bed, the empty urn lay on its side, its lid some feet away on a crimson rug. Neatly tacked into the polished wood, engraved on a sterling-silver-plated label the words ROLAND GAYLORD K.B.E. glowed eerily in the strange bluish light. They seemed to be clamoring for attention.

But Lady Dorothy's wet eyes were closed tightly, squeezing out what she imagined to be the terminal expressions of an unfathomable loss. Thus, the demand of the hollow vessel came to be nothing more than the vanity of discontent and the empty conceit of final dispossession. Slowly she shuddered into sleep wherein, though plagued by a terrible thirst, she found some measure of consolation amid whispers of triumph.

At dawn, she woke.

She felt hungry, but now not thirsty. For once she did not crave alcohol. *Bread and water*, she thought.

She rang the bell. Her servant came.

My Future is not so small after all, she decided, looking at him but thinking of herself.

"Make breakfast," she said. Then, for the first time in a long string of years, she added, "Please. And make the same for yourself too."

Lady Dorothy remembered a description that Future had used when, in her darkest hours of despair, he pulled aside the drapes that through her teary eyes seemed to be made of glass beads, opened the windows of the bedroom, and begged her to listen to the sounds rising from the wisteria and godetia plants that clambered up pergolas near the pond. They had been sent to her husband from Asia and Latin America by anonymous admirers. If not for Future's care, they would have run wild on the glorious terraces below that she never visited, never saw, until now. The Zulu had said it to her, in halting translation, so many times. Finally she understood.

"The 'Joy Birds' sing in the garden. Listen, Missus. Please listen."

She did and, at last, she stopped auditioning for hope. The furious battle with old memories had ceased. The selfish ambiguity of godlessness had withdrawn. The floodwaters of despair became shallow. She was not drowning. She no longer saw the amorphous statue deep beneath the sea. Adversity seemed to be converting itself into advantage.

Two words, "Thank you," were spoken clearly. Not muffled and indistinct, her speech emerged with a steady confidence that shocked and pleased her. There were no bubbles. No wish to drown in the fishpond.

Lady Dorothy had stopped fearing that the utterances of her inner anguish would burst forth. The sun shone, but it did not burn. The sugar trains still labored, but their groans were gone. The purposelessness that had clouded her life had begun to dissipate. Subtle intricacies of understanding were infiltrating her consciousness. Light looked different, softer, more illuminating.

She was sober.

She felt happy as never before.

Future entered the bedroom with a tray of cooked food. Steam rose out of the teapot's spout. There were two cups on the tray. She looked at him, as if seeing him for the first time. He put the tray down, turned, and left the room, a broad grin of pleasure on his face, his white teeth sparkling, his lips drawn back and a chuckle tickling in his throat.

∞ ∞ ∞

Ghost of the Ganges

> As I write these last words, my thoughts return to you who were my comrades, the stubborn and indomitable peasants of Nepal. Once more I hear the laughter with which you greeted every hardship. Once more I see you in your bivouacs or about your fires, on forced march or in the trenches, now shivering with wet and cold, now scorched by a pitiless and burning sun. Bravest of the brave, most generous of the generous, never had country more faithful friends than you.
>
> **Sir Ralph Turner, who served with the 3rd Queen Alexandra's Own Gurkha Rifles in the First World War, writing of the Gurkhas**

At the back of his Rolls-Royce Ghost, hidden behind drawn shades, a grotesquely fat man known only as the proprietor was reading *The Lloyds Register of British and Foreign Shipping*. The editorial concerned losses by the ultra wealthy Lloyds "names" to meet pirates' ransoms—the lucrative prizes for hunting modern oil tankers and cruisers off the Horn of Africa where naked soil runs red with the blood of drought that seems never to heal, and azure seas gleam beneath the burning, rainless skies of Somaliland's coastline.

His large lips tightened. A crooked smile wrought further havoc on his cruel face, scarred by syphilis. Vulturine eyes bored as he read. He shook his bomb-shaped head, which was too small for his large body. Shifting slightly, his suit of finest silk rustling, he crossed his legs and looked at his handcrafted shoes. The sight of the rippling snakeskin finish excited him. As he put the newspaper down, it caressed an emerald—the size of a bird's egg—set in his bulky gold ring. He leaned forward, opened the liquor cabinet, and reached for a bottle of Courvoisier. However, his restlessness continued unabated, for he was a man who craved pleasure from odious activities—the plying of "goods" that others would not dare to transport, and the trafficking in used armaments, sad children, and nuclear waste.

Freighters of the Old Ships Line are not targets, he thought as he considered the dozens of old ships in his private fleet, ferrying cargoes that none would suspect *because they are always departing, never arriving, and they look worn out*. He had arranged *disguises* for his vessels so that all appeared to be dirty tramps unworthy of inspection. Thus they were ignored, unlike big vessels in the shipping lanes.

"Mine may be old, but to me they are beautiful!" he declared in a loud voice. He did not care if his driver heard, *because he is expendable and speechless. My "girls" move across waters that cover two-thirds of the world. They work hard for me. There is always a customer, at the right price in the right place!* The proprietor smiled a selfish smile of entitlement, enjoying the comparison to prostitution, in which he also had significant "business interests."

Like a speeding box of steel and glass, black and immensely powerful, even at 110 miles per hour, the Rolls-Royce was rock steady. The seventeen-year-old finest quality VSO brandy in the Hungarian cut glass tumbler barely vibrated.

A Suzuki Hayabusa was behind the automobile and gaining on it as if challenged by solidity of form and function, pulled by a figurative winch of competition. One of the best standard production motorcycles in the world, the Hayabusa was accelerating fully. True to its namesake (the fastest-diving peregrine falcon known to man), the Suzuki GSX 1300R's rider immersed himself and his machine in the slipstream of the viper-engined Ghost. Concentrating on the moving mass ahead of him, the motorcyclist stalked his prey, devouring the distance between them. Helmetless, the rider was covered in leather from neck to shins. His rubberized goggles sucked blood from his pressed cheeks. Power surged beneath his buttocks. Zigzagging through the handlebars, the machine transferred its twisty shudders to his pelvis, back, elbows, and shoulders in a thrilling massage. The young man felt exhilarated. He was free, like a racing pilot maneuvering for victory.

Suddenly, beneath the engine cowl of the square Ghost, a hose burst. As the clips fragmented, the pipe tore away from its attachment, spewing oil downward under pressure. The massive rear tires of the heavy vehicle sprayed viscous liquid in a black cloud behind it. The Hayabusa's rider was blinded instantly. Letting go of the grips, he shot a hand up to rip his goggles off. The bike hit the streak of oil, skidded sideways, then took to the air in a somersault of spiraling aerobatic chrome, rubber, and garroting chain.

A red warning light flashed on the instrument panel of the Ghost at the same moment that its custom-installed rear video cameras recorded the leaping motorcycle. The proprietor looked into the monitor, set discreetly into the doors of the liquor cabinet.

"Do not stop!" he ordered. "Take the next exit!"

Alexander, the mute giant man in a black uniform at the wheel of the Ghost, obeyed, his gaze set on the lanes beyond. As death reached out relentlessly for the rider, the solid statuette on the hood barely swayed off its perpendicular base. Forward wind thrust beneath her sterling silver wings of "secret love." Although the statuette was retractable at the push of a button, Alexander, the Uzbek chauffeur, had orders to leave it exposed above the heavy radiator. His boss had been told that Sykes, designer of the Rolls-Royce emblem, *The Spirit of Ecstasy*, "had selected road travel as the lady's supreme delight, expressing her keen enjoyment with her arms outstretched and her sight fixed upon the distance."

∞ ∞ ∞

With long lazy wing beats, pelicans rode currents of rising air, apparently unaware that, when they grow old and lose the keen eyesight that enabled them to scoop up unsuspecting fish, they will fold their wings and plummet in a suicidal spiral from a lofty altitude to their death in the water that had provided them with sustenance since they were chicks.

Several cruise ships steamed out of nearby ports, the smoke from their stacks smudging the pristine backdrop of the horizon.

On the July night when the small body tumbled through the waves, like a piece of flotsam carelessly cast from a freighter out at sea, a wedding reception was in full swing in Coral Hall, the most ornate of venues in a private marina. Luxuriously decorated yachts bobbed gently in their secure berths. Crewed by lackeys, the brash and spurious toys of rich patrons waited with the patience of privilege. Murex Marina, with its bleached white sands, lay along South Ocean Boulevard, which wended its supple way along the Atlantic seaboard, running its tireless marathon for miles, flanked by parks, hotels, condominiums, resorts, and hotels. Some were ramshackle and others extravagant.

Beginning the ceremony, the officiating rabbi said, "Exile is temporary until the Messiah comes, speedily we pray in our times, if only we may be worthy of such a Golden Age." "Expulsion," he said, "is not a sojourn. Nor is it a destination. It is a place of temporary refuge. Our prayer is for this couple to reach 'home' together!" As he recalled the sacking of the temples, his beard shuddered. It looked grayed by distress, like a nesting place for birds of sorrow.

"The groom breaks this glass beneath his heel as a deliberate reminder of Tragedy, Destruction, Dispersal, and Banishment," the Rabbi explained. "It is imperative in a time of greatest joy to recall adversity. Only once we understand the contrasts and connections of happiness and sadness," he said, "may we begin to assemble the perplexing fragments of existence."

With a shaky hand, he signed the marriage contract, as if he were personally experiencing the throbbing ache of millennia.

Thus, a young man and a young woman were joined in

matrimony. Bride circled groom beneath a canopy topped with a meandering vine. Seven blessings were chanted.

A raucous party followed. Strobe lights on the stage flashed in time to the thumping and jumping of the eight-piece band. Dancers gyrated. Liquor flowed. Waiters and waitresses weaved between tables. Multicolored paper streamers straggled across the floor and clung to the ceiling in tails of crinkled crepe. Tall flower stands garlanded with Ecuadorian pink peonies, white lilies, mauve roses, and hydrangeas in columns of opaque glass overflowed in abundant floral splendor.

Draped ceramic towers, like miniaturized replicas of the Hanging Gardens of Babylon, proclaimed the affluence of the hosts. From fat wax bases, votive candles wicked into licking flames. Across the dance floor, sensuous and wavy reflections prowled in seductive swirls. Lushly decorated walls seemed to skip against the backdrop of maddened color. Amid it all, gold backed chairs rattled their skeletal frames to the boom and bash of drumming merriment.

In no mood for festivities, a man left the hall. His pain was intense. A sense of inevitability, a wound of realization, hemorrhaged somewhere within him. Outside, beyond the immediacy of the nuptial celebration, he moved slowly along the edge of the black ocean. Water licked sand in a continuous search for an everlasting wet kiss of translucent enchantment.

His shoulders were rounded, his back humped, his footfalls unevenly long. He pressed the heels of his shoes down first, making deep and deliberate depressions. As he watched their repetitive motion, cobalt boundaries of waves fled before him. The flashing lights of celebratory illumination plunged recklessly onto the beach. But they did not last. Each burst was quickly absorbed by the darkness beyond the hurricane resistant window panes, sucked up by greedy sea lips, and leaving behind only scattered patterns of vanishing confusion.

He wore a tuxedo with a silver cummerbund, a pleated white dress shirt, pearl cuff links, and a puffed velvet bow tie shot with tiny yellow moons. Down each trouser leg, smooth satin stripes divided the material. Inside thickly padded woolen socks that he liked (even in summer), his feet felt warmer than the rest of his body. The toecaps of his patent leather shoes glistened with the luster of stars that seemed to walk the beach with him as if in a parade of reflections.

Death, he thought, *takes on a life of its own! How bizarre!* Alone he wandered off, like a moon man, away from song and laughter, beyond the collective cries of pleasure and the scattered sounds of enjoyment, along a white beach visited by breaking water. Wry thoughts sent a smirk to his mouth as if it had been afflicted by sudden and high voltage. He felt cold. Notwithstanding the oppressive heat of the night, his teeth chattered.

At that moment, his glittered shoe encountered a soft, swollen carcass that had tumbled free of the surf.

∞∞∞

Even with a burst oil hose, the Ghost cruised with confident power. Auxiliary pumps fed its engine the fuel and lubricants it required. Alexander had taken the exit as directed. The proprietor wished to avoid the nuisance of witnesses. *The more they see, the more they are endangered by the knowledge!* Despite his self-assurance, the curdle of ill-begotten power trickled through him, and yet he had suddenly become hungry.

A neon sign caught his attention:

FONDUE FANTASTIQUE

"Stop in front! Go in!"

He handed his chauffeur a note written starkly with a Star Walker Midnight Black Mont Blanc pen, its ruthenium-plated 14 karat gold nib gliding silkily over the surface of the embossed stationery that bore a silhouetted black ship as a logo. Beneath that appeared the simply stenciled letters "O.S.L." There was no following address.

Nothing he did was without intention. *The platinum alloy discovered by Karl Klaus has been aptly named after "Ruthenia,"* he thought, *located in the core of Russian territory! My Motherland!*

"Sorry, we're closed between lunch and dinner," Jacques, the owner of the establishment replied, handing back the paper with a dismissive shrug. Alexander, whose head was elongated like that of a workhorse and whose sluggish thought processes extended only to the matter at hand, reached over the desk. He grabbed the owner by the throat, an enlarged thumb pressing into the notch below the man's Adam's apple, under an artificial silk knot. Alexander pushed until the cartilage threatened to snap.

"Now you're open!" he tried to mouth. But no words could emerge. Importuned temper turned into menacing intimidation. His color rose. His predatory eyes bulged in bursts of pulsing aggravation. Capillaries in his full cheeks, remnants of his heavy drinking days, threatened to rupture. Thus, despite the permanent muteness that afflicted the chauffeur, the owner of the restaurant understood his message as loudly and clearly as if it had been announced.

While his driver took the Rolls-Royce for repair, the proprietor dined indolently. Heaps of precisely cut bread squares dripping with liquefied Raclette cheese had been placed before him as a starter dish. The main course of pickled ham had been prepared to his taste with paprika, gherkins, onions, chives, and milled pepper. Alone, he drank an entire bottle of Pinot Gris 2004 La Côte imported from the French canton of Switzerland. He ended his meal with a chocolate soufflé and black coffee.

The mechanic did not need to be instructed orally by the chauffeur. He respected the subcompact Beretta that Alexander flashed more than the bundle of rolled dollars handed to him by a man whose fists were thicker than the Haitian's thighs.

That same afternoon Vitus Řòezníček arrived at Jackson Memorial Hospital. Usually he had the "graveyard shift," but he had swapped work hours so that he could make up time to attend a wedding ceremony scheduled for the following night.

The hospital, he thought, cited as "a tertiary medical teaching facility" in a "Best U.S. Hospitals List," is in "the northernmost South American city," as some sarcastically call Miami. Fluent in Spanish, Vitus did not care that many of the people who lived and worked there did not speak English. *Quite the contrary. If I can remember the complexity of Czech grammar, it is not a problem for me to discern and imitate the nuances of slurred accents, distorted dialects, sibilant s's, and the breathy innuendo of inherited lisps.*

As he walked the long, disinfected corridor to the Extreme Trauma Unit, or ETU, he could hear the clatter of the emergency airlift "hawk," a particularly adapted French Aérospatiale Dauphin, landing on the helipad above. He entered the scrub room and began his routine. By the time he passed through the swing doors to the ETU, a gurney bearing the fractured body of a motorcyclist was on its way down in the high speed elevator. The emergency medical services field attendants could do nothing more than convey the patient quickly and wonder that one so shattered in bone, muscle, fiber, and nerve—almost dismembered and looking partially decapitated—could still draw breath.

Vitus was the first in the trauma theater to attend. As he rushed through the preparations for the surgeons who had been summoned on their beepers, he saw flickers of movement on the lips of the lacerated face. Vitus leaned forward. He could not be entirely sure what the man was saying, but he thought he heard the words, "A black Ghost killed me."

Then the patient died.

Just as the surgeons burst in, Vitus left the operating room. "Too late," he said.

In the *Herald* that night, the proprietor read of the gruesome occurrence on the turnpike.

"Owner of the Ghost unknown!" he growled. "Corruption, bribery, greed . . . and silence!" He knew there would be no repercussions for him.

Vitus had never married.

It was not that he had never loved, but just that he felt he could not share. He lived alone in a two-story building called Azalea Gardens, which he had found after looking at dozens of apartments in buildings where he might reside without drawing very much attention. *The name is more appropriate to a cemetery than a condominium block with open catwalks that attract blowing rain into their corridors throughout our never ending summers.* He was the youngest resident by far. Despite his reticence, the old people appreciated having him around. It made them feel more secure.

"He's a nurse, you know," many whispered, always loud

enough for him to hear. Some of the old ladies even winked at him, and more than one beckoned with a finger. Yes, despite their fascination, they left him largely alone, which was the way he liked it. However, he made some exceptions to his general rule of privacy.

Vitus attended one of the clubs at Azalea Gardens. It was the German Organization. There, groups of Second World War survivors, Jewish and non-Jewish, gathered monthly to exchange stories. It was an eclectic group of former enemies and former friends—now all old, some tired of hatred, others of forgiveness. Soon after he took up residence at Azalea Gardens, a disabled veteran had collared Vitus and asked him to attend a meeting.

"We need to replace a member of our team," he said. "None of us is getting any younger," he added, stating the obvious.

Reluctantly, Vitus agreed. They had found out that he knew German, and soon they made him the secretary. One of his duties was to be "keeper of the files." Thus he had read the profile of each member in detail, including, as it turned out, a woman from Munich. It was recorded "according to first-hand testimony" that she had "saved one boy many years ago, by unusual means." But it did not say how.

The solitary widow, who had joined that club believing that only Azalea Gardens offered her the sanctuary of "her own kind," resided in the apartment above Vitus. She was sick and almost totally blind.

Since he had moved in, every night before he went to work he made the same dinner: two organic eggs fried in light olive oil, slices of toast, and tomatoes slit in half. He listened to her weep. As he ate, the sobbing continued. He could hear her over the sound of televised news. He thought, *I observe enough mayhem every day of my working life. They never tell us anything good. Why has conversation become rivalry—a contest of will— and why is propaganda spewed relentlessly in lieu of reportage?*

On a separate plate he set aside exactly half the meal; he made two cups of boiling hot tea, adding lumps of sugar and a spoonful of milk to each. This night, he supplemented with a treat that the old lady loved: very ripe bananas. *They are stippled like sleeping leopards that protect their kills until the flesh rots off bones and falls to the ground.* Then he put the food into a large serving dish. In a plastic bag, he carried an electric blanket. He walked up the stairs.

Vitus had a key.

When he let himself in, she was sitting at the kitchen table wearing slippers and just a thin cotton housecoat. Her frailty filtered through the garment. Her angular bones projected outward like thorns of age that refused to be dissevered. *She finds no rest on the march to the grave,* he thought as he placed the meal and the tea in front of her. *Do the blind cry tears?*

She faced him as she reached for the knife and fork, her thin wrists emerging from drooping sleeves, dark patches of blotched papery skin beneath her blurry eyes. He watched her eat and drink, heard her sob between gulps, her chest heaving dryly. Then he understood the self-evident answer to his rhetorical question.

Some time ago, she had told him a little about where she was born and a man she had loved, but lost to barbarism. She stopped in the middle of the telling. Then she said, "I am a *Muenchnerin.* You are a Jewish man. Why are you kind to me?"

The bubbling reply turned to dry ice. It froze and blocked his throat, though it burned rampantly in his mind because he knew from her file some, if not the full details, of her former life's story. *Is a connection with my own childhood possible?* he wondered, but quickly put the question out of his mind as if it were implausible . He gave no reply, for he had none that could render the truth. Not yet. She asked her question again. All he said was, "Shh, shh ... Gertrude ... Trude. Did I tell you that I have been invited to a wedding?"

She tried to say something more about that which had troubled her for decades. But the words would not come out. They seemed log-jammed in conscience, warped by time, trapped in memory.

Instead, with great difficulty she rose and tottered into her bedroom. When she returned to the kitchen, pushing her walker ahead of her, she had something in its front basket. It was wrapped tightly. She sat down and continued to eat the remains of her meal, then sipped the rest of her tea. At the end of her dinner after the mushy banana that Vitus irrationally detested (he called it "obsolescent fruit decay") had been consumed, she handed the item to him. He did not open it. He just took it from her hand and thought, *How life withers away.*

"Dear Trude" (he hardly ever called her Gertrude), Vitus said, as she finished chewing, his mode of expression sounding alien to him, as if he were writing a letter, not speaking. She showed no apparent interest in what he was saying. He wondered if she listened. *It doesn't matter*, he concluded. So he never completed the sentence.

The next evening, before the wedding, he delivered the meal to her much earlier than usual. With some haste he checked her bed, this time leaving the electric blanket between the sheets on a footrest made of loosely strung beads, thinking *her feet always get cold, despite the temperature, much like my own.* He pressed "medium," not "high," so that her thin skin would not burn. As he went downstairs, heading for his own apartment to dress for the gala occasion, silence announced itself to him. He hoped he had not been too offhand with Trude, in his haste.

She had stopped crying!

The realization was a happy shock unto itself.

He wanted to shout with joy. However the self-control that was the hallmark of his adult life intervened, so he refrained from any outburst.

In her bathroom, the *Muenchnerin* released her hands from her walker. She liked it much more than the old device. This one made her more "mobile" than her old rusted creaky aid, as Vitus said it would when he gave it to her, adding, "It's a present from my hospital." Slowly, she moved closer to a magnifying makeup mirror. With a shaky finger outstretched, she slid the switch on its plastic frame. A bright light sprang to life. Her lined face touched the glass surface. It felt cold, flat, and deadly smooth. She blinked hard. Her milky eyes suffused with the beams. An internal partition separated her from the reality of present surroundings. As her gray eyelashes brushed against the mirror, she imagined sparks of silvery light. They seemed to flicker momentarily, as if not daring to persist. Then they retreated beyond reach, into her imagination, from where they had come.

In their stead was a memory.

When she first came to Azalea Gardens, a man, old but steady, took an interest in her. He owned an apartment on the second floor of the building opposite. When he held her hand she could not see his smile. But she knew it was there, on his soft lips as he kissed her cheeks, one after the other, and the tip of her hooked nose. He confided in her a secret about the mangoes he picked illicitly from his window using a makeshift gaff, but only when other residents were already in bed and could not see him do it. He asked her to be his helper!

"How can I?" she responded.

"Stand below the tree with a bucket and I will aim them in," he replied, before he assisted her with her white cane, down the steps and into the garden. She could feel the sun setting on her skin as if it belonged there. She could smell the fruit on the trees and the perfume of summer blooms.

A blind woman, she stood as he guided falling fruit into a pail held in her arms. *How funny that was! But oh, so kind!* As her reward he brought her a bouquet of roses and a corsage from a wedding he had attended. He himself had married three times, he said. The bouquet had a handle bound by florist's tape around its base to blunt the thorns. Through the middle of the corsage, a knob-headed pin had been plunged. She could feel its roundness, like a marble.

Trude sat on her bed, her bare feet over the edge of the mattress. She wiggled her wart-covered toes. Her tactile fingertips sought the old corsage and the shriveled bouquet, its vibrant pigment long since decayed into friable, brown curls. They were dry and brittle. The pin was still in the withered spray, barely holding fragility together. *He used them. Then he presented them to me. I knew it. But better something than nothing!* she thought, recollecting his affection.

From a hairpin, the Muenchnerin released the white tresses of her hair. It was surprisingly long and rather thick. She buttoned a discolored cardigan that she called "a bed jacket" around her bony shoulders. She missed some of the buttonholes. She lay down, wishing that her bed socks were warmer, having forgotten that the electric blanket awaited her. She was ready to sleep through the restricting mesh of memory, after another day deprived of the blessing of authentic vision.

∞ ∞ ∞

A Gurkha, just a small boy, came to the Ganges. He wore a loin cloth. All he had was one possession. It was tucked into his waistband, formed by a roll of dirty cloth wound around his pelvis. Uneducated, destitute, utterly impoverished, he remembered the legend told to him by a beater of cloth after he traveled, barefoot, from Kathmandu to the banks of a river in India.

> The tale is told . . . so it is said . . . that while he and his friends, from whom he had separated, were hunting in the jungles of Rajasthan, a boy called Bappa Rawal found someone. By the sight of the man, who looked to be unconscious, Bappa's heart was moved. "Perhaps he is injured?" the boy guessed. So he remained with him until the adult revived, for he was neither sick nor injured, and had only been in a state of deep meditation. He appeared to be lifeless when, in truth, by the filament of profound contemplation he was connected to a higher plane. The saint, Guru Gorkhanath, awoke from his trance. The first sight that greeted him was the boy who had watched over him. Such devotion stirred the sage profoundly, for the fidelity of Bappa, a stranger who believed in the gift of friendship, had been granted to the mystic like a miracle revealed. The guru, who understood what it meant to be a true "warrior" in life, gave the boy a knife. "May it protect you from all who bear you ill will," he said before they parted. Then the saint and the boy went their respective ways.

That Khukuri knife with its curved blade, which Bappa Rawal received from the master, passed from Bappa Rawal through generations as a symbol of courage and good faith. Such a knife, albeit a cheap copy, came with a boy who worked on the banks of the hallowed Ganges, to whom a laundryman told the legend.

"You are now to be known as *Bappa*," he said.

"The river boy," who had no family of his own, felt the thrill of identification. As he learned from the man who, amongst multitudes, taught him how to beat cotton, striking it against stone, bending like a reed to the wind: "Your heart commands you to recite the Gurkha war cry."

> *Jai Mahakali, Ayo Gurkhali*
> Glory be to the Goddess of War.
> Here come the Gurkhas!

It seared his lips and focused his mind. Although immature, the boy carried with him the seeds of all the bravery that was sown on countless battlefields strung across imperial lands where his forebears had fought and fallen, only to rise and fight again. Without yet knowing it, the laundry boy would, one day, confront his own courage inside a rusting freighter carrying an illicit cargo of shame.

The river was brown, polluted with orange waste matter from countless sources, filled with floating and sunken muck, contaminated, and nevertheless holy! Its spirit gave optimism to the hopeless. It cleansed the sick, restored sustenance to the starving, emaciated masses, and rendered solace amid wreckage to the dying. Its waters became the stuff of life and the currents of death.

As they burned to ruined ashes on the sluggishly flowing stream, funeral pyre boats constructed of cedar wood for the sole purpose of flaming destruction gave off their peculiar perfume reminiscent of the high, sweet odor of rotting roses. Light converted from color to substance when the glow of the sun struggled to break through the contaminated haze, emerging at dawn and at dusk as purple fragmented clouds. They floated, lingered, appalling and delighting, their dewy vapor drowning slowly amid the deceptive drapery of sultry condensation and the oppressive expectation of implausible consolation.

A man from Bangalore found Bappa working on the banks of the Ganges.

Anutthara, whose name may be interpreted pretentiously to mean "something beyond any answer," decided on the spot to take him. *He is small, lithe, and skinny, with black-pebbled eyes. He is fearless!* He urged some frayed rupees into the hand of the laundryman. Thus a child on the steps of the Ganges, a young beater of rags, became a slave; passing through the rough hands of ownership and beginning victimhood as part of a shameful rite of passage.

∞ ∞ ∞

Vitus's Great Uncle Goldmacher knew that he was going to die. *Unnaturally*, the elder thought, but he did not permit fear to triumph.

"The Jews of Europe are doomed," he told his Gentile neighbor, a fellow storekeeper, as he boarded up his own shop in the small town of Dinkelsbühl. The habitation crouched on the Romantic Road southeast of the Rhine, which is dotted with medieval villages.

In the last quarter of 1938 Goldmacher had witnessed the mindless fury of Kristallnacht, when Gauleiters urged their bigoted thugs into paganistic violence, smashing the windows of Jewish properties, looting valuable contents, and expelling their owners—ultimately to their deaths. Every time he thought of it, Goldmacher could feel the fine particles of glassy dust still cutting his lips and irritating his lungs, the air befouled by hatred when they broke into his place. The sounds of shattering glass, squeals of jubilant annihilation, and choked-off protests of anguish would not leave him until his dying day some time later, when he heard screams of despair, defiance, protest, and disbelief in a ghastly, crowded, sealed chamber.

Without anyone to accompany him, Vitus, at the age of eight, had been sent alone on a train from Czechoslovakia to Germany to live with his uncle, a goldsmith. Vitus had been born to parents late in life, who protected him until they realized that they had no choice, because, although their only living relative, Uncle Goldmacher (who told them in a disguised Yiddish letter that he now had a new, "Gentile" name), was in Germany, they were sure he would find a way to save their son. *Otherwise, if the rumors can be believed, he will be starved and worked to death in the "east" as a factory laborer.* Their fearful nightmares, that he would die as the pall of war wound its relentless web over Europe, called them to action.

"An only child, serious, intelligent, a loner," Goldmacher

described him, speaking aloud to himself in his deliberate manner.

Uncle knew that his last name was too dangerous to keep. A kindly Lutheran father had said to him, "If you are to survive, I suggest that you take the name *Eberstark*." He said, "There is a grave in the yard with that name on it. It is not mine to give," he said, "but you should nonetheless assume it in the hope that it may become a defense. At least we can pray for that."

Uncle had asked, "Why are we sought out for punishment, imprisonment, torture, eviction, and death in the country of our birth where we have lived, contributed, and even acculturated for centuries?"

The cleric, who had begun to despise his fellow countrymen, wrestled with the hatred that threatened to fill his gentle being. He did not smile, but blinked repeatedly as he fell into otiose silence.

The newly renamed big man, strong as a bear of the forest lands, saw the glistening teardrops in Father Niklas of Dinkelsbühl's blue eyes. He knew what they meant. So Goldmacher took the name.

One of Vitus's earliest memories was of a bizarre custom of Bohemian peasants in a village called Skalany, not far from his parents' home. The outing was intended to cheer him up, though it had the opposite effect, leaving him instead with a distressing memory. At springtime men and boys beat women and girls with decorated whips—the *pomlázka*—made of plant fronds. The women were rewarded with strong slivovitz in return for the bestowal of good luck. This experience struck a phobia into Vitus.

"Am I next?" he asked, but he spoke so softly that nobody heard him.

Even his parents' tenderness and their enormous sacrifice of deporting him to his uncle had not eradicated his dread; and thus the fear of whipping had also never left him. *Our mothers make us the people we ought to be,* Vitus thought wistfully, years later when he became an adult and realized that perhaps his own mother would have been whipped by the same peasants had she not been Jewish. Instead she was ignored, which allowed him to have her a while longer and helped to root gentleness into his being.

After the train brought him there, Vitus lived with his kind uncle in Dinkelsbühl. Their neighbor had a store called "Der Hund," which dealt in "the business of dogs." The neighbor's specialty was small puppies. "Purebred miniature dachshunds and affenpinschers, considered rarities for collectors by the Reichsmarschall," the shop owner said, acting proud. But Eberstark, in his intuitive way, felt that the man was hiding some truth about himself.

"These are highly prized," the dog shop owner added, as he patted the most diminutive one and spoke to the goldsmith. Then, by way of afterthought and with deliberate sarcasm, he stated, "Eberstark, isnt it a pity about those Jews." In a moment of overemphasis and putative compassion for his dogs, in case someone overheard him, the breeder used Goldmacher's fake name because he knew why the Jewish man had become "Gentile."

The dog breeder flinched, almost imperceptibly. Uncle saw the movement. He knew that he was right about this man. *He has more courage than he knows!*

Undeniably, Eberstark "the Jew" was big and powerful, *although, not long afterwards, he died in Dachau, where his size and strength could not save him from inhaling Zyklon B,* Vitus reminded himself. Out loud he said to himself, trying to use speech to ease the pain of loss: "My Uncle was 'Goldmacher,' a 'preserver' of gold."

In the end, strong as he was, Vitus's uncle could not fight and he could not flee. However, he was determined to save the boy who had been entrusted to him. The idea that struck him was as unique as it was audacious.

Eberstark returned to his shop one night, when others cowered or simply deluded themselves into thinking that a ghastly pogrom was not about to descend upon them. *As if safety can be found in faith alone!* Wearing soft-soled shoes for walking quietly on cobblestones, he left his modest dwelling. He did not know that the pair would be his last, or that before too long he would see a large mound of plundered footwear with interwoven laces like monstrous works of art. Nor could he imagine the day when his own ashes would blow in the winds of howling lamentation.

Tiptoeing through the alleyway, he came to the back of the workshop. Nailed boards crossed the doorway in a crude X. He had left them deliberately loose in the framework. He removed an iron claw, hidden under his black coat, and used it to pry the wood loose. Deep inside the room, where it was pitch dark, he lit a forbidden Sabbath candle.

He opened the lowest drawer of his roll top desk, reached in, and pulled something out. The black velvet bag lay in his hand like an inert proclamation of faith. The word *tefillin*, written in Hebrew, was embroidered on it.

"As it is said in Exodus," he whispered as if speaking directly but most humbly to the Almighty:

> And it shall be for a sign upon your hand, and as a protection between your eyes.
> For with a mighty hand did the LORD bring us forth out of Egypt.

Eberstark shuddered with the presage that there would be no deliverance for him. *But my little Vitus, only child of my Czech sister, yes, I will try to save him, and so shall I seek to be worthy of You.* He remembered that the concept of *totafot*, "to guard, to protect," was older and wiser in meaning than the ancient Greek interpretation of the word. *Maybe it was spoken by God Himself?*

Emptying the velvet bag, Eberstark said, now in a stronger voice (but not loud enough to be heard outside): "O Lord, preserve my nephew, the last in our line, I beseech Thee!" The softly spoken plea, he prayed, would be heard not by the God of men, but by God most High.

He shook, steadied himself, then began his self-assigned task.

The bag contains symbols that remind us of our humanity. It had passed down to him as an heirloom of faith everlasting. He marveled at the beauty of a rare and valuable shell that he had recently gilded. He would soon place that work of art, with diamonds inside it, vouchsafed like a body in the protection of its coffin.

"God is the Great Designer of all things! Praised be His ineffable Name forever and ever!"

As if riding on a cushion of air, with the shell in hand, he moved quietly to the workbench. He carried the candle, borrowed in excusable need from its real purpose. He set it down on the hard surface. Steadying the shell firmly in his left hand, with his right he gripped his fine-toothed jeweler's saw. The blades were grained finely with diamond dust. Slowly, with the greatest of care, he made a perfect cut.

∞ ∞ ∞

That evening before he left to bathe, dress, and attend the wedding, Vitus was cleaning up after the old lady in Azalea Gardens. As he quickly put the plates, cutlery, and cups in the unreliable dishwasher, and hurled the banana skin (*leopard pelts*, he thought acerbically) into the trashcan, he whispered, almost surreptitiously, "My invitation to the wedding occurred for a reason *extraordinaire*." *I saved the bride's mother from death by choking! But, is this a sop to Cerberus, the three-headed dog that guarded Hades and could only be bribed by cake left in the hands of the dead?*

Vitus had taken a rare holiday.

The flight from Miami to Nassau was short and would have been routine, had it not been for a bizarre event. A woman in the first-class cabin was chewing on sweet Jamaican rum cake. The Boeing 730-200 airliner was heading down its glide path on the approach into New Providence. Safely past Bimini and the northern tip of Andros Isle, the cabin crew was ordered to begin preparing for landing. Just then a piece of gold broke loose in the woman's mouth!

As she gagged and coughed reflexively, the crown became lodged in her trachea. She was already starting to asphyxiate, her face changing color, when the captain called over the PA system for a doctor.

"Very urgent!"

Nobody rose. Vitus had no choice but to volunteer his skills. He stood up and was escorted into the front cabin. Compelled by professional training, as he reached her he immediately pressed the hollows of her cheeks to force her mouth open for resuscitation. *No time!* The aircraft had been cleared to bank quickly for an emergency landing. Passengers were buckled up. He kneeled before her, reached behind her back with both hands, and thrust her sharply into his chest. She gasped and took a huge inhalation, her lungs and heart desperate for oxygen. From his jacket pocket Vitus removed a small penlight and shone the beam into the back of her throat.

"Bolus and gold!" he exclaimed, plunging his fingers in, using a quick but incomplete clearing motion.

"Fork!" he demanded.

A flight attendant ran to the galley, returning in leaps and bounds.

Vitus thrust the metal into the woman's mouth swiftly and accurately, aiming for the glinting object. The tines trapped it. He yanked the piece back toward her lips. With his other hand, he caught it as it came out. She coughed hard, then breathed through her nose as he clamped her jaw with one hand and dropped the crown into his trouser pocket. Her consciousness seemed to re-engage with a sound like a clutch locking in a gearbox.

"Who are you?" she spluttered.

"Vitus Řòezníček, RN," he said softly, with a look of compassionate relief as he forced her mouth open again, just in case.

"Thank you for saving my life." She spoke hoarsely but coherently. Her words of gratitude complete, the woman slumped back into the leather seat, staring up at Vitus, her eyes sprung wide.

"You're most welcome," Vitus replied. He turned and walked back to his seat, as the woman and her husband watched, along with an awed group of passengers on their way to splash, gamble, and play on Paradise Island. "A naked society, a bastion of privacy," the travel agent had called it facetiously with a conspiratorial smirk when Vitus had made his reservation.

"Heimlich be praised!" someone nearby yelled.

"Good old American doctor!"

In the aching muscles of his arms Vitus could feel the aftereffects of the abdominal thrusts he had delivered to the choking woman.

Using their wealth and influence, the couple made sure

that "the good Samaritan" was located. A fortnight later, a gilded invitation to the black-tie wedding of their daughter arrived in the mail at Azalea Gardens.

Vitus was at the wedding. Having listened attentively as the Hassidic rabbi joined bride and groom in holy matrimony beneath "the canopy that represents your future home, unfurnished because people, not possessions, make a Jewish home . . . where God shall always be present and all visitors shall be welcome . . . as is predetermined by our ancient tradition," Vitus felt twinges of doubt and disquiet deep within. An intense desire to escape filled him.

There was an intermission for "*Yichud*, which in times gone by," the Rabbi explained to the guests, "had been a private interval of consumation." Now, Vitus realized, *it permits the gathering of the beautiful, who toy with privilege, to enjoy the cocktail hour.* He stood to one side. He did not know any of the guests. The party followed. Vitus stayed a while in the uncomfortable company of strangers whose platitudinous conversation he found stressful to hear over heavy thumps of dance music. Inanities did not interest him. He took his leave. At the main table, the mother of the bride saw him rise to go. She followed.

Beyond the doors of Coral Hall she caught up with him, the hem of her long dress pulled tightly around her ankles. Breathlessly (*again?* he thought), she curtseyed. It was not a presumptuous or obsequious gesture, but rather a display of genuine grace. Then, without a word, she reached for his empty hand, drew it upward, kissed his fingers and the insides of his wrists. He remembered her mouth. *This time it has been put to better use*, he thought, as she let him go without a word spoken. He put one hand in a pocket of his suit jacket. His fingers touched the gold crown lying there.

Vitus left the party behind.

He walked the length of the boardwalk. At the rear, set within a rhombus now in shadow, the hotel's swimming pool glimmered. To his great relief, music had become a dull beat behind the sets of tall doors separating giddy people on the dance floor from the world beyond.

From the beach, in the marina of the yacht basin, he watched as sails billowed in the breeze. Numbers stitched into manmade fiber flickered illegibly. Pennants at the mast tops flew. Like maritime chickens, seagulls pecked in the sand, looking for tidbits discarded by sun worshippers. A depressing query came to his mind. *Perhaps I never belonged here . . . or anywhere,* he thought. Vitus's saturnine expression turned bleak. At that moment of stark realization, the party seemed to define his overwhelming sense of depression.

Watching through the semi-gloom of night's veil, he saw a pelican cut loose from the delta formation in the sky, fold its wings, and plunge toward the surface of the sea. Absurdly, he wished he could swap places with it. *That way I too could fall into the oblivion of the last dive.*

The events of the trauma theater—so many of them—and then the worst of all when the motorcyclist had been carried in beyond repair, flooded his memory. He felt his gut roiling. At that instant his shiny toecap hit something that had rolled up onto the sand. From another pocket of his tuxedo, he withdrew the same little penlight that he had carried on the flight to "Paradise."

He was looking at the swollen body of a boy! The corpse was distended grotesquely, waterlogged from its time at sea. Beyond putrefying lips, teeth protruded, the brittle whiteness of enamel catching a moonbeam. *Surprised in death by drowning? Why and from where did he come?*

Vitus could not help himself. He used his foot to roll the body over. Staring in horrified fascination he noticed that the boy wore a torn and stained undershirt. It had lifted. Bound around his hips, groin, and in a line between the cheeks of his buttocks, a loincloth twisted. In the waistband at one hip, a short plastic scabbard held a bowed knife. Around the head of the corpse, like a crown, a garland of bluebottles had gathered. He wondered how the knife had remained in place as the body tumbled at sea.

He suddenly remembered something he had read in a printed letter of acknowledgment from a Christian charity that he supported:

> Another little face of need
> Another open mouth to feed.

He removed a mobile phone from his suit and called the emergency number.

∞∞∞

Anutthara, the man from Bangalore, was without conscience. A lissome child with deft hands and keen eyes, acquired cheaply from a river laundryman, although stunted by malnutrition, was still highly desirable.

"Good for cash," he declared when he bought the boy.

"How much?"

The Arab trader who plied wares—spices, silks, gold, silver, copper, girls, and boys—in the stifling cargo hold of his stout dhow was a man of few words, deep sighs, and tight fists. His arms drooped to the sides of his soiled robe. Within the folds, a dagger was hidden. In one hand he held filthy paper money. Blood spots covered the image of a crowned head, blotching the words "Reserve Bank of India."

Anutthara (known as "Annut") uttered a price as he held the boy by a wrist, his long fingers handcuffing the child's narrow bones. The Arab opened his hand, revealing the pre-counted bundle of rupees. He shook his leonine head. The Arab met "eye-with-eye." His was stronger, unblinking, and blazing with the fiendish look of one who conducts an odious trade.

Muttering, Annutt handed over the boy. "I can get many more." Quickly grabbing the tainted cash, he marched away, feigning the superiority of victory.

The dhow was ready to cast off. A cruel man, who worked on faltering turbine engines in the bowels of tramp steamers for a secretive Russian owner (who paid more than others, but was "the least of men"), known and feared in the port community as "the engineer," saw the boy being led up the primitive gangplank towards the sloping deck of the boat. It listed severely under the unevenly balanced cargo, its lateen sails limp. The Arab had already bound a rope around the boy's thin chest, restricting his breathing into hard coughs. From the fly-bridge of the SS *Karanja* of the Old Ships Line, the engineer had watched the sale of the child to the Arab. Before master and slave reached the barrels of dried beans and impure water lashed to the deck with sisal, he made his move.

"I'll pay you double what you paid," he shouted. "Wait!"

He rushed to his grungy cabin and grabbed a tight roll of money. Running on long legs down the splintery plank that connected ship to quay, he sprinted up to the Arab dhow moored nearby. He thrust the money at its captain, who had seen him coming, and in his free hand gripped the double-sided *Jambiya* attached to his broad belt. Such a weapon was needed by one who had many enemies and no friends.

The engineer did not wait for a response. He knew that he was paying an extravagant price. He also had a weapon. An antique Arendt Brevete revolver loaded with bullets banged against his chest, strapped in a leather brace. He had left it in the half-cocked position. Now he shifted it somewhat.

"Never wear it near your left armpit," the pawnshop owner in Madras had told him. "One wrong movement and it can fire by itself like that, leaving a leaking hole where your heart once beat." But the engineer was in a hurry to get his boy. So he took a chance with both his heart and his gun.

"Go!"

To his surprise the Arab released his grip and loosened the rope. He shoved the boy forward. Thrilled, the engineer felt the sharp bones of juvenile scapulae under his fingers. *Cherub's wings!* he thought, congratulating himself on his new possession. *He will do nicely for my needs!*

He pushed the wad of money into the slave trader's large dirty hand.

The SS *Karanja* (OSL) was a work-donkey of the Old Ships Line. Launched in the decaying naval shipyard at Madras, capital of Tamil Nadu on the Coramandel coast of the Bay of Bengal, it was illicitly flagged in the Nicobar Islands (formerly known as Pygmalion Point) at the southernmost tip of the subcontinent. The ship's owner never seemed to appear when his vessels came or went, nor did he personally communicate with his rusty freighters. Yet his presence always loomed in a cloud of sinister influence wherever his ships docked, loaded, and discharged their sordid cargoes. By the power of bribery the steamer had made many blood journeys. It once carried sick and injured troops of the Indian Army during the war. But none of its sailings was as hazardous as the last.

Once, in the Port of the Everglades, a notary accompanied by a sheriff's deputy had tried to impound the ship for nonpayment of a charter fee. The official, with heavy round glasses, a stained jacket, and pudgy fingers, glued a deed of hypothecation on it. Alexander, the speechless chauffeur, drove up in a Rolls-Royce Ghost. He stepped out of the car and plucked the paper off the steel hull. Then he balled it in giant fists and hurled it into the dirty water between wharf and beam where it joined rubbish floating on the oily surface.

When he was younger, Alexander, the Uzbek, drank undiluted vodka until his brain froze as if locked into ice cells of stupor. The proprietor had found him face down in the trough of a muddy ditch running the length of a filthy port. Like a phantom of stifled consciousness, a bulky vessel of the Old Ships Line had loomed out of Alexander's haze of incomprehension. Soon thereafter, the proprietor arranged for surgery to be done on the man. The barbaric operation assured that the torrent of foul invective, which had flowed from the Uzbek's mouth like a river of slime, was gone—for never did he speak again or drink alcohol again, which was exactly what the proprietor wanted in an expendable chauffeur.

Chugging doggedly off the coast of the channel that separates Cuba from Florida, the SS *Karanja* moved slowly, limping like an injured sea mammal. Its tired turbine turned sluggishly, whining in protest. Black soot puffed from its stack. Its propeller thrashed like the hooves of a drowning beast beset by predators, stronger and more tenacious than its urge for survival.

Small sea birds darted in and out of the smoke, challenging its dirt and warmth with swift and daring patrols. The little creatures seemed to ignore the acrid odor belching into their air space as they looked down on the grimy carcass below and flashed the shiny undersides of their wings for all, or none, to see.

The engineer in charge of keeping the SS *Karanja* moving was worried. He had come up on deck to refresh his lungs. But the air had the tang of a brewing storm. Off the bow he saw great clouds forming in multiple accumulations. Lightning ripped through them.

She's too slow! There's something wrong!

He thought of his home port. Superstitious and possessing a barbarous nature, he worried that the Aryans were seeking a final vengeance far from base, because he knew that Madras was the only Indian city to be attacked by the Central Powers during World War I. It happened when an oil depot was shelled by the German light cruiser SMS *Emden* as it raided shipping lanes. However, as he caught sight of a funnel cloud, the engineer took no more time to dwell on that long-ago attack. The waterspout swirled menacingly across the horizon. The engineer sprang off the deck, pulled a steel hatch door open, and ran down the iron steps to his engine room, a last breath of forewarning sea air expanding his chest.

The boy lay on a corded mat on the greasy floor in a corner covered with excrement. He wore a soiled shirt that matched the décor of scattered muck around him. In the engine room the smell was fetid. Although he liked engines, the engineer hated the sea, the ship, the cargo, the boy, Captain Arnav, and, most of all, without acknowledging it, he hated himself.

Two crude iron bowls sat next to Bappa. One contained a greasy liquid. The other brimmed with the remnants of a solid substance. The engine sounded much rougher than usual, protesting its forced labor. High pitched, irritating knocking noises filled the hot space. Nothing could cool the rising heat as steam hissed from the endangered boiler.

The drive shaft, feeding power to the propeller from the turbine, shuddered threateningly. The engineer knew that he might have to shut down the engine. *But, if I do, we'll lose propulsion and drift in a raging storm. We are dead in the water if I cannot start it again!*

"He can do it!" the engineer exclaimed, looking at the warped little body.

Lying curled on his mat like a half-starved cat, Bappa felt beneath his hollow stomach, for the knife, which gave him comfort during the nights at sea, when the engineer had "finished" with him. He kept it beneath his mat. Bappa realized that something terrible was about to happen. So he pushed the knife in its plastic scabbard into his loincloth quickly and deftly before the engineer could see him do it.

The engineer always cursed him. "Damned untouchable!"

he screamed after the "touching" had stopped for the night. The man who abused him had no idea that the boy was a Nepalese Gurkha.

"Get in! Pull whatever is in there out!"

He ordered the boy toward the crawl space. The shaft spun erratically, but it still possessed the power of generation. *There's an obstruction. Perhaps a loose tool inside!*

The engineer's interest lay with tarnished metals, fuel, pipes, switches, plugs, contraptions, and machines, not a pathetic scrap of discarded life that he owned and could do with as he pleased.

The captain, damn him, is an old sea dog dredged up from the slums of Calcutta. I can't wait to shoot him one day with my Arendt Brevete! He considered the option of becoming master of the *Karanja* himself, *due to a sudden heart attack of Captain Arnav!* However the need to remove whatever was causing the extreme vibration overtook the dual temptations of murder and mutiny. So he set the temporary thrill aside for another time and glared at the wretched little creature on the "swine mat."

The boy rose onto all fours, crawling forward dog-like. The engine noise increased, its pitch rising and rendering wrenching screams of mechanical protest. The engineer pointed with a hooked finger. The boy entered the trapdoor, squeezing and tightening his muscles as he prayed that his meager skeleton would get even smaller and flatter. Terror rose within him. He struggled to breathe. But then, in a clear voice addressed to the humming clatter and spin of dangerously failing machinery, he spoke the inherited words of courage: "Glory be to the Goddess of War. Here come the Gurkhas!"

In places expected and not, Nature's rawness manifests. The ship lurched convulsively, then rose at the whim of the coming storm. An instant later Bappa's left hand touched the shaft as he reflexively sought to steady himself. It grabbed his fingers, rolling them like a meat grinder, consuming flesh and bone.

The hand was gone.

The boy did not scream. He just bled.

He was a Gurkha!

The engineer saw blood coming from the hatch. It spewed onto his overalls.

"The boy is dead in there!" he exclaimed. "A further hindrance! I have to stop the engine!" He reached for the brass handle, pulled it down, and was about to set it in the STOP position when he impulsively decided to eject the boy's body. He thrust the lever to REVERSE. As the engine obeyed, he yelled into the communication tube.

"Arnav!" As always he refused to use the title "captain." "We have a problem. I am reversing the propeller before I stop the engine."

On the bridge, Captain Arnav was sound asleep, stooped over the wheel. A whisky bottle rolled across the floor and hit his foot.

The little body ejected, gushing blood. Kicking it aside with his rubber boots, the engineer re-engaged the lever. He pushed it to STOP and barked, "All engines stopped!"

The old vessel was now a plaything of the ocean, her propeller no longer thrashing. Waves immediately set it adrift.

The captain woke and began shouting incoherent commands into the voice tube. The engineer ignored them, his fury rising like a monster released. He lifted the body of the small slave. Even in the waning light of the engine room, where no sun could shine the light of truth, the sight of the boy curdled in his mind from eroticism to revulsion.

He rushed up the iron stairs without a thought that Bappa might still be alive. Nor did he care about the gushing of blood from the stump or feel the knife under the boy's waist.

I must throw this obscenity overboard!

"Shark bait!" the engineer screamed, hurling the Ghurka boy into the sea, just as the ship tossed and turned head first into the darkening storm. He felt a flush of heat.

Then, unaccountably, a vision came to him of a golden orb shining over one of the seven holy rivers of India, the Godavari, which begins its tireless journey in the hills of the Western Ghats and finds its way to the Bay of Bengal. The engineer had no god and he had never bathed in a river that would blot out his sins. Yet, at that moment of reckless carnage he saw the sun. It seemed to blink as it shed its liquid broth, lighting the way where long boats plied the river, birds flew in motioned silhouettes, and temples blended between the transparency of sky and the shimmering disappearance of water.

∞∞∞

When the storm troopers came into her little town, the Muenchnerin, who lived in Dinkelsbühl and knew what had happened to some of its inhabitants, threw her ring down a well. *They must not find this loop of gold with its compressed Star of David, which my husband gave to me on the occasion of our betrothal! If they do, it shall become the signet of death!*

Her husband, Adolf, tried to hide his half-Jewish origins on his father's side. The dog shop helped by creating a disguise and reflecting the image of a "good German" who wished to benefit the officers of the Reich by providing pure-bloodline "Aryan" pups. The little dogs frolicked, to the delight of German children and their generous, happy parents. Adolf's German wife, Gertrude, known as Trude, told him that "to hide in plain sight was better than to submit like a coward."

I must protect him from becoming meat for Gestapo mongrels, she thought, using a simile that pained but encouraged her to act. *I shall do it using the only weapon I have: my love for him!* The thought turned her legs to slush, like the trodden snow of winter on a village road. With a racing heart and raging mind, she sought the frenzied power of righteousness. So she kept the secret and whispered a soft prayer of praise. "Thank you for creating me a woman so that the 'Hounds of Hell' cannot tell by my simple nakedness that I am married to their prey." *They may assume that because Adolf is married to me he is a German who is not circumcised. It is utter madness that a man may be sent to his death because he has no foreskin!* The thought was horrendous and outrageous. But she was sorely mistaken.

Before the "Night of Broken Glass" had shattered his world, Goldmacher walked up behind her in the alley.

"Do not turn around," he said. "Continue walking. I shall speak to you as you go. I knew your husband's parents. He must no longer be 'Adolf.' He must take the name *Adalwolf*, 'Noble Wolf.' That name may save him. It is a trick that some of 'us' must play." *Me too*, he thought. "But I fear that it may not help him, for they know all the intricacies of our ancestry. I have watched. You know how to deal with danger. Trude, listen please. Vitus, my great nephew, is young. He must live! I need you to save him!" Uncle was not accustomed to asking for the assistance of others, especially Gentiles, albeit that he respected Father Niklas, the distraught priest, and many of his kindly neighbors. Yet now he no longer had any other choice.

"There is a loose brick next to the back door of my shop. I shall leave a corner jutting out slightly to mark the spot. Come tonight. Take the bag that I shall place behind it. Inside will be an object of great beauty and high value. If you twist it carefully it will come apart."

"Trude, when I am gone, use the contents to buy the life of the boy. I shall know when the day has come that I must hide him in the false base of my bathtub. He will be quiet because he has been taught that silence can save his life." Before she could react or reply, Goldmacher disappeared into a doorway and was gone.

That night Gertrude did as she was asked. She removed the brick, took the bag, and went home. When Adolf was asleep, snoring louder than his little dogs, she untied the string and removed the contents from its velvet wrapping. A gilded object shone as if possessing its own source of internal radiance. Carefully, as she had been told to do, she twisted it, applying light pressure with her refined fingers. It came apart, splitting into two perfect halves as Goldmacher had said it would. Inside each faultless chamber she saw pure white diamonds that sparkled with a hard light of their own. Translucent reflections danced as she gazed at the perfection before her eyes.

"Gott in Himmel!" she exclaimed.

On the day that men broke down the door of Goldmacher's shop and took him away, an erect major with perfectly squared shoulders came into Der Hund to buy a puppy and find some Jews. He appeared not to hear the commotion next door. "Adalwolf," the breeder and seller of dogs, politely asked, "How may I assist you, *Mein Herr*?"

The officer replied with a question. *"Was bitten Sie?"* he said, asking how much the breeder wanted for a particular pup, a thin thread of menace in his voice threatening to break as he petted the soft ears of the one he had chosen for his children.

Before Adalwolf could reply, the officer paid handsomely for the dog with reichsmarks. As he turned to leave, the woman in the shop spoke so softly that he had to ask: *"Was?"* She moved over to where he stood. In one small palm she held a few of the lesser diamonds. She reached for his gloved hand. She had noticed his wedding ring.

"A present for your wife," she stammered, not daring to suggest a direct bribe. "Please tell your men not to smash the bathtub . . ." Her voice trailed away erratically. She feared she might have said too much. He looked down at what lay in his palm. He stared long and hard at her, forcing her to flinch. She averted her eyes from his. He flicked his swagger stick against his thigh. Then he stepped outside.

"Komm!" he commanded, his voice curdling as they dragged away the elder Goldmacher who was bigger than any of the storm troopers, so that it took many of them to subdue his violent resistance. An astonished silence filled the void behind the tumult of seizure. They did not search the bathtub where the man who was strong as a bear of the forest had hidden his great nephew in a false bottom.

Vitus, the solitary registered nurse, remembered the present that Trude, the Muenchnerin, had given him before the wedding, which coincided with the anniversary of Kristallnacht, as well she knew. He picked up the small parcel, wrapped in multiple layers, and started cutting. When he reached the last covering, he saw words written on parchment:

> Goldmacher, Eberstark, your great uncle the goldsmith, made me take this one dark night in a German village called Dinkelsbühl, where he was born and you were saved. It belongs to you, dear boy.

A date followed. It was faded and difficult to read, but he thought it said "October 1941." Below it she had penned her name.

Trude (wife of Adolf the dog breeder and half-Jew, who died not a half but a full death in Auschwitz).

The day of the month was blank.

When he read it, he marveled at the coincidence that he had been befriended this particular old lady, *Of all the people in the world!*

He felt a surge of enlightenment. Now he knew more certainly, at last, who he was and from where he had come. He also knew who had saved his life. Thinking of frail Trude in her upstairs apartment, he said to himself, "It is not the guilt of survival that has plagued her all the years since her husband and my uncle were killed, but rather the survival of guilt."

Vitus turned to the task at hand: rewrapping the package containing the shell and its magnificent diamonds within for special delivery across the ocean to a venerable institution in the United Kingdom. Living in a place filled with flowers and trees, and being a nurse, Vitus had become interested in nature. He subscribed to magazines about all types of living things, including marine specimens and seashells. That is how he learned of the famous Professor Poch.

∞∞∞

Outside the imposing stone building, the messenger parked his scooter, strode up the stairs to the doors, and trotted into the foyer. It looked like the loggia of a palace: grand, spacious, echoing with the sounds of constant foot traffic on the stairs from the entrance on Cromwell Road in South West London. Near the large visitor information island in the center, another sweeping staircase led to exhibition halls.

> Special Exhibitions: Blue Whale {the Largest Creature on Earth}; Dynasties of Dinosaurs; Children's Butterfly Bounty; Flora and Fauna of the Pleistocene Epoch.

Pamphlets in printed colors, plentifully displayed, lay in trays on the counter tops appealing to the visitors. Behind a bank of attendants, on a swivel chair, a white-haired lady with round tortoiseshell spectacles sat alone. She looked at the crowds with a sense of achievement, as if she were personally responsible for their presence. She glided in semicircles across her island space, the hard nylon castors of her chair rotating silently. She did not deal with the general public. Her special secretarial services were reserved for one employer only.

On that "Observation Day," as Emeritus Professor Henry Poch, her boss, termed it, the courier arrived with an envelope. He said to an attendant, "I need to speak to Miss Handley privately." When the professor's aptly titled "personal assistant" stopped her perambulating and stepped to the front desk, the messenger said to her, "Please hand this to the curator."

The retired curator of the Natural History Museum looked up when Miss Rebecca Handley entered his room with the parcel. He had been poring over an article on seashells. His office was in darkness, except for a single bulb under a plastic shade that stood on his desk. It glared from its green cover like some bizarre Cyclops with an oblong, illuminating eye. The two hundred and fifty watt halogen bulb cast a piercing white beam onto the printed page. When once asked, "Why?" by Miss Rebecca Handley (who, although pensioned, stubbornly refused to leave the museum), he replied, "It assists my perfect concentration, which you are now disrupting!" He deliberately omitted any mention of his macular degeneration and keratinized cataracts.

"What is it?" he asked, referring to the interruption.

In one corner of the desk (where his hand now traveled as if autonomically motivated to stroke its cover) lay the only extant reference book by George Rumpf, known by his quill name, "Rumphius," whose long life began in the early part of the seventeenth century and ended just as the eighteenth began. *Now there was a scientist of old, a man who, though blind, could still work by touch when his sight failed*, the professor recalled as he turned his attention rather reluctantly to his "young lady." The first known volume of mollusk taxonomy felt good to the touch as if the knowledge it contained could be absorbed by tactile communication.

"No wonder his nomenclature was used by Carl Linnæus, extolled by the great luminaries Rousseau and Goethe!"

"I beg your pardon," Rebecca asked, perplexed.

"Nothing," Henry Poch replied, with a flicker of annoyance.

"I was thinking about Darwin's *On the Origin of the Species* when you interrupted me." The tightness of his voice gave way as he realized that there was no need to be rude to the woman who had assisted him for more than forty-five years.

"A courier brought this. I thought you should receive it personally," she replied.

Henry Poch pushed aside his reading material.

"Alright. Let me see it, please."

His hand now covered with a tight rubber glove, he took the letter and brought it into focus beneath a hanging magnifier as if he were examining a specimen. Although more than ninety years of age, Professor Henry Poch could neither be emulated nor replaced. "The greatest conchologist of all time" was how the *British Journal of Nature* extolled him. As such he still had his room in the basement of the Natural History Museum.

A fellow at the British Museum had given Henry a metal helmet. "Strictly on loan," he said. But he never asked for its return. "I believe it was once worn by Cromwell himself," he added at the time. The conchologist had a light fitted to the top. It now boosted the harsh beam.

"This one helps my brain," he told Rebecca Handley. Unperturbed by the shackles of retirement, she still stood guard like a sentinel in the public enquiries island and came in to work every day, except on Christmas, as a "personal volunteer." The emeritus professor sought her assistance in opening the package. First he found the note inside a simple envelope. He read it.

The sender had written, "Your museum houses one of the greatest collections of 'God's Acts' that exists anywhere." The writer was not referring to twists of nature, but rather to "marvels of creation" and had appended an enigmatic conclusion: "I sincerely hope that this may add to that!"

There was a printed addendum:

This is a rare form of nautilus shell that is chambered, decorated with distinctive white, brown, and gold-striped lightening ridges, running in jagged lines across the spiraling upper and outer ridges, establishing an impression of two opposing dimensions. Its formative creature is not certain. However scientists assume it to have been formed by either a large mollusk or more likely a cephalopod predatory squid that caused the shell to be rejected when it died or its protective shield was no longer required.

The professor had no idea who had written the note. He did however think that it had been added to the package for good reason. He uncovered the shell. He studied it under his light and magnifier. For a long while he said nothing.

Then he announced, "Certainly such a specimen from the depths, its casing hard and thick to withstand pressure, has the properties of aerated chambers that were added from the original single cell as the host grew to maturity. Presumably it could float and submerge by inflating or flooding the partitions and it could use the top, flared opening to catch wind. Such an amazing shell could sail upon the surface of seas or with its animal protected within, disappear beneath the waves, and sink into the depths of the primordial ocean."

Seriously intrigued, Henry Poch cast aside his suspicion. "Amateurs send me pieces, whole shells, fragments, fossils . . . usually rubbish," he said. "But occasionally there is something of real value amongst them."

Looking more deeply now with the added light of Cromwell's helmet, he gasped. *This specimen is so uncommon that it was believed never before to have been seen. I had heard of it and done extensive research to find it, but nobody knew who owned it. Now I am looking right at it!*

The professor declared, "I believe that this shell constitutes a hybrid worthy of its own classification. It needs a name. Perhaps the 'Poch Nautilus.' But no."

As always when absorbed by his love of seashells, he ignored Rebecca. But he was aware that she was listening, and in his heart he could not avoid the knowledge that they shared uncommon intimacy. "We give each other things to do. We make each other useful," in a weak moment of sentimentality he once said to Miss Handley, then immediately regretted his exclamation because it had the ring of delicate, personal reality.

***

Moving the letter to another location on his desk, he noticed the strange wording on the address label: "From Gertrude (wife of Adolf) who befriended Eberstark and saved Vitus Řoezníček, RN, Azalea Gardens, Coconut Creek, Florida, U.S.A."

Puzzling, Henry Poch thought. *Four people referenced. Is there a story here?* Henry had heard many tales of discovery. *Objects inside fish, buried in chests, locked away in vaults, found on beaches or in wrecks, dredged up in fishing nets and cast skeins, in diving bells . . . the list goes on.*

Rebecca gathered up the packaging. Professor Henry Poch began a more detailed inspection of the magnificent object. He had examined many species. Tiny nipple shells. The *Moneta*, used as money by Africans to buy goods from Arabian traders. Heavy *Strombus* from deep waters. The graceful thin *Calcarovula*. The thick-walled *Pteropurpura*. Rare and highly poisonous *Conus geographus* shells that look like they carry inaccurate sketches of ancient cartographers on their back. Even the cowry called *Tulerei* that few human beings have ever seen. During his long career he had studied, measured, described, illustrated, photographed, catalogued, and displayed them all.

"Keep the label for me," he said.

She did, although she threw out all the rest.

The golden nautilus lay uncovered. Like a surgeon, Henry Poch reached for it gingerly. Even with his bad eyes, clouded and misty with age, he realized immediately that it was unique. *It has been covered with gold leaf! Thin as a layer of friable skin, the epidermis is nonetheless fully intact. The gold layer can be removed by a jeweler without bleaching the shell into worthlessness as a museum specimen.*

Rubbing it gently like a bottle that houses a genie, he detected a thin crest in the midline. Rebecca Handley had not returned to her self-appointed station. She stood loyally beside his desk. She used its edge for support as she tried to straighten up from her retrieval activity in the gloom of his room and hoped that the ray from Cromwell's helmet would not let the professor see her struggling. *Even with his bad eyes, he never fails to observe everything, although he pretends otherwise.* As she recovered her posture Miss Rebecca Handley wished that this time she could rely on the disguise of her own behavioral etiquette to avoid embarrassment for her frailty in front of the man she so admired.

He twisted the object slightly. At the touch of pressure its secretly interlocked miniature hinges, almost invisible to the naked eye, slid soundlessly apart into two perfectly matching halves. At first he thought he might have broken the exquisite specimen.

In the quiet of his room he could hear the rumble of footsteps through the big halls above. Relief flooded him as no ineptitude on his part had caused the shell to be broken. Inside, the partitions were perfect, rotating from very small at the vertex to very large at the apex, and wider still at the operculum opening. Something glinted. He thought that perhaps the implanted lenses in his eyes were playing prismatic tricks. Turning his head, he reached up and thumbed a focal dialer on the helmet. The beam contracted, becoming pencil thin and sharp.

"Diamonds!" he exclaimed, stopped in the very process of thought. "Most are held in place by small jeweler's claws . . . but some are missing." He felt the small concave holes, counting as his fingers moved along in enquiry, like a reader of Braille.

"I beg your pardon?" Rebecca Handley queried, wondering if he wanted to dictate his observations. "Is there anything you require of me?" Rebecca Handley's voice was solicitous and her mode formally English as it had been throughout the decades.

"Nothing. Thank you," the professor replied. "This, indeed, is all!"

Although he sometimes thought that he was as old as a Dutch clog, this time he felt invigorated. Rebecca was taking her leave when Professor Henry Poch added, "The rotten deprivation of right and wrong. Once we were weak, now we are strong." He was known for his fluttery enigmatic rhymes sometimes grandiloquently spoken in an old-fashioned style. She smiled at him but did not stop. After all, her back was already turned.

∞∞∞

Swept by a great storm, the stricken cargo ship had been blown out into the deeper ocean, beyond the busy lanes where commercial vessels labored in their endeavors to fetch and carry goods of all types from and to the "New World." The tempest had long since passed, dragging its energies to wreak havoc elsewhere.

The SS *Karanja* had not sunk entirely beneath the surface. It had been overturned so that its rusting screw stuck up above the waves, cells of air trapped in its steel dividers keeping it afloat.

Inside the engine room that had flooded when giant waves struck its side and sent it over, the decaying body of the engineer floated in liquid entrapment. Like an alien marine specimen it twisted restlessly. As it moved with the flow, it seemed as if the body had been harpooned in the moment of sudden death.

Migratory birds flew over the ship's hulk, ignoring its obtrusive presence as an insult to nature, unaffected by the masthead of disgrace below the sunken bow where black water flowed like octopus ink.

A bloated, vulgar man, the proprietor sat in the black Rolls Royce. He spoke to his replacement chauffeur, another Uzbek. The former driver's glossectomy, some whispered fearfully, was ordered by his employer to make him silent. Yet others, more thuggish, preferred the gory rumor that it was bitten off in a drunken brawl. "Alexander" (he called this one by the same name, disregarding his real name), the rich man ordered, "drive me to . . ." He told him where exactly on the stretch of motorway he wanted to go.

The Russian oligarch was referring to the spot where the hose blew in the Ghost's engine and its trailing oil cloud consumed a racing Hayabusa rider. Hated by many and feared by most, the proprietor continued his endless quest for wealth. As usual when being driven from place to place, he reached for his Courvoisier. Then, as they reached the area but did not stop, he read a letter from the Rolls-Royce manufacturers in Goodwood:

> We regret the inconvenience.
> All expenses are ours.

The script, signed by a British peer, was followed by the famous intertwined *R*'s, sheltered within the shield of their square logo.

On a day of heat and thunder, a park ranger had caught Alexander (the "first" so named) fishing without a license on state land near an exclusive residential island.

"This is PRIVATE property!" the official announced sternly. Such a minor offence would not have sent a man to jail. However, when the proprietor decided that his erstwhile chauffeur (although a brutish semi-illiterate ruffian) had seen and heard enough about himself, the real owner of the Old Ships Line, he let it be whispered in the ears of a certain elected judge in Miami that the Uzbek was "really an illegal Cuban exile" who had "murdered three prostitutes in Nueva Gerona, capital of the largest of the three hundred and fifty islands of the *Archipiélago de los Canarreos* in the Gulf of Batabanó!" It was a certain way to get rid of Alexander under the guise of legality. *Even though he is tongueless, he knows too damn much!*

"In case he remembers the names of some who 'disappeared' in mysterious circumstances off one of my freighters, now he has found a kennel for expatriates!"

"Forcible removal of undesired persons!" the record of judgment had been euphemistically phrased. *A wise judge knows what is good for him, his wife, and his children!* The proprietor took another slug of brandy. Inside the forbidding Panopticon, which its English designer, Jeremy Bentham, cleverly conceived to prevent "the watching from being watched," on the *Isla de la Juventud*, the Isle of Youth, lying to the south of Havana, Alexander tried to spit up on the concrete floor of his moldy, dank cell. Without a tongue, full ejection of sputum was impossible. Gloom surrounded him. He tried to scream, but was thwarted by despondency about his imprisonment.

"Ogh" was the one deeply guttural sound that left his mouth.

Offshore a coast guard cutter nicknamed *Madonna of the Night* (because an imaginative midshipman who served on her once quipped, "with her black eyes she protects sailors, even in the cursed Bermuda Triangle") cruised beyond the shore of the communist island. It was a so-called "special municipality" under the aegis of the central Cuban government. International maritime law prevented the cutter from engaging in threatening actions.

But *Madonna's* "eyes" were her spinning radar antennae that incessantly transmitted blips of greenish data to monitors. In her darkened surveillance room the porthole shades were always drawn. Listening devices hummed in monotonous harmony.

"Commander, you need to see this!" the radar officer stated emphatically.

The night duty commander looked closely, then immediately stepped across to the captain's station. Miles above the earth, a spy satellite in geostationary orbit maneuvered into position. Blobs of luminous emission pulsated on the monitor. The captain and the commander returned to the radar monitor together and peered at what the officer had observed. The captain stepped back, having seen the phenomenon for himself. The coordinates vectored a floating position in busy sea-lanes not too far from their current patrol route.

"RAM!" Captain Arnold Bolderness of the cutter *Madonna* declared in a clear voice of authority. On the bridge, silence followed, until the captain added: "Encased in lead, radioactive material . . . RAM . . . 'lives' up to a million years!"

"Inside, what is this?"

Captain Bolderness did not yet know that he had been looking at the poorly encased cargo of the SS *Karanja*, which had been bound for Havana when the storm smashed into its drifting hull and inverted it quickly and effortlessly, as if with a magician's sleight of hand.

Trude was now approaching a century of age. Her long lost

husband had been hunted and chopped down by the axe of fascism despite all she did to save him with her courageous love. By now Vitus knew her life story and how his own fate had miraculously intersected with hers. He was still the secretary of the German Organization. His sense of responsibility towards her, as if she were a surrogate mother whom he had discovered by sheer chance, had not left him.

For more than a dozen years she had not worn anything but a cotton housecoat. This day, however, as a spur-of of-the-moment reward to herself for the gift of memory, she felt her way through the few dresses that hung in her closet. She found one she thought she liked. To her touch the fabric felt soft, feminine, and attractive. She could not remember its color. Slowly, she put it on. *It has become too big*, she thought, and then laughed at the size to which her body had shrunk.

Although alone, she sat dressed that way in a her pink reading chair upholstered in Draylon, beside her single bed with its waterproof cover (also provided by Vitus) arranged as a barrier against incontinence. The fear of age had long since left her. The unraveling twine of time that cannot be woven, cannot be rewound, had outreached her.

She did not doze. She remained clothed in the same "fine" dress.

Darkness was as much a friend as it was an enemy.

Although she could not witness it, light had risen. The flower of a new day opened its petals. She could hear the birdsongs. They sounded like Japanese bamboo flutes as they floated through the folds of daybreak, fulfilling their task as the forerunners of hope and energy.

How shall another day promote itself? Trude wondered, feeling peaceful.

She fumbled her way to the jalousie window. *The air of newness, the tones of sweetness*, she thought. Rough pain had given way to smooth acceptance. *I am calm and reconciled to the inevitability of my death.* A quote came to her. It had been said at a lecture on acceptance of one's discomforts that she once attended at Azalea Gardens. *No obedience to blind desire, no icy feet to the burning fire.* Its aptness was understood by her, a sightless widow, often lonely, who yearned for love, for forgiveness, and whose feet were always cold, except when Vitus warmed them with his electric blanket *at just the right temperature to make me feel comfortable.*

The despotism of habit seemed to evaporate. She had not seen any movement for a long time, but she remembered once the silky images of stingrays eyeing and gliding through crystal waters on a poster advertising Grand Cayman. *They were at one with their element.* The metaphor comforted her as she sought, found, and used her walker to help guide her through the pitfalls of domestic dangers. The memory of holding a bucket for the man who was stealing mangos on common property with a blind woman as his accomplice struck her.

Ridiculous, but then, perhaps not entirely?

She recalled the innumerable meals during all the years of kindness that Vitus Řoezníček, who had been born in Bohemia to the sister of Eberstark and made it alive to America, had prepared for her. She had no way of knowing that he had continuously tested himself against the immodest temptation of pity and still did daily, even in his late fifties. "His name means *Life*," she said.

She had not used the golden shell and its rare diamonds to buy a passage to liberty for the boy whom Uncle Goldmacher had urged be saved when he vouchsafed it to her care. Her own money had been enough, although she had used up almost all of it for that purpose.

Long ago, it seemed like a past lifetime, she had stopped praying for the restoration of her sight. But she saved the boy. "Indeed I did!" she said aloud to the walls of her apartment. Then, as she tried to recall where the kettle sat on the stove, she remembered a German poem from her childhood. She had heard it spoken by, of all people, a retired circus wrestler. In translation Trude recited:

> A better friend I needn't seek
> > Among the strong, amidst the meek
> In my wounded soul doest lie a trick
> > Of help, gifted to the ailing sick
> Blessed be "Invincible Might"

> Moving through the Darkest Night
> For whom does "The Spirit" weep?
> And where is found its hidden "Keep"?

The rest was obscured by the passage of time. She closed her sightless eyes, took a deep, single breath . . . and surrendered peacefully.

For a long time Vitus did not know that Uncle Goldmacher had acquired a seashell of beauty, rarity, and value in his landlocked little town of Dinkelsbühl by buying it from a weak-minded tinker. The unfortunate man had arrived from a place on an isolated coast. He only visited the small village once a year, spoke little, and asked for almost nothing. Uncle paid well for the object.

"You are welcome to food and shelter in my house for as long as you wish," he said. The strange tinker did not accept. Pushing his cart, mumbling to himself, he left the village and went back the way he had come. Trude only told this to Vitus much later during—as it transpired—their last meal together.

Vitus had inherited his uncle's great loving kindness, but part of the price he paid for it was the frustration of seclusion caused by the long hours of his ceaseless job as a specialized trauma nurse. As he parked his trusty Peugeot Familiale model in the staff lot outside the ETU at Jackson Memorial Hospital where he worked most nights, he thought, *there's no end to tragedy*. He had no other job. "This is it," he said to nobody in particular as his beeper buzzed to summon him.

When he saw an ambulance burst around the corner of the hospital entrance, almost tipping over in its urgency, and heard its strident siren, he began to run. Its screams added to the anarchy of injury despite the lessening of suffering to which Vitus knew the driver and staff were devoted. Although in a rush to save another life, Vitus suddenly realized what had plagued him since Trude had passed on: *Love has been hibernating! I must find someone of my own age to love, to marry me, because I am ready to love her!*

Vitus, a taciturn, lonely man watched as a pretty nurse ran by him in the opposite direction. He turned his head to observe the alluring sway of her hips, something he had never done before. Then, faced with yet another crisis, he smiled. As if a coiled spring had finally been released inside him, the irrepressible urge to laugh, adore, believe, and hope, to enter the flowing stream of life, compelled him forward. As usual, ahead of the surgeons, he entered the operating room. Only this time, he felt in charge of his destiny.

Although the RN had never seen it at the Museum on Cromwell road in London, *Nautilus Vitusensis* lay on its velvet base inside a case all of its own. Named by Professor Henry Poch who had suppressed his own ego and titled it after the person who had been saved, according the parcel's label, the shell was without its gold coat, which had disintegrated on removal. Its finely cut halves had been so closely mended as to be almost invisible to the naked eye. Visitors who gathered around the glass enclosure, protected by converging alarm rays, could not see the diamonds inside.

However, its startling beauty told a story all of its own.

On the secluded seashore, in the early twilight where late tourists frolicked in the gentle wavelets that lapped the sand, as the magnificent sun began its slow tropical fall and light turned into crystal sparklers, the ghost of the Ganges rolled at one with the tide.

It spread laughter to children and chuckled each time the toecap of a shoe turned it over and over again. Bappa, a Ghurka boy, carried a curved knife that seemed to have pried body loose from soul, and its one-handed gestures called for all who would see it at play in the sea where it gamboled in idyllic emancipation.

∞∞∞